THE DAWN OF DESIRE

"Tarik, I thought you hated me." Her words came out in a rush as she tried to comprehend what he was saying. How could she have misunderstood him so badly?

"Oh, no." He caressed the side of her face, smoothing a loose wisp of hair away from her cheek, while his other hand still held hers enfolded in his grasp. "I never hated you, Narisa. And I want you still. You must know that...."

Their mouths met in a warm, lingering kiss that went on and on until Narisa imagined he had drawn her very soul out of her body and made it his own....

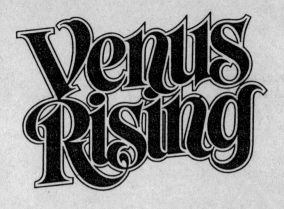

FLORA SPEER

For my father,
Ralph Philip DeGroodt,
Who worked on the early space program,
Who believed in space travel.

Book Margins, Inc.

A BMI Edition

Published by special arrangement with Dorchester
Publishing Co., Inc.

Printed in the United States of America.

Chapter One

Narisa thought she was awake, but she could not open her eyes. Slowly she became aware that she was lying on a lumpy couch. Her head ached, and her eyelids seemed to be glued together. She could feel the hot sun on her face. Beltan sun.

She knew where she was; she was at home in the garden of her parents' house, and in a moment or two her mother would come to scold her for lying in the sun so long, and tease her about tanning her skin into fine Denebian leather. Narisa could sense her approaching, and waited with laughter in her heart for the gentle, loving words she expected to hear.

Her mother's shadow passed between Narisa and the sun, moved away, then came back again, but she did not speak to her daughter. With great effort, Narisa lifted heavy eyelids, searching for her mother's beloved face.

"This isn't Belta!" The dream gone, she reared upward suddenly, only to be pulled firmly downward. Without thinking, she released the safety harness so she could sit. That automatic motion brought her to complete wakefulness, to the memory of where she really was—in the Empty Sector, where it was said dreams could be so real they led humans to madness. This, the computer on the rescue pod had told her, was the only planet within many parsecs that had a breathable, although thin, atmosphere. She had had no choice about where to land, for the pod had almost run out of air. A thin atmosphere was better than none at all, she had reasoned, but it had made landing difficult.

There hadn't been enough air friction to slow the pod properly, so it had crashed and bounced several times before the entry door had broken open and the little ship had suddenly stopped moving. An instant later Narisa had lost consciousness.

She was lying in the open pod, face upward toward a brilliant orange sun, and the shadow that had passed over her was not her long-dead mother, but a large bird. It soared through a deep blue sky, turned gracefully and flew back above the pod. Narisa squinted against the bright light, trying to follow the bird's path.

The creature was blue, almost the same

shade as the sky, which made it difficult to make out the details of its body. The blinding sun didn't help, either. Narisa's eyes began to water. She braced herself on one hand in an effort to shift positions so the sun wouldn't glare in her eyes as badly, and she could get a better look at the bird.

It wasn't a lumpy couch she had been lying on, it was a man. In her confusion she had forgotten about Commander Tarik. He lay perfectly still, his eyes closed, his pale, sharp-featured face serene. Was he dead? Was that huge bird a scavenger, come to make a dinner of Tarik, and possibly of Narisa, too? Frantically, she felt for a heartbeat, a pulse, a sign he was breathing.

It was there, she discovered when she flung herself down on him and pressed her ear to his chest. His heart was beating slowly and steadily, and he was taking shallow, steady breaths. She resisted the impulse to stay there, stretched out on top of him with her head on his chest, and weep from relief and fear. She was surprised at herself, and a little ashamed. Narisa never wept; tears were a sign of weakness.

She had not wept when her parents and sister had been killed by Cetans ten space-years ago. Nor had she cried when Cetan pirates had attacked the *Reliance* and their first blast at the space ship had killed everyone on board except herself and First Officer Tarik.

They had been together in the Navigator's Area, which had extra shielding. As usual,

Tarik had been trying to find some excuse to criticize her work. He had been standing when the blast came. Surprised, without any time to catch the guard rail and hang on, he had been thrown around the Area and badly injured. Narisa had been strapped into her navigator's seat and so had suffered only a few bruises.

She did not like Tarik, but she knew what her duty was. Somehow she had rescued him from the wrecked, drifting ship, had dragged his unconscious body through the corridors and wedged him into the only rescue pod left functioning. She had ejected the pod from the *Reliance* just before its automatic self-destruction system had exploded the ship into atoms.

Then she had brought them here, to an uncharted planet in the Empty Sector, where Service personnel definitely should not be, but where the Cetans would probably not follow them. The Cetans would assume a small pod that had gone into the Empty Sector would never get out of it.

Now she was solely responsible for the safety of the unconscious Tarik, and for herself. She scrambled to her feet, disregarding her shaking knees. After all, two people had spent long space-hours cramped into a one-person pod, breathing from a limited air supply. No wonder she felt weak and trembly. It would pass. She could tell the gravity on this planet was a little less than she was accustomed to. That would help her to recover. She took a deep breath. The air was hot and very dry.

She looked around, turning slowly to scan the entire horizon. There wasn't much to obstruct her view. The pod had landed in flat, desertlike terrain marked by occasional formations of gray rock. Some were spectacularly high. A few straggly gray-green plants grew on some nearby rocks. The surface of the land as far as she could see was covered with tan and gray pebbles and gravel.

"Not very hospitable," she said softly, glancing upward. The bird had disappeared, leaving the sky empty. Not even a cloud marred that perfect bowl of blue so dark it was almost purple at the zenith.

"That's because of the thin atmosphere," she said into the silence. There were no artificial structures at all, no signs of life save that one departed bird and the few plants. There was just the burning sun and desolate isolation.

"Is there intelligent life here?" Narisa continued to speak her thoughts aloud to counter the silent emptiness. "Will we be able to contact the Capital? Will we ever get off this planet?"

Not in the pod, certainly. It was made for escape from a ship in space and had the capacity to dock with another ship or to land on a planet's surface, but it could not take off again. If she and Tarik were to leave, they would have to find another ship.

A moan brought her back to the pod, where

Tarik still lay entangled in the safety harness. Kneeling on the stony ground, she removed it. As she did so, he caught her right hand and held it to his lips. His eyes were still closed.

"Suria," he whispered, his mouth warm against her fingers. "Suria, my sweet."

"Commander Tarik!" Narisa's spine stiffened. How dare he not know her from Suria? Suria was his lover, who had been navigator of the *Reliance* before Narisa had been assigned to that post. Unreasoning anger filled her. "Let me go—*sir*!"

Her hand was free. Narisa stood, watching him and nursing her resentment. Then she began to realize Tarik was having the same trouble getting his eyes open that she had had. Perhaps he, too, was deep in some beautiful dream. She regarded him a little more sympathetically. After a while his lids rose, and he stared up at her with eyes as purple-blue and impenetrable as the mysterious sky above them. It took a moment or two more for recognition to fill those eyes and his usual coolly assessing expression to return.

"Help me to stand," he ordered.

"I think you should lie still until you have adjusted to this atmosphere."

"Lieutenant." It was a command, no doubt about that, and his right hand was raised in an imperious gesture. Narisa braced her feet, put out her right hand to his and pulled. Once upright, he stepped out of the pod. Still holding his right hand and supporting that arm, Narisa put her left arm across his shoulders to help him steady himself.

"Where have you brought us?" he demanded. Before she could answer, he collapsed onto his knees, nearly dragging her down with him.

"I told you to lie still," she cried, watching him gasp for breath. His face was tight with pain, but he crawled back to the pod and sat leaning against its side.

"I believe," he said, measuring his words and his breath carefully, "that I have a broken rib. Possibly several. Where are the medical supplies?"

"They should be inside. I'll check." Leaning over the entrance, Narisa reached in to search the various compartments. "This is all I can find. There are no medical supplies." She held up three packages.

"Why," Tarik asked, "were the two of us in one pod?"

"It was the only one that was usable."

"Where was the rest of the crew?"

"Everyone else was dead." She made her voice flat and clipped so he wouldn't know how deeply that had affected her.

He stared at her, his eyes wide, and she wondered what he was thinking, if he felt the horror of those last moments on the *Reliance* the way she did. Of course he didn't. He had been unconscious.

"What's in there?" He indicated the packages Narisa held.

"A small tool kit, compressed food and water," she told him, reading the labels. "Enough for one person for five days."

"Or two people for two and a half days."

"Not in in the desert. We need more water."

"The last thing I remember," Tarik said, gently massaging his sore ribs, "I was in the Navigator's Area. How did I get to the pod?"

Narisa told him, adding, "When the *Reliance* exploded, all the instruments in the pod malfunctioned. By the time I got control again, we were in the Empty Sector. I don't understand how that happened." As soon as the last sentence was out, she wished she hadn't said it. He would use it against her. She knew he would.

"We were still close to the *Reliance* when she blew?"

When Narisa nodded, he looked thoughtful. Her tension eased a little. He might come to the same conclusion she had, that the horrendous explosion had had something to do with where they were. She hoped he would also decide that it didn't matter how they had reached this planet, that the important thing was how they were going to leave it.

"The Empty Sector," he said softly.

"We shouldn't be here, Commander Tarik."

"We shouldn't be alive, but we are. It's not your fault, lieutenant. Assuming, of course, that the instruments really did malfunction and you didn't go off course through inexperience or incompetence."

"How do you suppose . . ." Narisa responded heatedly, then stopped. Trying hard to keep her temper under control, she began again, speaking more calmly. "How could I possibly have gotten so far away from where

we should have been? It would take an
amazing degree of incompetence and a very
long time to achieve that."

"Just so. Have you any idea how long I was
unconscious?"

Indignation at his suggestion that she had
failed to navigate the pod properly, anger
against the Cetans and sorrow for dead shipmates, concern for their own predicament—
all the emotions she had been so rigidly re-
pressing now burst in a wave of furious rage
aimed at her immediate superior. Insubordination or not, she could hold it in no longer.

"You arrogant, cold-blooded, hard-
hearted . . . You have resented me since the
day I came aboard. I am an expert, accredited,
fully licensed navigator. The Service never
would have assigned me to the *Reliance* if I
weren't. I'm just as good a navigator as your
beloved Suria. I'm sure you would rather she
were here with you now. I'm sorry she's not. I
wish I were back on Belta, or at the Capital, or
in the next galaxy. Anywhere but here with
you." Narisa tossed the packages she was
holding into his lap and started walking away
from him.

"Lieutenant." Years of training made her
stop at his peremptory tone, but she kept her
back toward him. When he spoke again, his
voice was softer. "I haven't thanked you for
saving my life."

"It was nothing." She was so angry she
could not hear properly, and of course the
thin air played tricks with sound. Commander

Tarik could not possibly know how to laugh, though the noise she thought he made was suspiciously like one.

"Nothing to you, perhaps," he said, "but I do value my life. I also value loyalty. I know you dislike me. Thank you for what you did." He paused, and she heard a sound halfway between a chuckle and a groan. "Will you help me again? I need medical aid, and I can't do it myself."

"What is it you want?" Narisa turned to face him, and met his purple-blue eyes fixed full upon her. His face was serious, but his eyes were filled with a soft light.

"We need to find shelter," Tarik said. "Also water and more food than we have here. To do that, we will have to walk, and I know I won't be able to move very far. It hurts every time I take a deep breath."

"I don't know what to do." Narisa spread her hands in a helpless gesture. "I've had only the basic medical training for emergencies, and we don't have any supplies."

"Long ago," Tarik said, "injured people were bound tightly until their injuries healed."

"Do you mean," Narisa interrupted, unbelieving, "that a broken bone will heal itself without sonic instrument treatment? That can't be true. And even if it were, how do you know about it?"

"I just know." Tarik sounded weary. "Use the safety harness. Cut it out of the pod and wrap it around my chest."

There was a simple knife in the tool kit she had found. She used it to cut out the harness, then knelt beside him.

"Put it under my clothes, next to the skin," he told her. "You will have to help me take my jacket off."

The closures were pressure-sensitive, so it was easy enough to release them and peel the heavy dark blue fabric off his chest. It was harder to get his arms out of the sleeves. Narisa realized he was in a great deal more pain than he had revealed to her. She tried to be gentle, but he winced more than once, and finally he groaned.

"I'm sorry, Commander Tarik." She laid the jacket on the ground and picked up the harness.

"Can't be helped. Now wrap it. Do it tightly. It's elastic; I'll be able to breathe. I need the support."

She could guess by the short, clipped sentences how much it must hurt him to breathe and talk. She could also see the large blue bruises over the broken bones on his left side. Dislike him or not, she had to admire the courage it took for him to cry out in pain yet not give up.

She held one end of the harness against his chest with her hand flat on his warm skin, and reached her other arm around his back to catch the loose end and draw it forward. Except for their ride in the pod, she had never been this close to Commander Tarik before. She had avoided him as much as possible.

Now here she was on her knees next to him, and her arms were around him in an awkward embarce while she fumbled with the harness. She kept her head down so she would not have to look at him, but that meant her face was pressed against his chest when she reached behind him. He smelled so nice. The scent of his skin reminded her of gentle sunlight and cool breezes, and the tangy fragrance of moist green leaves.

"Pull the strap tighter," he said, his lips almost touching her ear. She could feel his warm breath on her neck, and she suddenly recalled how he had felt in the pod, pressed closely against her back during all that dangerous ride. "Tighter, lieutenant. Ah, that's good. Now wind it around again, and then another time if it's long enough."

She had to put her arms around him once more to do as he ordered, and this time she made the mistake of raising her head. They were cheek to cheek, so near she could almost feel the faint stubble on his chin. Poor Tarik, he had no more pills to take to keep his beard from growing. His hair was so dark he would probably look like a Cetan before long, with untidy beard and sweeping mustache. She almost smiled at that nasty thought. It took her mind away from Tarik's firm mouth, too close to her own, the corners pulled down hard in a grimace of pain. For one lunatic moment she wanted to kiss the pain away and smooth the deep lines that ran from nose to mouth, run her fingers along them and watch them disappear into laughter.

She must be going mad. It must be the sun and the unfamiliar air. This was the despicable Commander Tarik, not a friend. She finished wrapping the harness about his rib cage, fastened the end with one of the clips from the neck of her own uniform, and sat back on her heels, looking anywhere but into his eyes, or at his mouth, or at the chest and shoulders and upper arms that had proven to be remarkably hard-muscled in spite of his slenderness.

"Thank you," he said softly. "Now, if you would help me with my jacket again."

It was easier to get it on than it had been to take it off. He did not seem to be in as much pain now, thanks to the support provided by the harness. By the time he was covered and the closures fastened, Narisa had herself under complete control once more.

"Drink some water," she told him, handing over the largest of the three packages that made up the total of all their supplies.

He took a mouthful, swallowed, then inhaled deeply. She could tell it hurt because he doubled over and nearly dropped the water container.

"Be careful." She snatched it away from him, hastily reclosing it. "If you spill this, there isn't any more."

"Exactly. We must find more. Help me up, lieutenant."

She looked down at him doubtfully. He had a long, narrow face, the cheekbones high, the chin pointed. His nose was long and straight, his mouth a thinned line of pain. His eyes

were large, their purple-blue depths fringed
by thick black lashes, and above them his
heavy brows were two dark lines across his
pale skin. His hair was blue-black, straight,
and cut a little shorter than her own. He had
the stern look of an ascetic priest of some
ancient religion, yet Narisa thought if he
would only smile, his cold, sharp face would
soften into warm humanity and he would be
quite attractive.

"You should not stand up yet. You should
lie here and rest until you are stronger,
Commander Tarik." Strange how the formal
address lingered, even here on this foresaken
planet. Narisa wondered if they would die
here, still calling each other *commander* and
lieutenant. She shivered at the thought. If
they were the only two humans on this world,
then she would have to try to make a friend of
him. "You may have been more badly injured
than you realize. Have you pain anywhere
else, besides your ribs?"

"My head aches." The blue eyes were fierce.
"And elsewhere, but I'm not going to tell you
where."

"Then you must stay where you are until
you recover." She bit her lower lip, trying
hard not to laugh at him. She could guess
where else he hurt. She had seen him
thrown against the guardrail and then the
bulkhead on the *Reliance*. Did he think she
didn't know how the male body was constructed? Didn't he know that on Belta boys
and girls were schooled together, played all

sports together, and swam naked and unembarrassed in the warm, silvery Beltan rivers?

Narisa was familiar with the male body, though she had seldom gone into quiet corners or leafy glades with boys, as many of her friends had done, and she had never yet found the courage to do the thing the other girls giggled and whispered about, the thing that hurt at first and then felt so wonderful that boys and girls alike wanted to do it over and over again. Narisa had seen how her parents had dealt with each other, and watching them, sensing their deep love, the thing that happened between male and female had seemed to her too solemn and mysterious, too important to be indulged in casually. Someday she would love a man as her mother loved her father, and they would come together in mutual joy that would last all their lives. Until then, she was content to wait. Meanwhile, she had to deal with an irate Commander Tarik, who was determined to disregard her very sensible advice.

"Rest here?" he snarled at her. "Lie broiling in this merciless sun until all the food and water is gone? That would be insanity, lieutenant. If you won't help me, I'll get up by myself."

He pushed himself to his knees, got one leg under him and nearly made it to his feet before he crumpled. Narisa caught him, breaking his fall, but she was driven to her knees by his weight.

"You see, commander? You are too weak."

That angered him. He put a hand on each of her shoulders with such pressure that she thought he would break both shoulders and spine, bearing down hard until he was completely upright. He stood by himself at last, swaying a little, his legs planted wide apart for balance.

"If you fall," Narisa said, brushing off her uniform as she, too, rose, "I won't pick you up again. You are not a very sensible person, *sir*. You are plainly too injured to travel."

"Better injured and trying to walk than dead of dehydration. Is there anything in there I could possibly use for a crutch or cane?" He gestured toward the pod.

"Nothing." Except for the broken and useless navigational instruments and the artificial air system, the pod was molded of one piece of flexible metal with a single movable unit, the entrance hatch, which had been blown off at landing and was nowhere to be seen. "There isn't a thing there we could possibly take with us."

"Then if it becomes necessary, I shall have to lean on you."

They ought to have had a head covering of some kind, but at least their uniforms would protect the rest of their bodies from the heat and the sun. They both wore the standard Service uniform of dark blue jacket and trousers made of a specially formulated material that would keep them warm or cool, whichever was necessary. The only color on the uniforms was the red and silver braid stripes on the

high collars and sleeve cuffs. The four-pointed
star of a lieutenant gleamed gold on Narisa's
upper left arm, the eight-pointed star of a full
commander on Tarik's. Both were shod in
low-heeled black boots. The additional
elements of the uniform, used only for formal
occasions—ornamented belt, wide, red-lined
cape, and silver helmet—were lost with the
Reliance. Narisa regretted only the cape. It
would have made a useful blanket when night
came.

She noticed Tarik was staring at the
horizon, much as she had done earlier,
shading his eyes with one hand.

"Do you see that?" He pointed, but Narisa
could see nothing save the deep blue sky
where it met the desert at the edge of the
world. "I see some green in that direction.
And I thought I saw something moving."

"A bird?" She told him about the one she
had seen earlier, and he nodded, looking
excited.

"If there is something that big living here,
there must be open water. We go that way."
He started walking slowly and none too
steadily. Narisa picked up the food packet,
the water container and the tool kit, and
followed him.

Chapter Two

Tarik had started walking slowly, one arm held tightly across his chest as though to stabilize his rib cage and thus lessen the discomfort he must feel with every movement. But as he continued, he seemed to draw strength from some interior reserve. His steps became longer, firmer, and after the first half hour he was marching steadily along, both arms swinging rhythmically, aiming directly toward the green spot he had claimed to see on the distant horizon. He did not speak at all.

Narisa suspsected he was conserving every bit of his energy for the act of walking, and she wondered how long he could keep it up without dropping. She was almost certain he had sustained other injuries besides his broken ribs. She silently cursed whoever had

removed the medical packet that ought to
have been in the pod. In it there would have
been a diagnostic rod to tell her exactly what
Tarik's injuries were, and how to treat them.

Narisa trudged onward, exactly three paces
behind Tarik, just as Service regulations
required for formal occasions. Commander
first, then Lieutenant Commander, Lieutenant last, that was the order. She stiffled a
giggle.

Never giggle on duty, Lieutenant, she told
herself. It was the sun. She was terribly hot,
and so thirsty she wanted to drain every drop
from the water container slung over her left
shoulder. She yearned to throw herself into a
lake of clear water and float there, her face
shaded by gently arching branches that
dipped silver-green leaves into the water and
gave off a soft fragrance when touched, like
Tarik's body when she had pressed her face
against it. She could almost feel the water on
her parched skin.

So entranced was she by this inner vision
that she did not notice Tarik had stopped until
she bumped into his back. He did not react to
her. He was looking at the sky. Narisa
followed his line of sight. High above them
was a bird, the same one she had seen before,
or one remarkably like it. As they watched,
the bird began a dizzying spiral, flinging itself
downward so fast Narisa thought it would
land on top of them. It pulled out of the spiral
a good thirty space-feet above them, hovering
just long enough for her to notice that the

deep blue feathers of back and wings faded to
a slightly paler shade on throat and breast
before it was gone again, heading in a
direction some forty-five degrees off the
course Tarik had set for himself and Narisa.

"It's so huge," Narisa whispered, awe-
struck. She had seen many kinds of birds
before. They, or similar species, were fairly
common on the inhabited planets, but never
had she been so impressed by feathered grace
and beauty. The wings were large and
obviously very strong, yet delicately scalloped
on their lower edges. The body was sleek and
graceful, and the head was proud, with a
bright, soft eye and an elongated deep blue
beak, which was marred by a jagged scratch
or scar on one side. "When it stands on the
ground, it must be nearly as tall as you or I.
Look, here it comes again."

She was still behind Tarik, very close to
him, and he spoke over his shoulder to her.

"There are two of them. See there."

A second bird had swooped toward them,
flying lower than the first. In the same rich,
lustrous, glowing way that the first bird was
blue, this second one was green. It came
directly at them, skimming only twenty space-
feet or so above the desert floor. Just before it
reached them, it soared upward, flying upside
down for a few moments before righting itself, reversing direction and flying off the way
it had come. Above them the first bird, the
blue one, circled a few times, then followed
the green.

"Guides," Tarik said softly. "They will show us where the water is. This way, lieutenant."

He changed course to follow the birds, and Narisa went with him without argument. Whichever direction he chose, it would make little difference, for the desert seemed unchanging. Narisa glanced back once, but there was nothing to see. The pod and the rock formations near where they had landed had disappeared into the distance.

And still they walked over the baren landscape. The sun remained high overhead, having moved only a few degrees toward the horizon. Narisa began to worry about the length of the day on this planet. With no shade at all, they might well be overcome by sunstroke or dehydration before the day ended. She could tell her face and hands were beginning to burn from the sun. Then, during a long night on the desert with the temperature falling rapidly as she knew it did in most deserts, she and Tarik could freeze to death.

She wanted to speak to him about her fears, but decided if she did, he would probably respond with some caustic remark about her lack of intelligence or her inexperience. She kept quiet. She felt hotter and hotter, and more desperately thirsty than she had ever been before. She could feel the heat of the desert floor through the soles of her boots. She could not continue walking much longer. Just when she thought she would drop and never rise again, Tarik stopped.

"They are coming back," he said, his voice so hoarse that Narisa thought he must be as parched and tired as she was.

There they came, the same two birds, blue and green, racing across the desert at the same low levels as before, swooping past Tarik and Narisa, whirling to circle above their heads three or four times, and then flying back the way they had come.

"They are guiding us," Tarik exclaimed.

"Your wits are addled from the sun and your injuries," Narisa cried. "Birds can't guide people. They aren't intelligent."

"They know we need water. I can feel it. And look, see where we're going. Look at the green ahead of us."

He was right about that much, at least. Narisa could see it, too, now: a definite shimmer of green, and much nearer than the horizon. She had kept her sight on Tarik's heels for so long, trying to shield her eyes from the bright glare of the sun, that she had not looked up to see where they were headed. On a world with an oxygen-nitrogen atmosphere, green meant leaves and grass. And water. She could almost taste it, almost feel it running down her dry throat. In her present situation the thought was unbearable.

"Tarik," she gasped, forgetting formality, "I am going to rest here. I need water right now. And food. You do, too."

She sat on the ground and broke open the food packet, extracting two compressed wafers for herself and two for him. He looked annoyed at first, then took the wafers, and a moment later accepted the water container, too. He remained standing while she ate. She drank from the container, taking more water than she should have, but she could not help herself. Every cell of her body cried out for moisture.

"Don't drink it all," he warned when she lifted it to her lips again. "It will be a while yet before we get more."

"Why don't you sit, Commander Tarik?" she countered, her spirits revived a little by the refreshment. "Are you afraid if you do, you won't be able to get up again?"

"I am impatient to be on our way," he responded, frowning at her. "I am merely waiting for you to finish resting."

"I've finished." She rose quickly, completely aware that his words had been meant to produce just that reaction. Somewhere inside her a small, honest voice admitted that without Tarik's verbal prodding she might well have stayed where she was, letting her aching, exhausted body tell her to rest in spite of the clear chance of reaching shade and fresh water. She could easily have died there sitting in the sun, leaving her bleached bones scattered over the desert. Heat or no, Narisa shivered at the thought, and when Tarik started walking again, she followed him gladly.

They were still a good distance away from that lovely green area ahead, but once they resumed their trek, having the goal in sight gave them renewed energy. They kept going.

The birds returned periodically, sometimes one, sometimes both. Narisa still did not believe they were acting as guides. No bird she had ever heard of could be that intelligent, but this seemed their only chance of survival. Besides, she recognized she was no longer thinking clearly. Perhaps Tarik wasn't, either.

After a while the ground began to change in character. First there were patches of dry, desiccated vegetation, dusty and gray and stunted, pushing up through the stones and gravel of the desert floor. Then they were walking through low bushes interspersed with clumps of grasses. As they went on there were more and more grasses, until they were ploughing their way through a savannah thickly overgrown with knee-high grass, and the few bushes they saw had green leaves and some even had berries. Ahead were the trees, green and cool, beckoning them onward. There was still no sign of open water.

"Underground," Narisa muttered. "It's all underground. We'll never find it." Tarik did not answer her.

They were both at the end of their strength by this time, stumbling through the grasses, thinking only of those alluring trees, not so far away now, shade and shadow and respite for burning eyes and aching heads.

They were there; they had made it. Tarik was bent over, hands on his knees, gasping for breath, while Narissa clung to a tree to hold herself upright.

"I told you," Tarik rejoiced, "told you they'd bring us to water."

"Where? Where is it?" She could hardly speak. She had never been so tired before in her entire life.

"Listen. Over there." He flung out one hand.

It was true; she could hear the sound of a stream trickling over rocks and tree roots. Narisa pushed away from the tree and staggered toward the sound. It was farther away than she had thought, but she finally found it, clean and cool and edged with golden moss. She stood looking at it, hesitating.

Tarik was right behind her. He did not waste a moment; he simply dropped flat on the moss, put his face down into the water and began to drink.

"No, wait." She pulled at the hem of his uniform jacket.

"What?" he spluttered. "Why wait? Drink, Narissa. Drink."

"How do we know it's safe? It could kill us."

"The birds brought us here. They wouldn't have brought us to bad water."

"Commander Tarik, that is the silliest reason I have ever heard for doing something potentially dangerous. It is not sensible to drink unknown water."

"Then don't. Die of thirst if you want." He put his head back into the stream, while Narisa stood watching him. When he finally took his dripping face out of the water and sat on the bank, wiping one sleeve across his chin, she dropped into a squat beside him.

"Commander, regulations clearly state that on a strange planet, all unknown food or drink

should be carefully tested before being
swallowed."

"Regulations don't matter in the Empty
Sector," he told her with simple logic. "The
writ of the Assembly does not run here. I for
one am glad of it. A planet on which sensible
regulations do not apply. Delightful."

Narisa looked from him to the tempting
water, and back again, not certain how long
she could hold out against her body's desperate craving for liquid. She was so thirsty, so
very thirsty. Still, she had been well trained
by the Service.

"Look there." Tarik pointed downstream. A
small creature had come to the stream to
drink, an oval shape of lavender-gray fur with
large round ears and six legs, and a lavender
tongue that lapped up the water fearlessly. "I
have drunk and am still alive. That animal
drinks and lives. You can drink without fear."

"That animal lives here," she responded
stubbornly.

"So do you, now. Drink, Narisa. That's an
order. If my ribs didn't hurt so badly, I'd push
you in. Drink, I said."

Regulations required one to obey a superior
officer. Narisa lowered her head to the
stream and began to drink. Then she put her
whole head in, feeling the sweet coolness on
face and scalp. She sat back at last, and
enjoyed the way the moisture from her hair
dripped down her back under her uniform.

"Feeling better?" Tarik sat propped against
a tree trunk, watching her.

"Yes. Sorry I was so rude before," she added, recalling her earlier decision to try to make a friend of him. "I wanted to drink, but I was afraid."

"I know. You weren't yourself. All that heat out there." He gestured back toward the edge of the forest, toward the desert's glare. "I've seen it before—starving men who wouldn't eat, freezing men who won't put on a cloak, something in the mind that won't adjust to sudden new circumstances. Like those in the Capital, never wanting anything to change."

She decided to disregard that last treasonous remark, since for the first time he was showing appreciation for her feelings. She sat down beside him.

"Commander Tarik?"

"Hmmm, yes." He was looking into the green depths surrounding them.

"You don't really think those birds led us here, do you?"

"It seemed to me they were trying to communicate something. We did find water."

She started to say it wasn't very likely that birds would try to communicate with them, but she was too tired to argue the point. She did not for a moment believe the birds had any interest in them other than an instinctive curiosity in case she or Tarik were edible or dangerous. Let Tarik believe what he wanted. The birds were gone now. She voiced her primary concern.

"We have to get back to the Capital. It is our duty to report to the Assembly what has happened to the *Reliance*. How are we going to do that, Commander Tarik?"

"I don't know. Are there any more food wafers in that package? You see," he told her gravely, "I am now following regulations. Until we know what food is safe, I will confine my eating to these tasteless things. Or until we run out of wafers and I get hungry. Then I may start experimenting."

"Perhaps we'll find a settlement before then."

"Of what? Humans? Cetans? Some other species, known or unknown? Or perhaps we are here alone, the only ones on a deserted planet."

"Don't forget your birds," she said between bites of wafer. "Or that thing, whatever it was, that drank from the stream. There must be other life forms here, and some of them may be intelligent. We must find a settlement. You need medical care. You look feverish to me."

Tarik slid down from his position against the tree to lie flat on the soft moss.

"I'm tired," he said. "You, Lieutenant, may follow regulations and keep watch, or you may sleep, too, whichever you like. It's pleasant here. I've had enough to drink and a little food to content my belly until I find something better. 'A loaf of bread, a jug of wine, and thou beside me in the wilderness . . .' "

Narisa glanced at him sharply, but his eyes were closed, and he seemed to be asleep. She

was certain, after that speech, that he had lost
his wits, and no wonder, considering the
events of this long, strange day. Well, the day
must be nearly over at last, for it seemed to
her the shadows were lengthening. She would
let Tarik rest for now, and when morning
came she would try to find help for him, and
some way to communicate with their
superiors at the Capital.

She drank from the stream again, then sat
peering into the increasing darkness. The
forest was quiet except for the ripple of the
stream and the gentle rustling of the leaves
far above their heads as a soft breeze skimmed
by.

Tarik was right, it was pleasant here. Too
pleasant for the Empty Sector. It would have
been sensible of her to be on guard, even
afraid, in such a place as this. But Narisa had
no feeling of danger at all, no fear, and she
was tired of always being sensible. It was nice
to relax and enjoy the peacefulness of the
forest.

How long she sat there, she did not know.
Slowly a gentle drowsiness stole over her.
Several times she caught herself nodding into sleep. She stretched out, lying on the moss,
which she discovered made a wonderfully
soft bed, and after a while her eyes closed.

She awakened from a sweet and remarkably realistic dream of home and parents and
sister to find herself huddled against Tarik
with one of his arms under her head. It

seemed to her it must be early morning, for a
few shafts of pale orange sunlight filtered
through the thick, leafy boundaries of the tiny
clearing where they lay, and a faint mist
curled upward from the stream. The air was
chilly enough to make her shiver and move
closer to Tarik as she sought to return to her
lovely dream.

   She had lost the dream. It was gone forever.
Perhaps it was because of Tarik's nearness.
Something about him disturbed her still
partially drowsy consciousness. In the coolness of the morning, he was much too warm.
In fact, he was feverishly hot. All thought of
returning to sleep vanished. She touched his
flushed cheek. He tossed his head from side to
side, muttering broken phrases that made no
sense to her. The fear she had not felt last night
flooded over her, not for herself, but for him.
She might not like him, but he was a fellow
human, and if he died, she would be alone on
this strange world. She could not let him die,
for his sake and her own.

   "Commander Tarik, wake up. Oh, please,
please, wake up."

   He opened fever-glazed eyes, looking at her
blankly, and she knew he did not recognize
her.

   "But soft," he murmured, "an angel comes
here."

   "Commander Tarik!" She drew back in surprise, her voice a little sharper than she had
intended.

   "Sweet lady, curse me not. I am ill and like
to die." He dropped back into the feverish

sleep from which she had roused him.

"What's wrong with you?" she cried. "I knew you were hurt worse than you would admit. Now what am I to do with you? I don't know where to get help, and I can't carry you, even if I did know where to go."

She sat there on the moss, trying to recall every bit of medical information she had received while in training for the Service. But it had all been about emergency treatment until a doctor was available, and it depended upon equipment she did not have. Narisa had almost never been sick. She did not remember what her mother had done for her when she was young and ill, and the few minor ailments she had suffered after going to the Capital to join the Service had been cured quickly, in a matter of minutes, with the latest treatments. What did one do with a sick man and no medicine?

Tarik thrashed about in some feverish nightmare, crying out loudly as he hurt his broken ribs. She touched his forehead. He was on fire with fever. Narisa had not felt so frustrated since she had received the news that her parents had been killed.

"I will not cry," she said aloud, as she had said on that terrible day. "Tears are a sign of weakness. I will find a way to fight this, and I will win. I will."

Water would put out a fire. She could put water on Tarik's face and torso. Perhaps that would help to douse the fever. She stripped off her uniform jacket. Beneath it she wore the regulation undergarment of all females in

the Service. This was a cream-colored shirt,
scoop-necked and sleeveless, made of a
stretchable fabric that molded the body
closely and supported the breasts. The
material was absorbent, as the heavier outer
jacket was not. Narisa pulled it off and soaked
it in the stream, holding it in the cold water
until it was saturated. Then she wrung it out
and brought it back to Tarik. She brushed the
straight black hair off his hot forehead and
laid the shirt across it, wrapping the ends
down around his cheeks and chin.

"Cool," he muttered. "So sweet."

She unfastened his jacket. She doubted she
could get it completely off in his present
condition, but she could open it and put cool
water on his chest and abdomen. The safety
harness from the pod was still wrapped about
his ribs. Narisa checked it, lifting the elastic
straps at several places. It did not seem to be
too tight, and the bruised skin under it
appeared to be unchanged in color, so she left
it in place.

The cloth around his face was warm already. She took it back to the stream to soak it
again. After she had replaced it on his head,
she opened his trousers and slid them down
on his hips to expose his abdomen.

Tarik was not as obviously muscular as
many men, but his body was sleek and trim.
She recalled his endurance of the day before,
how, injured though he was, he had led them
across that endless desert, made her go on
when she would have stopped, and with a

faith and determination she had not shared
had brought them to a safe resting place.
Strength, Narisa decided, did not necessarily
mean muscular bulk. His body was beautiful,
the skin unblemished and smooth. She ran
one hand along his side, from chest to waist to
flank, momentarily engrossed in admiration
and something else, something that began to
stir deep inside her. The only flaw she could
find was the injury covered by the harness.
Then he moaned again, and she withdrew her
hand with a guilty start and hurried to put
more cold water on his forehead.

It did not trouble her that she was undressed above the waist. On her home planet
of Belta, the human body was considered
beautiful, and children were allowed to run
about half-dressed during warm weather. She
had grown up unhampered by any sense of
shame about nakedness, and not until she had
joined the Service and met members of Races
from other planets had she realized that other
people might feel differently.

She took a few moments to splash water on
her face and shoulders before moving upstream to a quiet pool to drink. There she saw
her face imperfectly reflected in the deep
water. She did not need to see it exactly. As
she knew her own body, so she knew her face.
She had strong features to go with her tall,
strong body. Her face was oval, the skin
flushed to a rosy tan from the previous day in
the sun. Her mouth was wide, with firm lips,
her nose straight but a little too long, her eyes

a cool gray with golden flecks. Her hair, a
warm golden brown several shades lighter
than brows and lashes, was worn parted in
the middle and clipped straight all around
just below her ears. Service regulations
ordered that style.

Straight hair, straight nose, level eyes, strong
body, honest mind and heart, all trained to Service regulations. Willingly. Gladly. Straight,
straight, straight. A good officer. A superb, if
somewhat inexperienced navigator with
brilliant potential.

With her family dead on Belta, she had
dedicated herself to the Service. She knew one
day they would meet the Cetans in open warfare and win. Her family would be avenged. In
the meantime she gave all she had to her
work, to her navigational studies. She
adhered rigidly to all Service regulations,
forcing her once free spirit into strict self-
discipline, not letting herself consider the
questions about the Service, or the Assembly,
which occasionally came unbidden to her
mind. She had always pushed such questions
and the doubts they raised out of her thoughts
with ease. She had tried to make herself into a
perfect Service officer, and she had almost
succeeded. Sighing, she stirred the water with
one hand, breaking up the image of Lieutenant Navigator Narisa raDon, and bent her
head to drink.

Tarik lay burning with fever for the rest of
the day, and Narisa spent her time sponging

him with her dampened shirt. Her efforts
made no difference that she could detect. He
did not know her. When he spoke, it was to
utter strange rhyming phrases she could not
understand. Since he was an expert in
languages, Narisa assumed he was speaking
in some of the many tongues he knew.

So intent was she on lowering his body
temperature that she was only dimly aware of
the passage of time. She sensed rather than
saw that the orange sun had risen to its
zenith. Here beneath the thick canopy of
leaves sunlight penetrated only in scattered
shafts of orange-gold light, and where the
underbrush was thickest, dark shadows persisted.

Thus it was that she did not see their
companion at first. She took her undershirt
off Tarik's chest and carried it to the stream,
once more to cool it and wring it out. As she
walked the few steps back to him, she per-
ceived a flicker of movement among the
bushes at one side of the clearing. She looked
in that direction, but saw nothing.

"Rustling leaves," she told herself,
rejecting the first stirrings of fear. "Good. If a
breeze comes up, it will help to cool Tarik."

She laid the cloth across his abdomen,
remembering how, when she was swimming,
cold water on her belly chilled her whole
body. Perhaps it would work for Tarik, too.

She leaned back. Reaching behind her without looking, she drew forward and opened the
package of compressed food. She took out the

two wafers that made up a complete meal, then put one of them back. She was hungry, she hadn't eaten since the previous evening, but she felt she should conserve their supplies. They might be without food for some time, and if he recovered, Tarik would no doubt need plenty of nourishment to regain the strength he had lost to fever and injury. She laid the food package aside, preparing to eat the single wafer.

It was then that she became certain she was not alone. Someone or something, some unknown presence, had moved from the bushes to stand directly behind her, looking over her shoulder at Tarik. Narisa turned, and then stopped, half sitting, half kneeling, the food wafer still clutched in her right hand. Stunned, she looked up at the creature who stood there.

It was the green one, an emerald splendor of a bird, its rich, thick feathers gleaming in the dim light. Its shining black eyes were fixed on Tarik. Its long green beak was slightly parted, enough for Narisa to see that it had teeth, neat rows of them, top and bottom. They gave the creature a sinister look.

Leaping to her feet, Narisa took a defensive posture between the bird and Tarik. The bird was nearly as tall as she was, and she was terrified of it, but she tried to cover her fear with angry words.

"Leave him alone," she shrieked. "He's not dead yet. You can't have him, or me either. Go away, you monster!"

Lacking any other weapon, she threw the wafer of compressed food at the bird. The bird caught the wafer in its beak in midair, then laid it carefully on the ground at Narisa's feet. The delicacy and control in that action stopped her incipient panic. She stood silently while the bird looked from her to Tarik and back again. If this creature wanted to kill them both, it could do so easily with either its beak or its large clawed feet. Yet now she was over her first fright, she could see there was nothing menacing in the bird's attitude. It was simply curious about them. Narisa thought she must be going mad to believe such a thing, but believe it she did. The realization lay firmly in her mind: This bird would not harm them.

Behind Narisa's guardian's back, Tarik tossed and moaned.

"He's sick," Narisa said. "He may die, and I don't know what to do. Why couldn't you have been an intelligent life form?"

The bird looked directly at her, cocking its head, then turned away. As it did so, one of its wings brushed against her bare arms and hands. The contact lasted only an instant, and when it was broken, Narisa felt an almost uncontrollable urge to put out both hands and touch the bird again. She did not, for she had just seen something she had not noticed while the bird stood quietly with folded wings. Now the wings were open, and Narisa could see that at the last joint on each wing there were three clawed fingers, which were separate from the wing itself and clearly capable of independent

movement. It seemed to her that the bird had
the bones for three more fingers, but those
were incorporated into the last segment of each
wing. She had ample opportunity to look, for
both wings were fully spread as the bird flew
to a branch of a nearby tree and, using the
three fingers on one wing, plucked a yellow-
green fruit. it flew back to land close to
Tarik and laid the fruit next to his head.

"What are you doing?" Narisa cried. It did
not seem at all strange to be talking to a bird.
This was like no bird she had ever seen
before, and much of her earlier fear of it had
dissipated.

Tarik turned his head toward the bird, his
eyes closed, moaning from pain and fever.
The bird bent down, and using its beak, gently
pushed the fruit toward Tarik's mouth.

"You want him to eat it?" Narisa had begun
to understand the bird's purpose. "But he's
sick. He can't eat."

"Chon," the bird said. "Chon-chon. Chon."

The sound was so sudden and unexpected
that Narisa stumbled backward a pace or
two. The bird waited. Narisa moved forward
again, and kneeling beside Tarik, picked up
the fruit.

"I wonder what it is?" she murmured,
turning the smooth yellow-green globe over in
her hands. It was perfectly round, with no
markings at all except the stem, and it fit
easily into her palm. "How do you eat it? Is it
safe?"

It contained juice. That knowledge lay as

solidly in her mind as had the earlier belief
that the bird would not hurt her. Juice. Tarik
needed liquid. The high fever was burning off
the fluids in his body, Narisa knew that much.
She had tried bringing him water cupped in a
large leaf, but he had refused to take it. Perhaps
he would drink the juice contained in this fruit.
Might it harm him? Did she dare feed him an
untested food?

She barely hesitated. Tarik was going to die
soon anyway. She might as well ignore
Service regulations and take the risk.

She found the knife in the tool kit and carefully cut a hole in the fruit. The smooth skin
was thick, and she had to press the knife hard.
When she finally got through to the liquid
center of the fruit, some of the juice spurted
out onto her hands. She brought a finger to
her lips. It tasted tangy, refreshing, unlike
anything she had ever encountered before.
Just the few drops that had touched her
tongue made her feel happier, more hopeful.

She sat beside Tarik, lifted his head onto
her knee, and when he opened his mouth to
groan, she poured a little of the juice into him.
He choked at first, then swallowed it, and she
gave him some more. Nothing happened.

"How will I know how much to give him?"
Narisa asked the bird, who stood quietly
watching her. Tarik opened his mouth as if
asking for more, and she poured the rest of
the juice into his mouth. The fruit was empty.
Narisa set it on the ground and cradled
Tarik's head in her arms, hoping she had not

killed him. She smoothed his hair, then laid her cheek against the top of his head, wondering what would happen next.

She had disobeyed Service regulations repeatedly, drinking untested water, treating a sick man when she had no medical knowledge, and now feeding him some mysterious fruit juice. She could be court-martialed and imprisoned for the things she had done in the last two days, yet the breaking of so many of the rules to which she had held so firmly for ten space-years was now unimportant. The Service to which she was dedicated, the Capital and the Assembly, Belta and the Cetans, were all part of a distant past that scarcely mattered at all in this strange new place. She still had sense enough to recognize what was happening to her.

"The fruit," she whispered to the watching bird. "It's the juice, isn't it? I only tasted a drop or two, and I'm so relaxed and sleepy I can't stay awake any longer. What will it do to Tarik? He had most of it. I've killed him. He was my responsibility, and I've killed him."

Chapter Three

Narisa wakened to find herself huddled against Tarik. It must be morning. The sun was still low, and a few shafts of pale orange sunlight filtered through the trees. Beyond her feet she could see wisps of mist drifting up from the stream. She stretched, feeling Tarik's comfortable warmth next to her, and turned over, pressing her back against his side. She sighed contentedly. She felt remarkably well for a woman who had trekked across a burning desert only a day ago.

No, not a day ago. She sat up. She had done this before, wakened in just this spot, and Tarik had been burning with fever, and she had tried to help him, and then had given him something . . . and killed him.

She looked down at the man beside her. He lay sleeping peacefully, his straight dark hair

tousled, his pale features untouched by any
feverish flush. He looked completely healthy.
His uniform jacket was open and her regulation undershirt was draped across his
abdomen just above his loosened trousers.

She glanced anxiously around the little
clearing. It was empty. Her eyes fell on an
uneaten compressed food wafer and a
smooth, yellow-green fruit.

"Narisa?" Tarik was awake.

"Are you . . . how do you feel?" she asked in
a trembling voice.

"Quite well. Why do you ask?"

"You were sick. You had a terrible fever. I
thought you would die."

"I don't remember." He stretched, then
rubbed his left side. "My ribs ache a little. I do
remember you wrapping them, but that was
back at the pod. Why are you undressed?" He
was gazing at her in open admiration, his
dark eyes lingering over her creamy
shoulders and softly swelling breasts.

Narisa, who had never felt shame at her
own nakedness before, began to blush. It
started somewhere down in her belly, and she
could feel it sweeping upward in a crimson
flood infusing her face and tingling her scalp.
Under that surging tide of hot blood she was
powerless to move or speak or even to think
clearly. She could only let him look his fill.

Tarik lifted his right hand and placed it
upon her left breast, cupping it gently, his
thumb flicking across the sensitive nipple.
Narisa drew in her breath, still immobilized.

"How lovely," Tarik murmured, pressing his hand a little more firmly against her flesh.

Narisa felt a sweet warmth curling inside her. She wanted to remain there, sitting beside him, with his hand on her breast, stroking it. She saw his left hand begin to move and knew he was going to catch her head and pull her down to him and kiss her. Her bare breasts would be crushed against his chest, his mouth would be on hers. The thought frightened her, and with that fear came release from the inertia that had held her in one spot while he caressed her.

With an inarticulate cry she leapt to her feet, snatched up her crumpled undershirt from his abdomen, her jacket from the base of a nearby tree, and fled the clearing. Taking long, deep breaths to quiet her pounding heart, she made her way through the forest to the pool she had found the day before.

It really had been the day before. She remembered all of it now. Every detail of that day came rushing back as she threw cold water onto her face and tried to scrub the touch of Tarik's hand off her skin. She was certain the juice from the mysterious fruit had caused her memory loss. It had had the same effect on Tarik. Fortunately, the loss was only temporary, and the fruit had apparently cured his injuries as well as his fever.

Having finished her washing, she dressed hastily, combing her hair with her fingers, tucking her damp undershirt into her trousers with a determined tug, pulling on and fastening her jacket with practiced efficiency. Back at the pod she had pulled off the top clasp at the neckline of the jacket and used it to fasten the wrapping about Tarik's ribs, nevertheless she knew she presented a professional appearance when at last she stepped into the clearing.

She found Tarik sitting indolently against a tree trunk, investigating the contents of the food packet. His jacket was still opened down the front, but she noticed that he had pulled up and fastened his trousers, and he had obviously washed his face, for his hair showed wet around the edges.

"Commander Tarik, I must tell you what happened yesterday," Narisa announced, standing at rigid attention.

"Sit down and eat," he invited, gesturing at the golden moss beside him.

"I prefer to stand while making a report," she stated stiffly.

"If I frightened you before, Lieutenant, I apologize," he said gravely. "I do not usually ravish the officers under my command."

"I quite understand, sir," Narisa responded. "You are still a sick man."

"Undoubtedly that explains it." His face was serious, but there was an odd twinkle in the purplish depths of his eyes. "Well, then, Lieutenant, make your report so you can eat."

Narisa watched him, disturbed. He was so relaxed and comfortable, munching on a wafer, leaning his head back against the tree trunk. He wasn't even looking at her. His eyes were on a pale blue winged thing that came fluttering across the stream and began flying around in circles between them. When it got too close to her, Narisa sidestepped it. Tarik put out one finger, and the thing perched on it a moment, before flying off into the bushes behind the tree.

"What is that?" Narisa asked. "I've never seen anything like it before."

"It's a butterfly," Tarik said, bemused. "There are none on Belta, nor would you have seen any at the Capital, or on any of the other developed planets. Lovely, isn't it? And remarkable, too. It begins life as an insignificant worm, only later growing into the magnificent creature you just saw."

"A worm? I'm not sure that's possible." Narisa sounded as confused as she felt. It wasn't just the butterfly, it was Tarik, too. He was not behaving like his usual self, and certainly not like an officer of the Service.

"If I explained it, you wouldn't believe me." Tarik dismissed the butterfly with a shrug. "Let me hear your report, Lieutenant."

Standing at attention, using the clipped, brief phrases she had been taught were the correct form for official reports, Narisa recited the events of the previous day.

"Have you finished?" Tarik asked when she stopped. She had given him the fruit when she talked about it, and he sat holding it, turning it over and over in his long fingers.

"Yes, sir."

"First, I want to thank you for saving my life a second time. I have no doubt I'd be dead by now if you hadn't tended me so well. But do be careful, Lieutenant Narisa. Save me a third time, and according to Demarian custom, you will own me. Have you ever been to Demaria? No? It's an interesting place.

"Next, will you please sit down? We have a lot to discuss, and it hurts my neck to keep looking up at you. Besides, it's bad for discipline to have you looking down upon your superior officer. Here, have some food. It tastes awful, but it's nourishing." When Narisa did not move, he added, "Well, what else have you to say? I thought your report was done."

"If you will forgive the impertinence, sir, I must state that your appearance is slovenly. There is a very sharp knife in the tool kit, surely you could use it to shave yourself. Then you ought to fasten your jacket. Secondly, your attitude is most unprofessional. There are Service regulations for situations like this, when one finds oneself on an unknown world. But you sit lolling against a tree, joking about discipline. You must recall that our first duty is to find some way to communicate with the Capital. Then we must—"

"I liked you better with your jacket off," he said.

Narisa stared at him, shocked.

Suddenly, inexplicably, he began to laugh. Before this day Narisa had never seen Tarik smile or heard him make a joke, but there he sat, holding his sides and roaring with laughter. The sound echoed around the clearing, while laughter continued to pour out of him and tears ran down his cheeks. It was a long time before he stopped and wiped his eyes.

"Woman," he said, still chuckling, "you function like the memory banks of a spaceship. Everything is done precisely, correctly, according to regulations, and no deviations are permitted. Ever."

"Sir." Narisa's spine was stiff, her chin high. She kept her expression blank, not letting her rising anger show. She told herself she ought not to be angry with him. He had been sick, and now he was clearly mad, and she would have to cope with that problem as best she could.

"Lieutenant," Tarik said, his mirth apparently under control, "sit down. Here, next to me. That is an order. Now, take these two wafers and eat them. That is another order."

He watched as she silently obeyed him.

"In spite of your *un*slovenly appearance and highly professional attitute," he went on, his lips twisting into a quickly repressed smile, "I do believe you are human and not the machine you appear to be. If the story you have told me is true, you admit to breaking a few rules yourself."

"Only because I feared you would die."

"It's comforting to know you are willing to

bend for my sake. Now, I want you to tell me once more everything you remember about that bird."

Narisa went over the story again, including every detail she could recall.

"The bird made no effort to communicate with you, no sound at all except for that one cry?"

"That's right, sir."

"Yet you knew, it was quite clear to you deep in your mind, that the creature meant us no harm, and later that there was juice in the fruit and it was safe for you to give it to me."

"Yes, sir."

"While I, out on the desert, was perfectly certain, deep in my own mind, that the birds would lead us to water. What does all this suggest to you, Lieutenant?"

"That we are very fortunate, sir."

"You disappoint me. I suppose I should have expected a lack of imagination. You can't help it, it's the way you were trained. I have a different theory. I think the birds have telepathic power." He watched her reaction, a glimmer of humor in his eyes. "Any comment on that, Lieutenant?"

"Are you suggesting those creatures are intelligent?"

"Haven't they been acting intelligently?"

"I would say it was instinct." She was determined to resist his idea.

"Indeed?" A cynical glint replaced the humor in his gaze. "Helping an unfamiliar species is instinctive behavior? Not in any

Race I've ever encountered. Why do you find
it necessary to resist my theory, lieutenant?"

The question took her by surprise. She
could almost have imagined he had strange
powers and had read her mind.

"Because," she said, "telepathy is illegal."

"I doubt the birds know that," he responded
dryly. "They have probably never had contact
with the Service, or the Assembly, or any of
the idiotic laws of the Jurisdiction."

"It's not only illegal, it's immoral," Narisa
insisted. "And for very good reason. Telepathy invades the mind of another being, and
that is immoral. All Races practicing telepathy were outlawed space-centuries ago and
their representatives banished from the
Assembly."

"Of course," Tarik countered mildly, "they
had to be banished. Because of their abilities
they were too well aware of what those in
power were trying to do. Telepaths would be
dangerous to those regulations you love so
much, and which the Assembly imposes on all
of us. And the Service, which was originally
formed solely to keep the peace, too often
uses certain of its branches to repress dissent.
Telepaths would understand that, too, and
perhaps protest and insist upon changes.
Change is terribly upsetting to the Assembly."

"Commander Tarik, I believe you are
speaking treason."

"I'm talking about freedom, Narisa. The
right to decide the simplest things for yourself. What, when and where to eat. Or read. Or

live. Or work, whether in space or on some planet. Have you never been free?"

"On Belta, when I was a child, I did as I pleased." Narisa was becoming very distressed by this conversation. Tarik was saying things that had occasionally crossed her mind, things she had always thrust away from conscious thought, finding them unworthy of a loyal officer of the Service.

"You were free as a child, yet you left Belta to join the Service. Why?" Tarik demanded, and Narisa, trained to truth, answered honestly.

"For my father. He wanted a son, but he had been assigned to Belta, and on Belta choice of gender for a child is not permitted. So he had two daughters. I chose to join the Service, to become a navigator to please him. To make him proud of me."

"Was it what you wanted to do? Are you proud of yourself?"

"Of course." She could not tell him the entire truth, that she had not known what she wanted to do and had never had the chance to think about it. She had obeyed always, wanting her father's approval. She obeyed still, following all regulations to the smallest detail. "I am a good officer," she insisted.

"You are the best navigator I have ever met," Tarik agreed. "But you do leave something to be desired when you are faced with totally new circumstances."

Before Narsia could protest, he raised one hand. "I'll call back some of what I just said.

You handled yesterday's emergencies remarkably well. Perhaps there is hope for you. Do you know why Belta is called Belta?"

"No, sir." She wondered where this change of subject would lead.

"It was originally Beltane," Tarik informed her. "The first settlers there many space-centuries ago claimed to be descendants of the Druids of Old Earth. The twin volcanoes erupting at each solstice reminded them of the ancient Beltane fires once lit on Earth, and so they named the planet. It was later corrupted to Belta."

"I've never heard that story before," Narisa said.

"You wouldn't know of it. It's not part of the approved history that the Races are taught. Change history and you change reality."

"I've never heard of these Druid people, either." Narisa was becoming angry at what he was suggesting.

"Of course not," he told her slyly. "Some of them with telepaths. Their descendants were forced to leave Belta after the Act of Banishment, and a new Race settled the planet. A Race with no unfortunate tendency toward telepathy."

There followed a deep silence.

"So we come back to the birds." Narisa had finally found her voice again.

"And to the fact that we are in the Empty Sector, on an unknown planet where Jurisdiction laws do not apply."

"I see. This has all been a lecture, some kind of lesson for me."

"Make of it what you will. Think about what I've said. Keep an open mind and follow your instincts, not the rules you were taught at the Capital." He caught her chin in one hand, holding her face steady to look directly into her eyes. "How very young you are, Narisa. How innocent."

"I am twenty-six space-years old," she declared.

"And I am thirty-two, and a thousand space-years older than you in experience." He released her and stood up. "It's time to go."

"Go where?"

"Where duty calls, of course. To find a place where we can communicate with the Capital, if such a place exists here. Fill the water container, Lieutenant, we may need it later. I'll take the food and the tool kit."

"Are you well enough to travel?" she asked, watching him rub at his ribs.

"Almost completely well, thanks to your good care and the bird's medicine. There is just a little pain in my side, and that will disappear soon. Ready? Then follow me."

Narisa had no quarrel with the direction he had chosen. He headed downstream, and that made good sense. A stream was likely to run into a river eventually, and a river into a lake or sea. If there were intelligent beings on this world, chances were they would inhabit areas near water. So said the Service manual written for those who visited unknown planets. Narisa had memorized it, as she had memorized everything given to her study during her training. She had an excellent memory, and was proud of her ability to recall the most obscure details. That was one reason why she was such a fine navigator. Even Tarik had said she was the best he had ever known.

She frowned, thinking of the other things he had said. She had been aware that there existed a large body of knowledge to which she, along with most other people, had not been given access. It had never bothered her because she had not needed any of it to do her job. Immersed in navigational charts, astrophysical computations and the latest course-setting instruments, she had convinced herself that what she did not know was unimportant. Now she began to wonder about all the things she had never learned.

She blew an errant lock of hair out of her eyes. While it was not as unbearably hot under the trees as it had been on the desert, it was still warm, and much more humid. Delicate red-winged insects darted here and there. She swatted at several, feeling irritable. She did not want to think about uncomfortable subjects. She wanted to get safely back to the Capital and be reassigned to another spaceship, to the life she had prepared for and accepted.

And enjoyed? a small voice in her heart asked relentlessly. No, she told herself, enjoyment had nothing to do with it. She was pledged to duty. The uneasy question was

Commander Tarik's fault. He had a way of
shaking her resolution with his artfully in-
sidiously suggestions.

Tarik. A walking puzzle. A man from an
important family who had attained high rank
in the Service, who freely spoke treasonous
thoughts. Under normal circumstances she
would have continued to avoid him as she had
done aboard ship. And yet, thrown together as
they were, he became more and more interesting, the disturbing things he said only increasing his peculiar appeal. As for the way
he had touched her as though she belonged to
him, she could not think of that without beginning to blush again while her blood raced
through her veins.

She watched him just ahead of her as he led
the way along the stream. He paused, holding
back a stocky bush so Narisa could squeeze
between it and the edge of the water.

"Have you noticed the odd assortment of
growing things?" he asked.

"No, I haven't." Squeezing by the bush
meant brushing against Tarik. When she
slipped a little on a patch of mud, he caught
her arm to steady her, drawing her closer.
Narisa caught a whiff of the body scent that
had so dazzled her while she had wrapped his
broken ribs, a fragrance compounded of sun-
shine and green leaves.

She pulled away from Tarik and stepped
onto a flat rock that overhung the stream. He
joined her and stood looking into the thick
growth surrounding them.

"Look there," he said, pointing. "That kind of tree once grew on Earth, and those, too, I think. Those over there are giant Demarian ferns, and that triangular bluish-green plant is from Ceta. There are others I recognize from other planets." He named a few, and Narisa followed his pointing finger to look at each in turn. Then he stood watching her expectantly.

"How can they all be growing on one planet?" she asked. When he did not answer at once, she found the explanation herself. "It's unlikely they would all grow here naturally. Someone must have brought them here."

"And?" He was watching her the way her favorite teacher used to do, waiting until she worked out the problem in her own mind and found the solution for herself.

"That means there are intelligent life forms here." She paused, looking at the tall trees. "Or once there were. Those trees have been growing for a long time. But if the people who planted them are still here, it means our chance of finding someone with communications equipment is fairly good."

"Can't you just enjoy the journey?" he asked. "Narisa, look around you. Are you blind and deaf?"

"I've been on guard, Commander Tarik." That was not entirely true. She had been thinking, and not paying much attention to where they were going. It was the journey's end that interested her.

"Being on guard means being observant." Tarik caught her shoulders and pushed her to the edge of the rock. She knew he was annoyed with her and briefly she thought he was going to throw her into the stream, but instead he held her at the very brink and made her look into the water. "Tell me what you see," he commanded.

"Water. And rocks. A few green things growing in the water. That's all," she said stubbornly. But something caught her eye. "Wait, what's that? That silvery thing, there by the round stone."

"Fish. There are schools of them in every quiet pool," Tarik told her, and turned her to look elsewhere. "See there? It's one of those creatures we saw the first evening, the little furry thing with six legs. I don't know what it is, but it seems harmless enough. And see that vine draped over the stream from one tree to another? We could use those yellow flowers for drinking cups, except they're too beautiful to destroy. And the blue butterflies, have you noticed them? I've seen at least a dozen."

"I haven't noticed any," Narisa admitted.

"Open your eyes, woman. This is an incredibly lovely world. I'm beginning to think someone deliberately planted it this way."

"Who? For what purpose? To trick us? Don't forget, we are in the Empty Sector, Commander Tarik."

"I haven't forgotten. I'm on guard as much as you are, but that doesn't stop me from delighting in the things I see here."

"There might be large predators." Narisa eyed the thick forest before them. "Or the birds might come back."

"I hope they do. Let's stop for a while, shall we?" Tarik dropped to sit on the rock, sliding off the straps of the packages he had been carrying over one shoulder. He pulled off his boots, rolled up his trouser legs and stuck his feet into the water. Then he took off his jacket and dumped it on top of his boots. Narisa stood watching him while he fumbled at the safety harness still wrapped about his ribs.

"You should leave that on for a few days," she said. "Just to be certain you have healed. That's the sensible thing to do." When he did not answer, she reluctantly sat beside him.

"Put your feet in," he advised. "We've been walking all morning. It's refreshing."

"Commander Tarik," she began sternly. He stopped her.

"No more commander or lieutenant," he said quietly but decisively. "On this world you are simply Narisa, and I am Tarik."

She absorbed that a moment or two, considering the implications and trying not to notice the way the sunlight played over the muscles of his shoulders and upper arms. It took a great effort to stop looking at his sleek, hard body and consider his words instead.

"You don't believe we will be able to leave here, do you?" she said at last. "What's more, you don't care."

He said nothing. He was watching the water flow across his bare feet and wriggling his toes in pleasure. Narisa remembered her childhood, and wading in Beltan rivers. She pulled off her own boots and stuck her feet into the stream beside his.

"This," she stated, "is dereliction of duty. We could both be court-martialed. We ought to be trying to find a way home, not playing."

"No one will ever know," he promised. Then, more seriously, "Narisa, you must understand, although we will keep searching, it is possible we won't find anyone here who can help us. We might find those who will be our enemies. In either case, it is unwise for us to quarrel. We will need to trust and depend on each other, whatever happens."

"I understand. It's just that you are so different now from the way you were on the *Reliance*, and you won't pay any attention to regulations. It's as though you are happy we've been marooned here."

"I suppose I do appear to be different. I'm certainly not pleased about the loss of all those lives on the *Reliance*, but there is nothing I can do to change what has happened, and I see no point in scrupulous adherence to rules that don't apply here.

"Did you know this was to be my last voyage?" Tarik heaved a sigh that might have come from inside his very soul. "The truth is, I ought to have left the Service long ago. I've always had an independent streak. One of my ancestors was an anarchist who was punished for his crimes by being pushed out the hatch of a prison ship into deep space without an air supply. My family has become more respectable in the centuries since then, but sometimes when I was naughty as a child, my father accused me of being like that ancestor. I suppose I did inherit a need to go my own way, and I have always been skeptical of anything I was told I ought to believe without question. Those traits did not make me a likely candidate for the Service, but somehow I managed to keep myself under control and not cause scandal to my family. I would have been captain of my own ship one day, but I've seen and heard too much, in the Service and in the Assembly. My older brother is also in the Service, and my father is a Member of the Assembly. Whenever we were all at home, I listened to them talking together. I want no part of Service, or Capital, or Assembly. Not any more. I'd like to find a quiet world outside the Jurisdiction where I could live, and someone to live with me, to be my companion."

"A world like this one?" Narisa wasn't certain she could live on a world without the strict regulations she was accustomed to after so many years in the Service. The thought was frightening. How could people know what to do without regulations to guide them? Yet somewhere deep inside, she felt strangely excited by the idea.

"Well," Tarik said with a crooked smile, "you must admit this world is outside the Jurisdiction."

He would want Suria to live with him, of course, not Narisa. Beautiful, flame-haired

Suria, with her sensuous body and her sultry voice that could make the simplest navigational instructions sound like an erotic invitation. Narisa had met Suria when their duties had overlapped for one space-day so Suria could fill her in on the eccentricities of *Reliance*'s navigational instruments. The woman had been friendly enough, but she had made Narisa feel totally unfeminine and incompetent. No wonder Tarik resented Narisa, considering what he had had to give up when Suria left the ship.

Narisa looked at Tarik. They sat shoulder to shoulder, and he was staring into the stream, presenting his profile to her. He had such sharp, clear-cut features, only slightly blurred by three days' growth of beard. Whereas Narisa was partly in shadow, the orange sun shone directly on Tarik's face, and his shoulders and arms glowed with the orange-gold light. Dark hair grew on his forearms and chest, and his hands were long and slender, and very strong. She remembered the touch of his hand on her breast, and began to feel the same warmth she had felt then.

He must have sensed her close observation, for he turned his head suddenly. They gazed directly into each other's eyes for a long, breathless moment. Then Tarik bent toward her. He did not have to move very far before his mouth lightly touched hers, withdrew, and returned for a deeper kiss. Narisa sat perfectly still, unable to respond.

It had been years since anyone had kissed

her in that way. The last time it had been one
of those laughing playmates on Belta, a boy
with silver hair and soft gray eyes, and he was
long dead, gone with all the others the Cetans
had killed ten space-years ago, and no man
had kissed her since. That had been largely
her own doing. She had wanted it that way. A
tear rolled down her cheek. Tarik wiped it
away with one long finger.

"I'm sorry," he said softly. "I didn't mean to
make you cry."

'I wasn't weeping," Narisa snapped at him
in sudden irritation. "I never cry. Tears are a
sign of weakness. It's the sunlight. I'm not
used to it after so long on a spaceship. It's so
terribly bright."

Tarik looked hard at her, opened his mouth
to speak, but what he would have said she
never knew, for suddenly one of the birds was
there. It was the blue one this time, and it
glided along the stream, its great wings barely
missing the trees and bushes on either side.

Tarik jumped up and stood on the rock in
his bare, wet feet, watching it. The bird flew
past them, heading downstream to disappear
around a bend. There was complete silence
after it had gone, as though the very forest
held its breath. Then they heard it far above
their heads, the beat of its wings followed by
the call Narisa had heard the day before.

"Chon. Chon-chon. Chon."

Then it approached again from upstream,
flying along the same route as before, till it
was hidden from sight at the bend of the

stream. A third time the bird repeated its performance, and by then Tarik had his boots and jacket on, and was urging Narisa to hurry with her own boots.

"We've been going in the right direction," he said excitedly. "Come on, Narisa." He grabbed one of her hands, pulling her to her feet and dragging her after him.

They reached the bend in the stream. There was no sign of the bird, but they kept going, and Tarik saw to it that they moved faster, as though he knew something important lay ahead.

Where they now found themselves, the forest grew ever thicker with no clearings at all. Underbrush constantly blocked their way, and Tarik and Narisa had to frequently hold back branches, or sometimes large bushes, so they could force their way through. Above them huge vines hung from tree to tree. Several times Narisa thought she saw movement among them, or between the bushes or trees, but she could not stop to investigate. She did not want to lose sight of Tarik.

The forest was so dense that there were long stretches when they could not see the stream, but had to listen for it so they could follow its direction. In spite of all the obstacles, Tarik pressed on. After an hour or so of the rapid pace he had set, Narisa was gasping for breath.

"Could we stop?" she panted. "Just for a little while, please. You should rest yourself, or you will be sick again."

"No, I won't. I'm perfectly healthy now. I feel wonderful. We might eat something, though."

He brought out the wafers of compressed food, and they sat between two bushes in a space so small their knees were touching. They ate quickly, then drank a little water.

"I'll leave you for a few minutes." Tarik rose.

"Wait." She wanted to say, *don't leave me*, but could not bring herself to admit she was afraid of the forest, which now pressed closely upon them. And she, too, wanted a few minutes alone to attend to personal needs. "I'll go to the stream. I'd like to put some cool water on my face. I'll stay there, right by the stream, until you come, so we won't lose each other."

Tarik nodded and moved off into the thick greenery. Narisa headed toward the stream. It was a short time later, when, on the narrow, muddy verge, she bent to wash her hands and then her face, that she became aware the bird was flying along the stream once more. She watched it, thinking this was no special guidance for herself and Tarik, but only the bird's daily habit. It was probably looking for food. Perhaps it ate the fish Tarik had shown her earlier. She knew little about birds, but it seemed to her this one's long, toothed beak would be well suited to catching fish. She wondered how they tasted, and whether she and Tarik might catch and eat them when their wafers were all gone.

She watched the bird as it disappeared downstream, then glanced around to see if Tarik had appeared yet. She saw that one of the thick green vines had dropped off a near- by tree and had begun crawling toward the stream. Narisa stared at it. She stood in its way, and even as she heard Tarik's tense voice, she recognized it for what it was.

"Snake," Tarik said from some distance behind her. "A poisonous one, I think. Stay where you are. It may pass by you if you don't startle it."

Narisa could not have moved if she had wanted to. There was no place to go in that tiny area between dense undergrowth and stream, and she was too frightened to do anything at all. The snake was large, with black spots along its green body, and she thought it was looking directly at her. It was big enough to strike well above her protective boots. She stood frozen, waiting.

"Don't move," Tarik said.

"No." Her own voice sounded surprisingly calm. "No, I won't."

From high overhead she heard the beat of wings. She could not look up. Her eyes were fixed with hypnotic intensity upon the snake. There was a flurry of blue feathers, and the bird stood perched precariously upon a rock in midstream. The snake slithered closer to Narisa.

The bird surged off the rock and pecked at the snake. The snake twitched, turning toward the bird, its path diverted from

Narisa. The bird pecked again, drawing blood this time, and the snake reared upward to strike its attacker. The bird was now standing in the shallow water at the edge of the stream, and as Narisa watched in horror, it stepped to one side, spreading its wings. The snake struck with lightning speed. The bird, equally as fast, took the blow on the edge of one extended wing. The snake fell back, stunned by the force of its own strike, and the bird pounced upon it with beak and outstretched talons. In an instant the snake was dead. The bird dropped it, but continued to stand over its prey.

Narisa felt Tarik's arms around her as she slumped backward against his chest.

"Don't faint," he warned her wryly. "There's no place to lay you down except in the stream."

"I'm not going to!" Terror was replaced by anger at his suggestion that she was weak and liable to faint. She pulled away from him, but staggered as dizziness overcame her. Tarik swept her off her feet and held her. "Put me down," she ordered.

At that he gathered her more closely to himself and pressed his rough-bearded cheek against hers, holding her captive in a warm embrace.

"If you weren't frightened," he said, "I was."

She felt her anger evaporating at his words, and raised her arms to circle his neck, finding safety and comfort in his strength.

The bird stood at the water's edge, watching them. Tarik loosened his grip on Narisa.

"Look at it." He set her down slowly, his eyes and mind now on the bird. "It saved you. That was a deliberate act, Narisa. You can't deny there is intelligence of some kind at work here."

Narisa was too grateful to be alive, and too touched by his open concern for her, to argue with him. She steeled herself and stepped forward. She did not want to go anywhere near the dead snake, but there was something she must do. She had recognized the bird by the jagged scar on its beak. It was time to say thank you, and to help if she could.

She put out both hands, reaching toward the wing the snake had hit. It was spread a little awkwardly, as though the bird was deliberately holding it away from its body, but Narisa could see no sign of blood or other damage. The three clawed fingers at the last joint of the wing were curled slightly and looked relaxed rather than tense with pain. Narisa should have been afraid of the bird's dangerous talons and beak, but she was not. She put both hands on the wing at the spot where the snake had sunk its fangs. Behind her she heard Tarik gasp.

There was no sign of injury. The feathers were smooth and stiff to the touch, their radiant blue color glowing against her own pale skin. Narisa stroked downward gently, then lifted her fingers and stroked again. The bird cocked its head, watching her closely,

but did not move away. Narisa wanted to
stroke its chest feathers, too, and wondered if
she would be permitted. She lifted one hand.
The bird side-stepped her, turned toward the
stream, and, opening its wings, took off, flying
straight downstream as it had done before.

Tarik was staring at her in amazement.

"What made you do that?" he asked.

"I don't know. I simply had to do it. I don't
think the wing was hurt at all. You saw how
easily the bird flew."

"The snake may have struck the outer edge
of the feathers instead of flesh. Are you all
right, Narisa? Can you go on?"

"Certainly I can. I'd like to get away from
that snake at once." Her voice was crisp, as if
she were in complete control of herself,
though inwardly she was intensely moved by
what had happened, and confused by her own
reactions. Deep in her mind she was now certain Tarik was right about the birds; they
were intelligent, and they did communicate in
some way. She had known the bird wanted
her to touch it, and she had not wanted to
resist. Accepting these factors meant going
against all her training, and against Jurisdiction laws. This strange planet, combined
with Tarik's dangerously subversive ideas,
were changing her thought patterns, and it
was most unsettling.

They resumed their journey downstream,
Narisa keeping a wary eye on the overhead
vines as well as looking for unfriendly beasts
on the ground, but they saw nothing, nor did

the bird return.

The sun had set into a lavender and orange dusk when the forest ended abruptly and they found themselves at the edge of an immense lake. In the far distance a purple mountain rose, crowned in white. To their left the stream they had been following turned into a low waterfall, then wended its way through a brief stretch of grasses and blossoming water plants, and at last emptied itself into the lake. Beyond the stream the land rose in rocky tiers until tall cliffs loomed over the lake. To the right of where they stood, the land was flat and heavily forested, edged all along the shore by clean white sand. Narisa thought there was an island in the lake, but it was getting too dark to see well. All was still. Not even a breeze stirred the placid water of the lake. There was no sign of life.

Narisa turned toward Tarik, looking at him through the deepening dusk. "What do we do now?"

Chapter Four

What they did was sit upon the soft white sand and eat one wafer each out of their dwindling supply of compressed food, washing down the inadequate meal with water from the stream.

"Half rations," Tarik said, measuring each bite of his meal carefully to make it last as long as possible. "We will continue in this way, one wafer at every meal for each of us tomorrow, and again the next day until evening, when we divide the last wafer in half and try to sleep hungry. In the meantime, we will look for something edible."

"How will we know what is safe to eat?" Narisa wondered. "We have no equipment to test possible food sources."

"We couldn't test the water, either, but that hasn't harmed us so far. We'll just have to take our chances with the food, too."

"Perhaps," Narisa began, scooping sand into a mound to serve as a pillow, "just possibly, what the birds eat might be safe for us, too. If we could discover what they eat."

"Why, Narisa, are you becoming flexible about regulations?" he teased.

"I see no reason to starve to death if there is food nearby," she replied stiffly. "Will you take the first watch, or shall I?"

"There's little point in standing watch," he said. "We are defenseless. But on the chance that danger might come, I'll stay awake first."

Narisa lay down on the sand, and Tarik moved to sit beside her, his knees drawn up with his arms resting on them. He was so close to her that she could feel the warmth of his body. She repressed the desire to touch him. There was no need for physical assurance, she told herself. She could be quite certain he would remain exactly where he was until it was time for him to waken her so he could sleep. Tarik had always been a dependable first officer.

"It's not so very dark," she murmured, letting her mind drift toward slumber. "There are two moons. That's what the computer said back on the pod. Two moons around this planet."

"How romantic." There was lazy humor in Tarik's voice. "But there are very few stars. Have you noticed? 'the night has a thousand stars, and the day but one.' From where we are, that appears to be precisely the case.

Only a thousand."

"Clouds of hydrogen gas blocking the light
from the others." Narisa heard his low laugh
mocking her matter-of-fact response just
before she gave herself up completely to
sleep. . . .

She was on Belta, and the silver river, edged
with gently drooping trees, flowed before her,
just as she remembered it. The sun was warm,
the breeze soft, and she could hear her
parents talking. Her little sister was laughing,
playing at some childish game. She could not
see any of them. There was only the river and
the trees and the sound of their beloved
voices.

The silver-gold Beltan sun disappeared
behind a cloud, and suddenly there were
other voices, loud Cetan words destroying the
peaceful day. Then came the screams, over
and over again. The very air grew darker, and
thunder rumbled across the sky. Narisa knew
she had to find her parents and her sister, had
to help them. She could not, *could not*, let the
Cetans kill them again. Not again. She almost
found them this time. She was so close. She
heard a last loud shriek.

"Mother! Father! Laria! No! Wait for me.
Wait!" She was on her knees, struggling with
some tall creature. "Let me go, you Cetan pig.
I must find them. Let me go, I say!"

"Narisa, it's me, it's Tarik." Strong hands
held her, pinning her flailing arms to her
sides, shaking her hard. "Wake up. You've
been dreaming. Narisa!"

She fell against him, breathing hard as though she had been running for a long time, clutching at him to reassure herself he was real and not part of her nightmare. They knelt together in close embrace while she tried to compose herself. Tarik pulled her head onto his shoulder and stroked her hair until her tearless cries had quieted and her breathing was normal again. After a while he eased her gently down onto the sand and lay beside her, still holding her.

"If you tell me about it," he said softly, "you will chase the dream away faster and be able to sleep again sooner."

She would never have breathed a word of her family tragedy to the cold and arrogantly superior Commander Tarik she had so despised aboard the *Reliance*, the man who had harshly criticized the most minor details of her work. But this was a different Tarik from the one she had known then, or rather, she had not known him at all until they had been forced together during the last three days. His peculiar ideas constantly threw her off balance, but he had been genuinely afraid for her when the snake might have killed her. He had kissed her, not once, but twice. And just that morning he had put his hand on her bare breast and held it there. She grew warm again at the memory, and snuggled against him. She felt his lips brush across her brow. They were lying so close, almost like lovers, their legs entangled. She thought if he kissed her brow again, she would raise her face and his lips might touch her mouth. What would he do then? Would he put his hands on her as he had before? What was it like to be loved by Tarik?

"Tell me the dream, Narisa," he urged, recalling her from her foolish imaginings. She began to talk, and before she was done she had told him not only the dream, but the terrible story of the Cetan raid on Belta, and the extermination of her family along with so many others that has caused the planet to remain devastated and nearly unpopulated for long years afterward.

"I was at the Capital at the time of the attack," she continued. "I was in the second year of training for the Service, and my superior officer would not let me return to Belta. As you know, recruits are never allowed to leave the Capital, not for any reason, until the training is over and they are assigned to a spaceship. When I insisted I had to go, they told me Belta was too far away, which was true enough, and they gave me extra duty to punish me for my insubordination. I have never been back to Belta since then. I've never seen the ruins of my old home."

"So, not having seen the material evidence, you find it hard to believe your loved ones are really dead, and you keep searching for them in your dreams, as though you could change what has happened."

"Yes, I suppose so, though I know full well in my mind that they are gone forever. It's my heart that won't believe it. I loved them so." She knew he was right. She had understood what was happening to her when she dreamed, and thus had never spoken of the nightmares to anyone until now.

"I often wondered why you cried out in your sleep," Tarik said. "Your cabin on the *Reliance* was next to mine, you recall, and I would hear you."

It had been Suria's cabin she had occupied. There had been a door connecting them. Narisa had kept it locked, sealed with her own private combination so she would have one place on the ship where he could not come. She should have realized sound would carry through the door. She ought to have been quieter.

"I'm sorry if I disturbed you," she said stiffly.

"It doesn't matter now." He gave her a quick hug. "You lost more of your family on the *Reliance*, didn't you?"

"How typical of Cetans," she burst out, "to attack and destroy a ship on a diplomatic mission of peace. Yes, the Beltan ambassador and his senior assistant were both distant cousins of mine. I didn't know them very well, but they were kin and all I had left. Now there is no one at all."

No one, she thought, *who remembers when Laria and I were little girls, or how happy a family we were. I have lost all of my past.* The self-pity lasted only a moment before her usual control reasserted itself. She would have pulled away from Tarik, but he held her firmly, and she sensed a tender purpose in his next words.

"Narisa, have you considered that we may be all alone on this world? Just the two of us."

"I have thought of it, but I can't believe it's true. We have to get back to the Capital."

"Ah, the Capital. I almost forgot your dedication to Service regulations." He loosed his arms, moving apart from her, leaving her feeling oddly bereft. "Sleep if you can, Narisa. It's still my watch."

But she lay a long time on the sand, staring up at the few stars, before she slept again. And she wondered what would happen if she were forced to spend the rest of her life alone with Commander Tarik Gibal.

He woke her when the night was half gone, and she saw by the distance the two moons had moved across the sky that he had timed his watch precisely. She went to the stream to splash water on her face to wake herself to full alertness. She did not quite trust the lake water, not knowing what else flowed into it, so, cautious as always, she preferred to use the water that had not harmed her. Not yet, she reminded herself. There might be long-term effects. Nothing was certain on any unknown world.

When she returned to the spot where Tarik lay, she sensed he was sleeping. She could see his pale bearded face and smooth black hair in the moonlight.

Narisa sat staring into the night, thinking about the events of the last three days. So much had happened. She still felt disoriented, not least by her constantly shifting reactions to Tarik. She was honest enough to admit to herself that she felt a strong physical attraction to him, but she was afraid of that attraction.

A faint breeze sprang up, ruffling her hair and rippling the surface of the lake. It was growing cooler, both moons had set, and it was so quiet, except for the soothing noises of the water. Narisa leaned back, bracing herself on both arms, to look at the night sky. The stars glittering brilliantly through the thin atmosphere were unfamiliar to her, and for all her training she could not tell from them where she and Tarik were.

Her training had been strictly in the sciences, and none of it had taught her to appreciate the natural beauty of any world, but Tarik's injunction to open her eyes and look had induced her to do just that. She watched the sky until it began to lighten into lavender and pale orange, as behind her the sun rose slowly above the forest in orange-gold splendor. The peak of the lofty mountain in the distance changed from gold to rose to pure white, and the mauve-gray mist lying over the lake dissipated into the clear air. While she looked, marveling at the loveliness of the landscape spread before her, the sky gradually turned to its daytime hue of deep purple-blue.

Far out on the lake she saw birds, six of them, flying high up, then diving straight

down into the water and out again, trailing
sparkling silver drops of moisture behind
them. So they did eat fish, Narisa observed.
Fishing was the only activity she could think
of to account for what they were doing. It
occurred to her that she knew nothing about
animal behavior in any species. It had been
one of the deliberate limitations of her
training. She might have learned on her own,
but she had not cared enough to do so, not
after her family was gone. After that, she had
adhered strictly to duty and regulations.

As the morning light grew brighter, she
realized that she had been right about the
island in the lake. It lay directly in front of
her, near the cliffs. It appeared to be quite
large. She could see the birds diving on the far
side of it, the water dripping off their wings
when they rose again, so the lake must extend
completely around that spot of land. An island,
edged in pale sand and covered with luxuriant
vegetation.

The sun rose still higher, its rays gleaming
on something white and smooth, set back
among the trees along the island's shore. A
building. She squinted to see better. It had to
be a building. They would find intelligent life
there. She knew it.

Before she could shake Tarik awake to tell
him of her discovery, something else caught
her eye. High in the steepest cliffs overlooking
the lake there were holes, niches, caves, and
deep folds in the rock, and the birds were
flying in and out of most of them, some

carrying fish in their beaks. They must have brought Narisa and Tarik to their home.

Beside her, Tarik stirred, yawning and stretching, then sat up and rubbed his eyes. Narisa smiled, thinking how unkempt a man looked with three days' growth of beard. She liked him better for it. It made him less intimidating. She probably looked almost as bad, though she had tried to comb her hair with her fingers and keep her face and hands clean.

"You were right," Narisa informed Tarik, dispensing with any morning greeting. She told him about the birds, then pointed out the building on the island.

Tarik leapt to his feet, completely awake now, and ran to the water's edge to get a better view. Narisa joined him.

"If there is communication equipment there," she said exaultantly, "we can call the Capital, and they will send a ship for us."

"Don't get too excited, Narisa. We don't know yet what we'll find. Can you swim that far?"

"I am Beltan-born," she replied proudly. "I can swim anywhere. Can you?"

"Easily." He frowned a little, his eyes on the island. "I see no sign of life, nothing moving over there."

Narisa's hope would not be dashed, not until she had seen for herself.

"Let's go at once," she urged.

"Not before food and a little preparation. I thought you were the cautious one of our expedition, Narisa."

"I suppose I am," she admitted. "Usually. It's just that I want to return to civilization. I'm not accustomed to wild places like this."

"Nor am I, but I find I like it, certainly more than I like the Capital."

They broke the night's fast with a single compressed wafer for each. Then they returned to the forest to pick up what fallen branches they could find and break off a few from living trees. Tarik climbed a tree to pull down several thick vines, while Narisa watched him fearfully, shivering at the memory of the vine that had proved to be a snake.

They carried their findings to the beach. There, under Tarik's instruction, they wove the vines around the branches to make a small, leaky raft. They lashed to it the watertight containers of tools and food, and the water container, now full of water they had taken from the stream. Next they took off their boots and uniforms and fastened them on top of the containers, using the safety harness from the pod, which Tarik insisted on unwrapping from his ribs, saying he felt certain they were completely healed. Narisa privately doubted that, but she was so eager to get to the island she did not want to waste precious time arguing with him.

"Our clothes will get damp," Tarik said, "but if we push the raft carefully, we shouldn't have to walk in boots that are completely soaked, and the uniforms will dry quickly."

He glanced at Narisa, his eyes glowing with

appreciation. She wore only her close-fitting
undershirt and the regulation lower undergarment, which was cut high on her thighs.
Her long legs were bare, her frame slim yet
strong and healthy.

Tarik wore a similar lower garment and
nothing else. He had a fine, supple body, so
well proportioned and sleek with taut
muscles that he looked much taller than he
was. He was not short for a man; it was just
that Narisa was so tall he topped her by only
two inches. There was a light furring of
smooth black hair on his chest and forearms.

They stood looking at each other, each
frankly enjoying the sight of a handsome
specimen of the opposite sex. Fearing she
would embarass herself by blushing again,
Narisa turned away and went to the stream to
drink. She knew his eyes never left her. She
could almost feel them caressing her
shoulders and back, buttocks and legs, down
to her slender ankles and narrow feet.

She wanted him to look at her, but she
wanted him to touch her also, and to kiss her
again. Her thoughts frightened her. She had
looked at other men, boys really, on Belta,
and they had looked at her, and there had
been a pleasure in the looking, and in the
touching, too, but never this kind of tension,
this shameless urge to throw herself into a
man's arms and let him bear her down to the
sand and do whatever he wanted with her. She
knew what it was she felt. She had heard
other women talk of it, and she had felt it her-

self once or twice before, though never so strongly. It was desire.

"Not Tarik," she whispered to herself, splashing cold water on her burning cheeks. "I can't want him, not for the first man."

"Are you ready?" Tarik called across the beach. She got off her knees and left the stream and went to help him launch their little raft.

The lake was cold. Narisa did not quibble about the possible composition of the water, or the possibly dangerous animals that might be living in it, as she ought to have done. She was too eager to get to the island.

She was glad to have the coolness swirling about her ankles, then her knees and hips, until she was shoulder deep and began to swim and help Tarik push the raft along. She let the chill water wash away the unhealthy desire she felt, leaving only a residual warmth deep inside her that she could easily control.

By the time they pulled the raft up onto the island beach, she was in complete possession of herself. She was not even daunted by the realization that their uniforms and boots had gotten wetter than they had expected and would have to be spread out on the sand to dry. After they had let themselves dry off a bit in the hot sun, they started to explore, wearing only damp underclothes.

They had come ashore a little beyond the spot where they had seen the white building. However, directly before them was an opening between the trees, and Tarik headed

for this. Once they were off the sand the
ground was covered with thick, soft moss.
Narisa stepped carefully.

"It's a road," Tarik said, showing her the
ancient stones set into the ground and disguised by the green-gold moss. "It looks
unused for a long, long time, Narisa."

They went on, until she estimated they had
reached the center of the island.

"Where is the building?" she asked.

"Right here." Tarik pulled back a branch
that obscured her vision, and let her walk past
him.

They came into a circular clearing. A knee-
high stone wall, broken in places and overgrown, was evidence that the clearing had
been made deliberately. Narisa could see the
entire space had once been paved with smooth
white stones. Moss lay on most of them, while
plants had sprung up in cracks between the
stones. In the exact center of the clearing
stood a white stone building. It was round,
with a domed roof and a row of columns all
around the outside. Behind the columns the
facade of the building was broken only by a
carved double door at the terminus of the
road they had been following.

"This is what you saw from the beach,"
Tarik said. "Look there, the trees are thin
enough in that direction to see through them,
but the underbrush is too thick for us to make
our way through it. We came by the right
path, the way the builders intended it should
be approached. See how the stones are laid

across the clearing. Their pattern leads directly to the door."

"Is it a palace, or some kind of religious temple?" Narisa spoke in a half whisper, awed by the simple beauty of the building before them.

It was overrun with vines, and wild shrubs had grown up close to it, but it was obvious that it had been created by the finest workmanship, and even now the still-smooth white stone surface gleamed luminously where the sun touched it. There was a scroll-shaped ornament at the top of each simple column, but no other decoration on the building save the wooden doors.

Three wide low steps led up to the colonnade and to the doors. Tarik climbed them, Narisa close behind him. The two panels of the door were dark wood, carved with figures of men and women in gracefully draped robes, apparently all bringing offerings to the building. Tarik pushed on the doors. They were locked.

"Perhaps there is another entrance," Narisa suggested.

Tarik had gone to his knees to examine the door more closely, and now he began to laugh.

"There may very well be another way in," he said, "but I think I can open this one easily enough. I see you brought the tool kit." He put out a hand, and Narisa gave him the kit. He riffled through the contents for a moment or two before finding what he wanted. He drew out a long, thin metal rod.

"This may do it," he told Narisa, flourishing the rod before her. "The simplest means may be the most effective, precisely because intelligent people always expect important things to be complicated. If my suspicions are correct, this very simple lock has held for space-centuries. And with this equally simple instrument, I will now unlock it."

He bent to the door, inserting the rod into a hole in the carving, which Narisa had not noticed before. He twisted and turned it, pulled the rod out and put it back in again, muttering a word Narisa would never have used. She was about to make a tart comment on his simple solution when there was a loud click from inside the door.

"Now," Tarik said triumphantly, replacing the rod in the tool kit, "behold." He pushed on the double doors where their two halves came together, and they swung open.

Narisa caught the scent of dry, imprisoned air, and of something else, something unpleasant that tugged at her memory until she recognized it. The smell of death. She stood hesitantly in the colonnade while Tarik threw the doors wide.

There was an anteroom with a smooth white stone floor and half columns carved out of the white stone walls. An ornate lamp of some discolored and corroded metal hung from the low ceiling. On the other side of the anteroom was another double door. Tarik strode toward it.

"Be careful," Narisa said, hanging back outside the first door.

"I need the rod again. This door is locked, too."

She stepped unwillingly into the anteroom and handed him the rod from the tool kit. It took him only a few seconds to open this one and push both panels back.

They walked into the central part of the building, a large circular room with a colonnade around its wall, exactly matching the columns outside. The dome high above them had a round window in its very top, and through it came brilliant light. The room was entirely white, the ceiling where the dome was set being decorated with a carved frieze in the same design that ornamented the tops of all the columns. In the center of the room was a round console, on which a primitive computer-communicator stood with two chairs beside it.

At one side of the room, on a carved wooden couch, lay the source of the unpleasant smell. It was the skeleton of a human, dressed in a simple blue robe and low blue boots. Its hands were folded upon its chest. On one finger a gold ring with a triangular purple stone hung loosely. Tarik went to the figure.

"Was it man or woman?" Narisa whispered.

"I can't tell. There is nothing left but bones and the clothing. Perhaps if we can get the computer working, there will be information in it. Before you start that," Tarik said quickly, seeing Narisa take a purposeful step toward the console, "let's explore the rest of this building."

There were twelve rooms around the circumference of the main room, all opening off the inner colonnade. Beginning at the anteroom through which they had entered, they turned left and worked their way around the building. First they found six personal rooms with two couches in each, all in perfect order with coverlets drawn up on the beds and garments neatly folded in chests and drawers. There was a bathing room with a deep tub carved out of stone, basins for washing, and toilet facilities, but no water. When Tarik manipulated the knobs and levers, nothing happened. There was a room that plainly had been a kitchen, though neither of them could find any evidence of a heat source for cooking. Lastly they found three rooms just like the personal rooms, but these had been used for storage. Preserved food filled one room. Some containers had been damaged, their contents crumbled to dust in the dry air, like the person in the main hall, but most of the food was still in tightly wrapped packets.

"This solves our most immediate problem," Tarik declared. "Look, see this sign on the packets. That was used in early Jurisdiction days. It means the food has been irradiated and is good indefinitely, for space-centuries if it's left unopened. It was developed for space flight."

"What is it made of? Can you read the labels on the packets?" When he studied one package and shook his head, Narisa added,

"We don't know it's safe for humans."

"Those are human bones out there." Tarik inclined his head toward the central room.

"Perhaps," she suggested, "he, or she, tried some of it. Perhaps that's what killed him. Or her."

"You may be right." Tarik put the food packet down. "Still, I'm getting awfully hungry on compressed wafers. If I don't find something more appetizing soon, I may begin sampling this."

Having finished their exploration of all the rooms, they went back to the main hall to examine the computer-communicator.

"It's very old," Narisa said. "The power source may be dead. We'll have to find a way to recharge it. I'm sure we could get a message out over this. We could be rescued, Tarik, and soon, too."

Tarik had been opening doors and pulling out drawers around the console. The doors simply gave access to the interior of the computer itself, in case repairs were needed. The drawers held the usual supplies and additional equipment. One drawer was locked.

"Use the rod on this lock, too," Narsia suggested.

"It's the wrong kind of lock. It needs a triangular insertion." Tarik stared at the lock a moment, then hurried across the room to the remains lying on the couch. He gently slid the ring off the skeleton's finger and brought it to the console. The triangular purple stone in the gold ring fit the lock perfectly, and the drawer slid open. Narisa moved forward quickly.

"A key!" With eager fingers, she picked up the flat metal artifact lying in the bottom of the drawer. "I remember about these ancient computer-communicators now. I learned about them in training. You have to insert the key and turn it, and then push the right buttons, and the machinery should start working no matter how long it has been disconnected. I think I can remember some of the common combinations of buttons, too. I'll try it."

"No, you won't." He snatched the key out of her hand.

"Tarik, give that back to me. We have to call the Capital."

"Not until I've read this." He held up the other item the drawer had contained. "Is this the effect the Empty Sector has on you, to make you reckless? We don't want any nasty surprises, Narisa. We are still unarmed, and we don't know if anyone else is on this planet. If you start sending out messages, who knows what may happen, or whether those you contact will be friendly?"

He was holding a book, the kind of notebook scientists sometimes used before they were ready to consign new and uncertain data to a computer's memory banks. Narisa could see as he flipped through the pages that they were thickly covered with writing.

"We could get more information out of the computer, and much more quickly," she said.

"No." He held on to the key.

"Don't you trust me?"

"I have no reason not to," he told her. "Your determination to do your duty to the Service is laudable. All the same, I will keep the key until we mutually decide to turn on the computer."

"You don't want to leave here," she accused him.

He did not answer. He was looking at the book, tracing a line of writing with one finger.

"Since you are the linguistics expert, I hope it's in a language you can decipher quickly," she said acidly.

"I can. It's quite simple, an earlier version of our own speech, in fact. Are you hungry?" He closed the book with a snap.

"Hungry? Tarik, don't change the subject. *I want to call the Capital!*"

"Later. Let's go get our uniforms off the beach. They should be dry by now. I suggest we hide the raft, too, and smooth over the sand. Let's leave no trace of our arrival on this island. Then we'll come back here, enjoy a midday feast of compressed wafers and water, and I'll start translating the book. I'll read it to you as I go along. Will that please you?"

"What should we do about him? Or her, whichever it is?" Narisa indicated the skeleton on the couch.

"We'll know that after we've read the book."

They did as Tarik wanted. While they had

been in the building, the sky had grown cloudy. By the time they got to the beach, the sky was black, and a fierce wind churned the surface of the lake into white-capped waves. Narisa retrieved their uniforms and boots while Tarik used the edge of the raft to smooth out the sand, eliminating their footprints. Then they ran through pelting rain, back to the building, Narisa carrying the clothing, and Tarik the raft.

The storm had raised a childhood memory in Narisa. She dumped her burden in the anteroom and went back outside to stand on the moss-covered stones and let the rain wash over her, rubbing her face and arms and shoulders. Tarik joined her, water dripping off his hair and rough beard.

"This is not wise," he shouted at her above the noise of the storm. "I thought you were always sensible."

"It feels wonderful," she called back. "We used to do it all the time on Belta. It's a rain-bath."

There was a powerful clap of thunder, and the downpour increased. Tarik caught her arm.

"Inside," he ordered.

When the thunder sounded again, she obeyed him. She ran laughing into the shelter of the colonnade, pausing there to watch him as he came up the steps to her.

"I haven't done that since I was a little girl," she said, lifting her sodden hair to twist it and wring out the water.

She was as wet as she had been when she had walked out of the lake earlier, her thin undergarments plastered to her skin. Tarik was just as wet, and his manly torso shone with moisture. The single garment barely covered his stiffening manhood. Narisa pulled her eyes away and met his intensely focused glance. The hands she had lifted to her hair were stilled by that look. She stood waiting, the damp locks twined in her fingers.

He took two steps, closing the distance between them. His arms slid around her, and hers around him, until they were locked in a close embrace. He covered her mouth with his, and she could feel the length of his body, his hardness pushing against her. She gave herself up to his kiss, her lips opening to his searching tongue, her hands wandering across his shoulders and into his wet hair, while her lips returned the pressure of his. The rain beat down around them, heavier and heavier, and the kiss went on and on.

Narisa was lost in a sea of glorious sensation. Tarik's near-nakedness against her own flesh was sweeter than she had ever imagined a man might be. She pressed closer, wanting every inch of her body to touch his, wanting to feel the warmth of him, and the sweetness. He responded by tightening his arms until she could hardly breathe. She revelled in the sudden unleashing of his need, and thrust her tongue against his repeatedly, feeling the moist heat of his inner mouth. He caressed her lower back, then moved lower still, pulling her nearer so his manhood rubbed against her. She could have screamed with the exquisite agony of that touch through two thin layers of wet clothing.

She wanted him. She wanted to offer to him that part of herself no one had ever possessed, and see in his eyes his joyful acceptance of the gift.

But he loves Suria, her better sense reminded her. *Suria, not you. He would not value what you would give him.*

She felt as though she had been tossed onto a cold, rocky shore after nearly drowning in rapture. She fought valiantly to recover her drugged senses. It took all her willpower and self-control, but she succeeded. She had begun to pull away from him before the sudden lightning flash and crack of thunder made him raise his head and loosen his arms.

"We had better get under cover," he said, giving her a last quick kiss before pushing her gently toward the door.

She fled to the anteroom, picked up their uniforms and boots, and continued into the main room, while he closed both sets of doors. Here the sound of the storm was muffled into a distant murmur. Tarik came toward her across the white stone floor, and from the flaming desire in his purple-blue eyes she knew what he intended to do.

"Here." She held out his uniform and boots with a hand that shook almost as much as her voice. "I'll dress in one of the personal rooms. You choose another room and do the same."

She did not wait to hear his reply or see his angry face. She was thoroughly unnerved by her own conflicting emotions. The only thing she was capable of doing just then was reverting to formal manners and treating him as she had on board ship. She ran into the first room she came to, swung the door shut and sank down on one of the beds, her damp uniform clutched against her chest.

She had never experienced anything like this. Her body had betrayed her mind. She wanted Tarik to come crashing through the door and pull her into his arms and tell her he wanted her and only her, and then take her until he had released the painful burning ache that still held her in its grip. But he did not come to her. There was complete silence on the other side of the door.

It took her a long time to pull herself together. When she could stand without trembling, she found a garment in one of the drawers, and dried herself with it, towelling her hair hard. There was a comb in another drawer, and she used it. Then she put on her uniform, and her professional demeanor with it, and went out to the round central room.

Tarik, fully dressed, sat in one of the two chairs by the computer-communicator console, reading the notebook he had found. The second chair had been pulled up to face him. Next to it on the console were one food wafer and the water container. Narisa slid into the chair. Tarik did not look up.

"Tarik," she began, leaning toward him, not

certain how to explain the way she felt, "I'm sorry."

"Stow it," he said harshly, and added a spaceman's crude epithet to the ancient phrase. This was the cold-blooded first officer of the *Reliance*, who did not deign to look at her when he spoke to her. "My mistake. I misunderstood you. *Again*." He went back to the book.

The silence between them deepened. Narisa looked at the food and water. If she tried to swallow, she would choke. She wanted Tarik to kiss her again, tenderly this time, and listen to her explanation. She wanted him to care about her, but he did not. He loved Suria. She sighed.

Tarik did look up at that, his eyebrows raised, and she believed what she saw in his face was contempt for her timidity in a matter that meant little to most people. She did not know another woman who would have refused him.

"I have begun to translate," he said, his voice cool and businesslike. "I deciphered the date. This book was written not quite six hundred space-years ago."

"Will you read what it says out loud?" she asked.

He nodded, his eyes falling to the book again. Narisa settled back in her chair, relaxing a little, and Tarik began to read.

Chapter Five

"My name," Tarik read, "is Dulan, though that hardly matters to the story I must tell. There were one hundred and two of us originally, eighty humans and the rest of mixed Races, all driven from our home planets in the Jurisdiction after all telepaths were banished. We were a difficult group, and sometimes quarrelsome, for our customs and needs were too diverse for easy friendship, but we were firmly united in one purpose—to find a place outside the Jurisdiction where we could live without fear.

"During the Time of Dread immediately following the Act of Banishment, when so many telepaths were being killed or hounded to the very edges of the galaxy and beyond, we maintained contact with each other, and finally assembled at a chosen place on a neutral planet whose ruler turned a benign eye upon our presence. Her own mother had been a telepath. She herself lacked the Power, but for her late mother's sake she would make no move against us, daring punishment by the Assembly if her kindness were discovered. From such acts of conscience is freedom born.

"Through means best not recorded here, we commandeered a spaceship large enough to accommodate all of us and our considerable belongings. There was not one soul who was not a telepath who dared to go with us on that perilous journey. Families were broken, and hearts, too, mine among them, for my lover deserted me.

"There was good cause for such trepidation on the part of those not actually banished. We had taken a vote and had agreed that the safest place for us to settle would be the Empty Sector. Jurisdiction ships were unlikely to pursue us into that forbidden part of the galaxy, though we knew we would be tracked until we reached it. When we disappeared, as we planned to do, we would leave debris and a last transmission pleading for help. The Empty Sector has such a bad reputation that we believed the Assembly would assume ours was one of the many ships mysteriously destroyed there, and would *promptly forget about us. So far as I know, that is what happened.*

"*Everything we had heard about the Empty Sector proved true. We had many remarkable adventures during which we lost too many of our number. We searched more than a hundred planets before agreeing to settle on this one. By then there were only sixty-four of us left. We were weary of endless space travel, and this world's gravity and atmosphere were acceptable to all of us. We explored the planet completely, mapped all of it, and chose the location of our settlement with great care. Then we removed from the ship all materials and equipment we could possibly use, including the two computer-communicators that we had brought with us. We set the self-destruct mechanism and sent our ship out of its orbit around this world, heading toward the very center of the Empty Sector. We believe it did explode on schedule, for we saw brilliant flashes of light across the sky for three nights afterward.*

"*We cleared land and built our settlement. We farmed the rich soil, and for the most part lived in harmony with each other. We had endured so much together during our long journey that unbreakable bonds had been forged that transcended individual or Racial differences. After a few years some of us wanted a quieter place where we could retreat into privacy or solitude from time to time, and so this building was created, half a world away from the main settlement.*

"I should speak about the flora and fauna of our planet. Some of us were botanists, and they brought with them familiar plants. Others brought beneficial insects, or small mammals as pets, not knowing where we would settle, but wanting some part of their old lives to survive in the new. Most of these species flourished, adding to the lushness of the plant and animal life we found here. There are no large predators, but there is one species of extremely poisonous snake. I urge you to avoid it. Most other fauna are small and harmless, and usually friendly.

"We come now to the birds. We call them the Chon, for their repeating cries. If you have seen them, you know of their large size. They are blue or green, native to this planet, and they are semi-intelligent. They have the ability to communicate by a primitive kind of image transference, which is just short of actual telepathy. Because of our own telepathic abilities, we have been able to train them to help and protect us. They appear to pass learned information on to the next generation, so each generation is more intelligent, and therefore more useful to us, than the last. No coercion was used in this process of learning. The birds themselves instigated it. They are curious and friendly, and since they can fly and we cannot, they are able to gather certain kinds of information more easily than we can.

"Children were born to some of us. I recovered from my broken heart and took a mate, and we had a son and a daughter. For one hundred of this planet's years we flourished in peace.

"That is not quite one hundred space-years, which is to say, time as it is kept at the Capital of the Jurisdiction and which is by decree used on all Service space-ships, whether it be the natural time of the spaceships' crews or not. Once we had landed here, we made our own calendars in keeping with the rhythms of this world, and ours is a shorter year with a slightly longer day.

"All the same, we lived more than a human's normal life span, and it was the same for the other Races among us. We believed it was something in the soil or the water. It scarcely mattered which. We were happy, most of us, and certain we were entirely safe.

"After a hundred of our years, we were found by a Cetan ship that had gone off course. They came to rape and pillage and loot, and we were defenseless against their savagery. They took much of material value, and all that was price-less—our young men and women. The old

*and the very young they killed. Twelve of
us, old folk all, survived by hiding, and
later made our way to this island, which
the Cetans had not found. We watched on
the computer screen as the Cetans left our
world, and we saw their ship explode
before it left orbit. We had received a telepathic message from a young man aboard
it. Our sons and daughters, though
captive, had found a way to sabotage the
ship and had chosen to blow it up and die
rather than live in slavery. Thus perished
a people who wanted only to live in peace.*

*"We twelve survivors lived on here. We
had no heart to return to the main settlement, and our friends the birds were nearby. They make their homes in the cliffs
next to the island. Many of them were
killed by the Cetans for cruel sport and
for their glorious plummage, or when
they tried to protect us. Their numbers
are now badly diminished, but they will
recover in time and reproduce again.*

*"We on the island were not so
fortunate. We were all too old to produce
young ones. I am the last of our group,
and when I die, we will be extinct. The
non-humans among us went first, six of
them, and then my dear mate and two
more within a day of each other. We remaining three lived on, adding the sum of
our individual knowledge to the computer's memory banks. At last there were
only two of us. Ten days ago my dear*

*friend Tula died, who stood by me
through heartache and joy for so many
years, and I dug the last grave in the
burial plot on the side of the island
nearest the cliffs. The birds will watch
over all of them.*

*"For myself there will be no grave,
unless the one who reads this when I am
gone will inter my remains. All is in order
here on the island. I have finished with
the computer. Its memory banks were
filled with information about the planet
and our lives here. But I have never
trusted machinery. I much prefer the
mind, human or other, and so I have
turned off the power and have hand-
written this very brief account of our
history. I do not know if anyone will ever
find it, but still I hope.*

*"I grow tired. I will rest a while, and for
safety's sake, I will lock the notebook and
the key for the computer into a drawer.
The couch looks most inviting."*

Tarik closed the book, his face solemn.

"And so," he said softly, "Dulan locked up
the book and the key, and went across the
room to rest. And very likely never rose
again."

"How lonely it must have been," Narisa
whispered, "to be the last, with such memories and nothing to do but wait for death.
Tarik, we still don't know if the writer was a
man or a woman."

"I suppose," he said reluctantly, "that information is somewhere in the computer. Or there might be medical information that would help us analyze the bones. I know men and women have different pelvic bones, and there are other skeletal differences. But I don't think I want to disturb Dulan except to bury the remains with proper respect. Does it really matter so much? That person on the couch, of whatever gender, was a victim of the Jurisdiction."

"No, of the Cetans." Narisa's eyes narrowed, her lips curled with the contempt and disgust she felt. "Always the Cetans, those vile creatures."

"The Cetans have been blamed for entirely too much. The people who died on this planet would not have been found here, totally unprotected, if the Assembly had not banished them from the Jurisdiction," Tarik said flatly. "They were only a few of the millions who died needlessly from one cause or other, not all of them having to do with the Cetans. Don't try to defend the Act of Banishment, or the Assembly that passed it, to me."

Narisa believed he was still angry with her for her earlier rejection of him, and that was why he spoke so sharply now. Perhaps, also, he had been as affected as she by Dulan's story and wanted to hide his feelings.

She had always been taught that telepaths were an immoral, wicked group, but faced with this tragic story, she could feel only sympathy for Dulan and the other settlers.

Surely, in all the wide galaxy, there ought to be room to accommodate those who were different from Jurisdiction norms.

She decided to overlook Tarik's remarks, as she had tried to thrust out of her mind other things he had said about the Jurisdiction and the Assembly that ruled it. She kept silent, not wanting to irritate him further, and not wanting to admit aloud her own sudden qualms about an important Jurisdiction law. The unsettled feeling she had experienced since landing on this planet had intensified as she had listened to Dulan's story. The possibility that the laws the Assembly made were sometimes wrong or even unnecessarily cruel had occurred to her before and had been rejected. She could not reject that possibility now. And if one law was wrong, others could be, too. She frowned, feeling that such ideas were disloyal to all her training.

Tarik's slightly raised voice broke into her troubled thoughts. She realized he had been speaking to her for a while and had apparently taken her lengthening silence for indifference.

"Have you no curiosity, Narisa? Wouldn't you like to see the main settlement Dulan's people built?"

"Yes, I would," she admitted, glad to discuss a neutral subject. "I admire their courage, Tarik. They could not help being born telepaths, and I don't doubt they suffered terribly for their talents. They must have built a remarkable settlement, but

wouldn't it have been destroyed to its
foundations by the Cetans? It's probably
covered with forest after so many centuries.
Why don't we investigate the information
stored in the computer before we start
exploring? Dulan said the main settlement
was half the planet away from here." The
thought of setting out on foot for another long
journey through thick forest or across dry,
stony desert was too much for her to deal
with after the last few days. She had not
realized just how worn out she was. She
couldn't help drooping in her chair.

Tarik noticed. "We both need a rest before
doing any more travelling,' he conceded.
"This is the best place to do that. You are
right about searching the computer's memory
banks. However, I think the first thing we
should do is bury Dulan, as he, or she, wanted.
He glanced upward toward the round window
in the high dome. "It has stopped raining. I'll
go look for the burial ground."

"I'm going with you," Narisa said.

"As you wish. But sit where you are and eat
that wafer while I try to find whatever Dulan
used to dig the other graves."

Narisa was content to do just that. She even
put her feet up on the second chair, and was
half asleep when Tarik came out of one of the
storerooms with a shovel in his hand.

"Isn't it interesting," he remarked, "that
there are some things that don't change? In
spite of all our technological advances,
Dulan's shovel is basically the same as the

ones we use today, and it is probably not so
different from the shovels used a million
years ago. Every Race with hands has something similar.''

"You look remarkably happy for a man
who's about to dig a grave," she noted.

"I prefer this to sending ashes into space
the way we do, and we know that it is what
Dulan wanted," he replied.

They had trouble finding the ancient grave
site. The island was larger than they had
thought, and Dulan had written only that it
was on the side nearest the cliffs.

"What we need," Narisa remarked after
they had tramped back and forth for a while,
unsuccessful in their efforts, "is a bird with
a long memory to help us."

"Call one." Tarik was testing the ground
around an oddly shaped stone that he thought
might have been used as a marker for the grave-
yard, and thus he answered her absently.

"I don't know how." Narisa wondered
whether Dulan had called aloud or had some
instrument to bring the birds when they were
needed.

Dulan used the powers of the mind. That
long-dead person had been telepathic, after all.
Narisa, lacking that power, could not sum-
mon them. She wished she could. How lovely
it would be simply to think of a bird, the blue
one with the scratched beak for instance, and
have it come. She could imagine it, blue wings
spread, gliding in to land beside her.

"Chon. Chon-chon. Chon."

Narisa spun around. The blue bird folded its wings and stood watching her. Behind her, Tarik laughed aloud.

"Did you call it?" he asked.

"No, I only thought how nice it would be if it came to help us. I'm not a telepath, Tarik," she added defensively.

"You are not, but the bird is. Why don't we both think about Dulan, and digging a grave near the other ones, and see what happens?"

Only a day before, Narisa would have protested that what Tarik had just suggested was against Jurisdiction law. But Dulan's story had changed her thought patterns until she could not believe there had been any evil, or any danger to the Jurisdiction from the settlers who had come to this planet. She thought about Dulan, about the eleven telepaths who lay somewhere near, of Tula, the only other one whose name she knew, and of Dulan's mate who had gone before. Dulan deserved to be buried with them. She scarcely noticed that Tarik, standing behind her, had put his two hands on her shoulders. The bird watched them both.

After a few minutes the blue wings opened. The bird flew to a low hill covered with bushes, and perched on top of it, looking back at them.

"Of course," Tarik exclaimed. "High enough to be out of reach of the waves in a bad storm." He moved toward the bird, his hands still on Narisa's shoulders, pushing her along before him. The bird flitted to one side as they drew near. Tarik hugged Narisa.

"This is the place, I'm certain of it," he cried.

"But I didn't do anything," Narisa said, confused. "All I did was think."

"That's all we needed to do. The bird did the rest. Look." He was on his knees, pulling up a layer of weeds and turf. "There is a stone here with a word carved on it. Let me get the dirt off and see if I can read it. *Tula*. This is it, Narisa. We've found it, the three of us together."

She saw in his excited expression that he had forgotten his earlier anger with her. For the moment at least they were functioning together in complete harmony. Tarik paced out an approximate size for Tula's grave, based on Dulan's height. Narisa marked the boundaries with broken twigs she stuck into the damp ground. They could find no sign of another grave next to Tula's, and the bird made no move to stop them, so they cleared away a small bush, and Tarik began to dig a hole of similar size.

"We will put the two friends side by side," he said.

The rain had stopped, and the sun was shining again, but the air was still very humid and growing hotter. It was not long before Tarik was drenched in perspiration and nearly covered with mud. When he paused for breath, Narisa took the shovel and continued the digging.

"That's deep enough," Tarik said at last.

"It's time to get Dulan."

They returned to the grave site a little later,
carrying between them Dulan's bones, which
they had gently wrapped in the coverlet from
one of the beds. The bird was still standing
near the grave, but when it saw them, it flew
away.

"We should have checked the computer to
see if there is a burial ritual," Narisa said.

"If we find one later, we can come back then
and say the correct words," Tarik told her.
"For now, this is the best we can do."

They laid Dulan in the grave they had dug.
Tarik had picked up the shovel to begin replacing the soil over the remains when there
was a rustle of wings and the bird reappeared.
In its beak was a flower, one of the yellow,
cup-shaped ones Tarik had noticed growing
on a vine in the forest. The bird dropped the
flower on top of the wrappings covering
Dulan.

Narisa began to cry. She could not help it;
the tears simply came, pouring down her
cheeks. She, who never wept, who believed
tears were a sign of weakness, sagged against
Tarik, feeling his strong arms holding her upright while she sobbed uncontrollably. It was
not only for Dulan's lonely end that she wept,
but for her own family and friends also, for
whose deaths she had not allowed herself to
shed a tear lest she never stop crying.

When Tarik lifted her into his arms and
carried her back to the white stone building,
she put her arms around his neck and her

head on his shoulder, and wept like some small, lost child. Tarik laid her on a bed in one of the personal rooms, pulled off her muddy boots and uniform, and covered her warmly, for she was shivering in spite of the heat. She was sobbing still, her face streaked with tears and dirt, her hair hanging in limp strands. Tarik sat on the edge of the bed, holding one of her mud-streaked hands in his.

"I'm sorry," she wept. "I can't seem to stop."

"Cry all you want and don't be ashamed." He squeezed her hand. "Perhaps it was time for you to weep." He stayed where he was, keeping her hand in his until her sobs finally stopped and she drifted into sleep. After a while, certain she would not waken soon, he went back to the open grave and finished burying Dulan.

Narisa woke later to a dim room illuminated only by the light shining through the partially open door. Realizing she was wearing only her undergarments, she sat up to look for her uniform. Not finding it, she went to the door and gazed into the main room.

Tarik stood beside the computer-communicator. She had to look twice to be certain it really was Tarik. She had never seen anyone so dirty. It was hard to tell he was wearing a Service uniform. He was encrusted from head to foot with mud and leaves. A few twigs, along with other more mysterious debris, clung to his untidy hair. His face was smeared with dirt. Even his beard was filthy.

"What have you been doing?" she asked.

"Making repairs." He diverted his attention from the computer screen to grin proudly at her. "I have fixed the plumbing. Some animal had made a nest in one of the cold water pipes and blocked it. I cleaned it out. Then I found the heat source and turned it on, so the bathing room is now ready for use, with a choice of hot or cold water."

"You need it," she murmured, but not unkindly. He was so enthusiastic about his accomplishments, she could not help smiling at him. She gestured toward the computer-communicator. "Have you got that working, too?"

"Just a little while ago. It controls the ventilation and heating systems for the building, as well as the lights."

"I can tell. It's much more comfortable now." The stale odor was gone, and the temperature was nearly ideal. Around the base of the dome a system of indirect lighting shone, illuminating the carved frieze and lending a soft glow to the white room. Narisa could see through the window in the top of the dome that it was night. Tarik had gotten the lights working just in time.

He had found furniture, too, probably in the storerooms they had only glanced into earlier. A table and two low, cushioned chairs had been set out near the couch where Dulan had lain. The original cushions were gone from the couch, as was the thick layer of dust. New cushions covered with blue-green fabric padded the couch. The large central room looked almost like a home.

"Have you been able to get much information out of it?" Narisa asked Tarik, who had turned back to the computer-communicator. She did not suggest trying to call the Capital. Tarik's earlier anger against her had vanished completely, and she did not want to annoy him again. Nor did she mention her tearful outburst at Dulan's grave. It would only embarrass her to speak of it now.

"I haven't had time to begin researching the history of Dulan's settlement," Tarik told her. "I've been more concerned with our practical needs. When I found the heat source for the water, I discovered it is also used for cooking and for heating the entire building. It's in a subterranean room and it's really very ingenious. There are hot springs on this island. The water from them is pumped into the room below this, where it's stored until needed. I'll show it to you tomorrow. Fortunately for us, Dulan had turned off the valve that lets the hot water into the tanks, and then had drained the entire system. Once I opened the valve and flushed out the pipes, it worked perfectly."

"Then we could make hot food. If only we had something to cook."

"That is just what I've been checking." Tarik indicated the console. "There is a record in here of everything in the storerooms. I'm certain the food we found is safe to eat. So is the water, in case you were worrying, both the lake and hot springs."

"How wonderful. I'm so hungry, and I never did like those compressed wafers."

"You won't have to eat them anymore. Why don't you use the bathing room while I finish what I'm doing here? Then I'll clean myself up, and we'll have a feast."

"Where is my uniform?"

"I spread it out in one of the storerooms until it's dry enough to shake off the dirt. Use some of the clothing left in the personal rooms. That's what I'm going to do."

Narisa nodded agreement and went to see what she could find. Service uniforms were made of a specially formulated material that kept the wearer warm or cool as necessary, and never needed to be cleaned. When a uniform got wet, as hers had, it needed only to be dried, then shaken hard to release any dirt trapped in the fibers. Aboard ship, with its clean, filtered air, Narisa had never felt uncomfortable wearing the same uniform day after day. But on this planet, after tramping across a desert and through a forest, she found she did not want to put it on again.

She quickly overcame any scruples she had about using the clothing of Dulan's long-dead friends, and selected a silvery gray robe from one of the drawers in the room she had been using, and a pair of matching low-heeled slippers that had straps only across the toes. They were a little small, but they would do.

Tarik had stocked the bathing room with cleansers, some of them scented, and after

washing her much-worn undergarments and
hanging them to dry, Narisa luxuriated in hot
water and perfume until she felt clean once
more. The silver robe she had chosen was
simply styled, with a wide round neck and
long loose sleeves, both edged with pale blue
braid. There was a matching braid sash,
which she fastened about her slender waist. It
had been a long time since she had worn anything other than a Service uniform. She found
she liked the feeling of the smooth, delicate
material against her skin and the way the
skirt of the gown moved against her bare legs
when she walked back into the central room.

"I've finished, if you want to bathe," she
said to Tarik.

He was still bending over the console. He
looked up as she spoke, then straightened
slowly. He stared at her like one entranced,
taking in every detail of her appearance, from
her freshly washed golden brown hair and
lovely face to the exquisite robe she wore and
the delicate sandals showing beneath the garment's shining folds.

" 'So fair she takes the breath of men away
who gaze upon her . . .' " he whispered. "You
are unbelievably beautiful, Narisa."

"Thank you," she whispered back, stunned
by his reaction. No one had ever called her
beautiful before. She was absurdly pleased by
the compliment. As for his strange, rhythmic
words, they reminded her of the broken
phrases he had uttered when he had been sick
and only partly conscious. She was going to

ask him about that, had her mouth opened to
do so, when he spoke.

"I had better use the bathing room at once,"
he said, rubbing his face with one hand and
thereby streaking mud more thoroughly
across his cheeks. "I'm ashamed to be in the
same room with you when you look so lovely
and I'm in this condition. I'll do something
about it right away. I even found something to
take off this beard. I won't be long."

He disappeared into the bathing room and
closed the door. Narisa was going to call after
him, to ask if he wanted her to begin preparing their meal, but she heard the water
running and knew he couldn't hear her.

Instead she walked across the room to the
console. Tarik had left the computer on. Dis-
played on the screen was an inventory of one
of the storerooms. It listed irradiated and
dried food. She touched a few buttons, easily
calling up more information on food supplies.
Listed in order were the dried herbs and
spices she would need to make a stew.

The simple machine was remarkably easy
to use, and she stood with her fingers resting
lightly on the buttons, wrestling with the
temptation they presented. The turmoil in her
mind was intensely painful. She wanted to
obey Tarik. He was her superior officer, and
she owed him her obedience. More than that,
she had begun to care for him and therefore
wanted to please him by doing as he wished.
She did not want to destroy the emotion that
had led him to call her beautiful, nor end the

tender mood that had enveloped them minutes ago.

And yet she, who had memorized the rule book, knew they ought to have sent a rescue call as soon as they had the machine working. It was wrong, and possibly dangerous, to delay any longer. Should she do what Tarik wanted and wait, or should she follow Service regulations and send a message?

Deep inside herself she felt she had betrayed the Jurisdiction by her admission that the laws could be unjust. Dulan's story had shown her how cruel the Act of Banishment was. She felt a deep sympathy toward the telepath, not only because of persecution by an unfair law, but because Dulan had suffered from Cetan depredations in much the same way as Narisa had, losing both family and friends.

But the Jurisdiction taught that telepaths were wicked. She felt guilty for caring about Dulan. Perhaps, she reasoned, obeying regulations by sending a message would alleviate her guilt.

Then there was the matter of what the Cetans had done to the *Reliance*. She owed it to her dead shipmates to return to the Capital and report what had happened. The Service might be able to use the information she could provide, to hunt down and punish the Cetan ship responsible for the attack. The crew of the *Reliance* deserved that much from her.

They deserved it from Tarik, too, but Narisa was convinced he would find excuses

to delay sending a message, if, indeed, he ever
sent one. She believed he had become so en-
thralled by this strange new world, and so
eager to remain, that he had forgotten his
duty.

She knew her own responsibility to the Service. It had been drilled into her for more than
ten space-years, and she had accepted it,
knowing the Service and its regulations must
come before anything else in her life. Regulations required her to send a message, and
send it at once.

Tarik would be furious with her if she went
ahead and did it. His tenderness toward her
would end as quickly as the mist evaporated
off the lake at dawn.

Tarik was wrong. He was disobeying regulations.

Narisa could hear the water still running
behind the closed door of the bathing room.
She forced herself to stop thinking any more
of those painful, conflicting thoughts. She
pushed to the back of her mind Tarik's insistence on waiting. She tried to forget her
feelings for him. She could allow herself only
one thought.

Duty to the Service first. Duty . . .

She punched in the standard rescue call and
held the *SEND* button down for as long as she
dared.

Chapter Six

When Tarik reappeared, the exact display he had left on the computer screen was still showing, and Narisa was just coming out of one of the storage rooms with an armful of food packets. She stopped short, staring at him in much the same way as he had looked at her earlier.

Tarik was not only clean, he was shaved. She thought how attractive his sharp-featured face was, long and narrow and rather pale, as though carved out of some fine, smoothly polished stone. He had chosen a deep crimson robe, made in the same simple style as Narisa's, but left unbelted. The neck and sleeves were edged with wide bands of blue and gold embroidery.

"You look splendid," Narisa said. "Like some grand ancient ruler."

"That's appropriate," he responded, smiling at her.

"Really? Why?" Narisa returned his smile, but nervously, as she moved toward the kitchen. She knew she had done the right thing in sending the rescue call, and searched for the relief she thought she would feel after having made that difficult decision.

Even now, somewhere far out in the galaxy, Service spaceships were receiving that signal and determining where it had originated. It was a good thing their instruments could do that, since she did not have an exact idea where she was. But she was certain that Service ships would find them soon.

"I'll tell you later," Tarik said, taking some of the food packets she was carrying.

"Tell me what?"

"Why it's appropriate for me to look like an ancient person." He laughed at her. "What are you thinking of, Narisa? Your mind is somewhere off in space."

"No, it's not," she said quickly. "I was only thinking about the stew I'm going to make."

"I'll help you." He followed her into the kitchen.

It was a small room, white, as were all the others in this building, and made even smaller by a wide ledge around three sides of it, upon which food could be prepared. A heating surface for cooking took up one section. Narisa reached for the button to turn the heat on, and bumped into Tarik.

"I'll do it." He leaned across her, his arm brushing her right breast as he did so. Narisa caught her breath at the contact and stepped back a pace. Tarik turned on the heat, then reached behind her to pick up one of the food packets she had laid on the counter. Narisa was still moving backward when she stepped on his toes.

"Careful, please." His face was very close to hers.

"I'm sorry." She turned around and found herself almost in his arms. "It's cramped in here."

"Yes, isn't it?" He made what Narisa believed was an entirely unnecessary reach over her shoulder toward the counter, which brought his mouth to within a millimeter of the sensitive place where her throat and shoulder met. She could feel his warm breath on her skin. "You used the scented cleanser," he murmured.

"Tarik, please, you're pushing me against the hot section."

"Then come here." Placing his hands on her shoulders, he pulled her against him. She looked straight into his night-dark eyes. His voice was soft, caressing her when he said her name. "Narisa."

She knew he wanted to kiss her. She wanted it, too, wanted to feel again the way the pressure of his hard body had made her feel when they had kissed in the rain. She fought valiantly for self-control.

"We will never eat," she told him severely, "if I can't prepare the stew. And I can't do that if we keep bumping into each other."

"Then you stay here." He moved her to face

the heated section of the counter. "And I'll work over here. We need a good meal first."

First? Before what? Narisa's heart began to pound. Did Tarik mean what she thought he meant, that he wanted to make love to her? Lovemaking would mean nothing for them, for he loved Suria, not Narisa. She should never forget that. Tarik might believe they would be marooned on this planet forever, and Narisa would be the only woman available. In that case, it would still mean nothing to him.

But the truth, Narisa admitted silently to herself as she tore open a packet of irradiated vegetables, was that she wanted Tarik to make love to her. She was already entirely too fond of him. She warned herself to be very careful, lest she give away her heart completely, and it be broken. She forced out of her mind the image of a naked Tarik lying next to her on a couch, and directed all her attention to the food she was preparing.

In a surprisingly short time, considering how unfamiliar both the food and implements were, they turned the food packets into an appetizing stew, which sent its delicious odor wafting throughout the building. There were round, flat loaves of dry bread to sop up the juices, and Tarik had discovered a supply of distilled spirits in one of the storerooms.

"It's not Falernian wine," he said, opening a glazed ceramic bottle and sniffing at the contents, "but it will do."

"What is Falernian wine?"

"The Romans used to drink it."

"Romans?" Narisa looked blank, then re-membered. "Oh, yes, on Old Earth. I see now why you said your robe is appropriate. It's because you can talk about ancient things."

"Only to you, Narisa. To no one else, not for long space-years. I love history, real history, not the censored and carefully molded ver-sion taught in the Jurisdiction. Most people have no idea what hardships our ancestors endured in ancient times, or how difficult it was for them to leave Earth and settle throughout the galaxy. It's a wonder the Race survived all the wars and the terrible accidents. There were times when whole planets died."

"You've said that before, that the Juris-diction doesn't teach the truth about our past."

"It doesn't."

Nairsa, still feeling guilty about her earlier defection from total loyalty to the Juris-diction, wanted to argue the point, but decided to let it drop in favor of not spoiling his agreeable mood or the meal they were about to eat.

They laid the food on the table Tarik had placed in the central room, along with spoons and bowls for the stew. Tarik found cups for the liquor, and larger ones for a hot herbal drink he had brewed according to a recipe Dulan, or someone, had put into the computer. He pulled out one of the cushioned chairs for Narisa, seating her with a deep bow and a wave of one hand that made her laugh at his exaggerated formality. He took the other chair, across the table from her, and tasted the stew she had ladled into their bowls.

"This is delicious. Far superior to wafers." He began to eat with the relish of a half-starved man.

"Tarik," she said, changing the subject, "when you were sick you kept saying the strangest things. The bread, and your talk about wine, reminded me."

"Of what?" His eyes were twinkling. "Did I tell you all my secrets?"

"Among other things, you talked about a loaf of bread and a jug of wine."

"Poetry." He took another mouthful of stew.

"Poetry?"

"It's like the words to a song, but without the music."

"I know what poetry is. What you said did not sound like any poetry I've ever heard."

"It's from Old Earth."

"Always Old Earth. You were born in the wrong time and place, Tarik." Narisa sipped the liquor. It had a sweet, fiery taste and made her head swim a little, but she liked it.

"I agree with you." Tarik broke one of the round loaves of bread into halves and gave her part of it. Then he poured a little more of the liquor into their cups. "I would rather have lived in ancient days, when men made their own destinies and were not forced to obey Jurisdiction laws, or follow the paths laid down for them by others."

"Do you want anarchy?"

"No, only a little freedom. I have always

done as I was ordered to do, Narisa. I had no
desire to rebel and be sent to a detention
planet. Had I been free to do what I wanted, I
would have been a scholar, not a spaceman.
I'd have written accurate history, and a little
bad poetry, and I'd have been content."

Narisa was silent, fingering her cup and
wondering if Tarik had had too much from
the ceramic bottle.

"And you," he went on. "You told me once
you became a navigator to please your father.
Had you pleased yourself, what would you
have done?"

"I don't know. I never let myself think about
it. I did as I was told to do."

"Have you been happy?"

"As happy as anyone ever is." She thought
for a moment, considering how much to
reveal to him, then said, "Ever since we
landed on this planet, I have felt strangely
confused. At first I thought it was the effect of
the crash. Later, I thought it was the desert
sun and lack of water, or the juice we
swallowed. Now I don't know what it is. I
watched the sun rise this morning and felt
happy just to be in the midst of that beauty. I
see one of the birds appear, and I'm filled with
delight at its presence. I never cry, yet I did
today. My feelings about so many things are
changing. Like the way I think of you. I used
to—" She stopped.

"Dislike me?" he finished for her. "Don't
deny it, I know you did." The lack of anger in
his tone gave her the courage to say what she
otherwise would have left unspoken. Or per-

haps it was the liquor that loosened her tongue.

"It was you who resented me," she said softly. "From the very first. Because of Suria."

"Suria? What do you mean?"

"Because I had been given her post. You wanted her as navigator, not me."

"Is that what you thought?" He caught her hand across the table and held it tightly. "Narisa, I did not want Suria. What was between us ended well before you came aboard the *Reliance*. Suria wanted to stop space travel and leave the Service so she could have a child. She had applied for permission some time ago, and since her family is highly placed on her home planet, the chances are good she'll be allowed to reproduce. So you see, she would have left the ship even if you had not been assigned as navigator. And, incidentally, we never discussed Suria having my child."

"Then why did you treat me so badly?" Narisa asked. She tried to pull her hand out of his, but he would not let it go. He leaned across the table, his face serious, his eyes locked on hers. She held her breath, waiting for his answer.

"Because I wanted you so much," he said. "I saw that you had nothing to do with any of the men on board. I thought you disliked men. You certainly seemed to dislike me, and I did not want to risk being hurt by you if you rejected me. So I made myself treat you with rigid correctness and nothing more. You can't imagine what you've put me through, how often I wanted to touch you when you were so distant, to say something funny so I could hear your laugh. I used to pace my cabin, listening to you cry out in the grip of a nightmare, and wished I could break through the door that separated us to hold you in my arms and comfort you."

"Tarik, I thought you hated me." The words came out in a rush as she tried to comprehend what he was saying. How could she have misunderstood him so badly?

"Oh, no." He caressed the side of her face with a slim yet very strong hand, smoothing a loose wisp of hair away from her cheek, while his other hand still held hers enfolded in his grasp. "I never hated you, Narisa. And I want you still. You must know that."

"Tarik?" Her voice cracked with emotion as she spoke his name. She hardly dared believe what she had just learned. "I thought I did dislike you. You were so critical of me, and so arrogant. But when I saw you after the Cetan attack, injured and likely to die, I knew I couldn't leave you behind on the *Reliance*. You make me so angry, you have no respect for Service regulations or Jurisdiction laws, and you make me think about things I would rather not think of at all. But something about you touches the deepest part of me, and when you kiss me, I know that I want you, too. Still, I'm afraid." It cost her a good deal to admit that, but she had to say it.

He let go of her hand to cup her face between both of his hands, then leaned over and kissed her lightly.

"My sweet Narisa, there is nothing to fear. I won't hurt you, no more than any other man has. Or is that it? Did someone hurt you once, perhaps the first time? Is that why you're afraid?"

"No." She caught at his hands, pulling them away from her face. "Tarik, there hasn't been any other man. No one at all."

"No one?" he repeated, his amazement plain to see.

Narisa hurried on nervously, looking anywhere but at his astonished face. "I know most people treat lovemaking very casually, but it seemed too important to me. There was never the right man among my friends, not even on Belta when I was fifteen, which is the usual age there to begin such things, and so I just waited. And kept on waiting."

"Yet you said you wanted me."

"I do." She made herself meet his eyes at last, overwhelmed by emotion and absolutely certain of what she was doing. "I don't want to wait any longer. Please, Tarik."

"Narisa, my sweet love." He meant those words. She had never seen such an expression on a man's face before, of wonder and surprise, and yes, love. It was not just physical hunger Tarik felt for her. She was wise enough to see that.

He rose from his chair and held out his arms, and she went into them, putting her own arms around him, feeling his strength beneath the thin red robe, and his need of her. She raised her face.

Their mouths met in a warm, lingering kiss

that went on and on until Narisa imagined he
had drawn her very soul out of her body and
made it his own. When the kiss finally ended,
she hung in his arms, her eyes closed, while he
covered her face and throat with more kisses.
He returned finally to her softly parted lips,
his tongue searching gently across them, then
plunging into the moist sweetness of her
mouth. Narisa moaned and leaned against
him, overcome with weakness. She felt him
lift her off her feet and was glad of it, for her
knees would not have held her much longer.

Tarik carried her to the grandest of the personal rooms, and laid her down upon one of
the beds. He leaned over her, brushing his
mouth across her cheek.

"In ancient days on Old Earth," he
whispered, "a woman preserved her virginity
until her marriage night, then gave it in love
and trust to her husband."

"Marriage?" Narisa's eyelids fluttered
open. Like her parents? Did he really care for
her that much? His next words answered her
unspoken question.

"I love you, Narisa. I have since I first saw
you. And because I love you, I respect and
trust you, as I hope you do me. Most of all, I
treasure what you freely give me now."

"Oh, Tarik." She could not meet his eyes.
She had already violated his trust by sending
out the rescue call. Wishing she had never
touched the computer-communicator, she
buried her face in his neck, hiding her guilt.

"If you don't love me now, perhaps you will
in time. But whether you do or not, I love you

and always will." He began to demonstrate
that love with his hands and mouth and with
murmured words. Golden lines of beautiful
ancient poetry caressed her ears as he
removed her gown and slippers, and told her
how beautiful she was, how priceless, how
dear to him.

She saw his naked body, slim and taut and
full with need of her, and her own body responded to the sight with a moist, aching
emptiness that cried out to be filled by him.
She was consumed by a deep longing that
sprang into life wherever he touched her. Her
fear vanished along with her lingering sense
of guilt over the message she had sent. She
would worry later about what she had done.
For now there was only Tarik.

He was gentle with her, touching her
tenderly, urging her to touch him in return,
stirring all her senses until she opened to him
as naturally as a flower in springtime. Her
discomfort at this first joining with a man
was brief, only an instant of pain, and a small
price to pay for the sweetness of complete
union with him, or the unbelievable ecstasy
that followed. Narisa lay drenched in
pleasure while he loved her, and told her he
loved her, until he could speak no more but
cried out his joy with gasping sounds that
spoke more of love than words could ever do.
And when they were both replete with love, he
cradled her in his arms and whispered words
again until she slept with her head over his
heart.

She woke to love again later, with no apprehension this time, his body more familiar to her now, as hers was to him, and it was more beautiful, more exciting and fulfilling than the first time.

"How strange," Tarik mused as they lay close together afterward, "that we who are not afraid to risk our lives in space travel should be so fearful for our hearts. How self-protective we have both been, and would have gone on being, had we not crashed on this blessed planet."

"I trained myself not to feel anything at all," she told him.

"And now?" He ran his hand over her with loving freedom.

"Now I feel too much, and my only fear is that it won't last."

"It will," he assured her. "To my life's end and beyond."

Would it last, Narisa wondered, past her telling him of the rescue call she had sent? She would have to do that soon. But not yet. Not until he had loved her once more and made her cry out in wild passion as he taught her yet new ways of delight.

She postponed telling him all the next day while they explored the island, and swam naked in the lake and made love on the beach under the hot orange-gold sun until they were both covered with sand. They fell apart laughing, lying side by side with his fingers woven between hers.

"I'm happy," Tarik said. "I have never been happy before."

"Not even when you were a little boy?" She envisioned a small, wiry child with dark hair falling into his eyes, who questioned everything.

"I was an odd child." He squinted into the deep blue sky, his eyes on a pair of circling birds. He seemed to be speaking more to them than to Narisa at his side. "I did not fit into my family very well. I made my parents uneasy, especially my father. My mother and my brother could always manage my father, but I only made him angry."

"Why?" Narisa asked, amused. "Too many questions?"

"Yes, and as I grew older, most of them about the intentions of the Assembly. Since my father is one of its foremost Members, my questions did not please him." Tarik sighed. "Then my older brother and I quarreled. We parted on bad terms. I'm sorry for that, because we had agreed the Assembly needs reforming and some of its most repressive laws must be repealed or there will be a great revolution in a few decades, which could destroy the Jurisdiction. Together, with our mother to back us, we might have convinced our father to take the first steps toward change."

"I'm sorry you and your brother quarreled," Narisa said softly. She did not want to talk about the Assembly or the Jurisdiction. Her mind was on more romantic subjects. She turned on her side and ran her hand across his chest. Tarik smiled suddenly, catching Narisa's exploring fingers and bringing them to his lips. The change in his mood from solemn to loving was startling.

"You are my peace," he whispered, "and my joy. 'True love is a durable fire, in the mind ever burning.' I burn for you, my love."

"More poetry," she teased. "I'm beginning to like it."

"And me?"

"And you." She had not yet said she loved him. She was still afraid to put her feelings into words, but she thought he must know how she felt by the way she accepted him so gladly when he began to caress her and then bent to nibble at one bare breast.

She could not tell him what she had done then, not while passion was rising so deliciously in both of them once more and he was pulling her on top of him to make her embrace him in rapturous frenzy.

After a while, she rose to plunge into the lake again, leaving him dozing on the sand. She scrubbed herself with both hands until the sand was washed away from her face and hair and body. Then she swam far out into the lake, slicing the water with long, sure Beltan strokes, glorying in the element in which, like all Beltans, she felt most at home.

When she finally turned back toward shore, she saw that Tarik had entered the water, too. He stood naked and knee-deep, watching her. She waved a leisurely arm and started toward him. After a few strokes she decided to show off a little, to amuse hm. She took the necessary three deep breaths and dove deep into the crystaline water.

She could not find the bottom at first. The water was a perfectly clear blue-green, pierced by long shafts of golden sunlight. There was no bottom to the lake, or at least none that Narisa could see. For just a moment she was lost, disoriented as she had never been when swimming on Belta, until she noticed the faint outline of a gray ledge. It rose precipitously, and she followed it upward. It must be, she decided, a continuation of the cliffs that edged the side of the lake nearest the island. Soon she saw pale sand and knew she had judged her distance well.

She stood up suddenly, coming out of the water in a surge of bubbles and laughter, flinging her hair back to get it out of her eyes, holding out her arms to Tarik, who stood close to her. His concerned, searching expression lightened at once.

" 'Thus,' " he declaimed, laughing back at her, " 'did Venus rise from out the sea.' "

"Poetry again! I recognize it now." She threw her arms around his neck and bore him down into the water, her sudden assault unbalancing him. But not completely. The next thing she knew, she was lifted high into his arms and he was carrying her ashore.

"Who was Venus?" she asked, nibbling at his ear lobe.

"An ancient goddess of love," he answered, holding her so that her body slid down his wet frame until they stood pressed tightly together from toe to forehead. "She was born of the sea. She was beautiful beyond all imagining. Like you."

"Did she have a lover?" Narisa murmured, her lips touching his.

"Many."

"Then I am not like her, for I shall have only one. Only you."

The look in his eyes when she said that was so deep, so glowing and warm and tender, that she knew she could not tell him yet about the message she had sent. Instead, she told him about the depths of the lake and her theory that it must be of volcanic origin. She talked on and on until he stopped her very reasonable scientific speculations with a shower of kisses that left her knees weak and her head spinning, and made her postpone the telling until later still.

But she did not tell him later, when, bathed and clothed again, they worked together at the computer-communicator, learning as much as they could of the planet's history and of the knowledge of Dulan and Tula and their friends. They walked along the shore at sunset, hand in hand, watching the birds fishing, and Tarik's love for her was so open and so precious to her that she could not spoil the moment. She would tell him the next day, she promised herself, after another rapturous night spent in his arms, learning more of the ways of love.

She put it off again while they ate in the morning. The day was gray and misty, with a steady rain, and Tarik decreed they would spend all of it at the computer-communicator.

"With appropriate pauses," he teased, kissing her nose. "Aren't you glad we haven't tried to call the Capital? We can explore the planet ourselves, without interference, now that we have all the information in here." He gave the console a little pat and moved to turn the machinery on. "Afterward we'll decide what we want to do, whether to attempt to communicate with the Capital or not. This machine is so old, the rescue signal from it might not reach that far. It might be more dangerous to use it than for the two of us to just live here. I have an idea about modifications, if we decide we do want to call, though I confess I wouldn't mind at all spending the rest of my life alone with you."

The time to tell him had come, and Narisa knew it. Her mind did not register all he was saying; she recognized only that she could wait no longer. He was making plans for their future, and a rescue ship might appear at any moment.

"I have already sent a message," she said, and waited for the explosion she was certain would come.

He did not react at once. He went on working at the console a little longer, as though he hadn't heard her. She watched as his hands went perfectly still over the buttons. He turned slowly, drawing himself up stiffly to his full height and facing her with a curiously blank expression.

"You did what?" His voice was almost a whisper, yet hard, a travesty of his gentle tones when making love to her.

"The first night we were here," she told him, the words tumbling over each other.

Now that she had started her confession, she wanted to have it all out and be done with it. "While you were bathing, I sent out a rescue call. You had left the machine on."

"I trusted you." He took a step toward her, clenching his hands. He balled them into fists and held them at his sides as if he were trying to keep himself from using them on her. The pain on his face, the cold fury in his eyes, tore at her heart. "How could you do such a stupid thing? And how could you not tell me about it?"

"I thought it was best," she said, trying to placate him. "You know the regulations, Tarik. I know you are angry now, but in time you will see it was the right thing to do."

"Regulations? Very well, if you want regulations, *Lieutenant Navigator* Narisa, I'll give them to you. You deliberately disobeyed your superior officer's expressed wishes. You are a candidate for court-martial."

"Tarik, my dear, don't you see why—"

"*Commander* Tarik!" he thundered. "Listen to me, *lieutenant*. Not only have you disobeyed me on a vital matter, but you may have killed us both. Weren't you paying attention to what Dulan told us? The Cetans found this planet once. They may find it again. And didn't you hear what I said just now? One reason I haven't sent out a rescue call was because I wasn't certain this communicator could send a signal strong enough to reach the Capital, or even a Service spaceship. I wanted to explore this planet to find the original settlement, where the other computer-communicator is located. I had thought if it is still in existance, it's just possible we might use parts from that machine and couple them with this one to produce the strong signal we need. That is the modification I was talking about."

"I didn't know that," Narisa faltered. "You hadn't told me. I didn't think."

"No, you didn't think, *lieutenant.*"

"Please don't call me that. Please call me Narisa."

He ignored her plea and went on, showing his hurt now, and growing more and more angry as he spoke.

"While I made love to you, and poured out my heart and soul to you in complete trust, you lay there, knowing you had betrayed me, and you never had the decency to tell me what you had done."

"I haven't betrayed you. I was trying to help us both. Tarik, I love you."

"How glad I would have been," he said, "to hear you say that last night, or even an hour ago. Now I don't know whether to believe you or not. How can I trust anything you say when you have been lying to me for days?"

"I'm sorry." She was utterly miserable. She ought to have known he would have some good reason for wanting to delay the rescue signal. She ought to have trusted him, as he had trusted her. She was afraid she had, by her own act, killed his love for her. She could see in his cold face nothing of tenderness, only contempt and dislike. At that moment Narisa would have given her soul, her life, anything, to have back those moments when she had sent the rescue signal. And she would gladly spend the rest of her life on this lost planet, if only Tarik would love her again.

For Narisa, the next day and a half were absolutely wretched. Rain poured down, confining them to the building. Tarik treated her with cold, silent disdain, and she was not certain which was worse, her own heartbreak or the misery she saw in his eyes and in his face when he did not kow she was watching him. They slept apart, Narisa in the room where she had taken a nap their first day on the island and Tarik in the room most distant from it. By unspoken consent they both avoided the chamber where they had lain together in love.

Narisa could only hope his anger against her would be dissipated by time and that he would come to understand why she had done what she had, and eventually forgive her for it. Except there might not be enough time. Every hour brought a rescue ship nearer, and once they were aboard it, Tarik would most likely remove himself permanently from her life. She could not bring herself to accept the possibility of anything other than a Service vessel answering her message. Tarik's concerns about the Cetans must be wrong. They had to be.

Midway through the second day, he called her out of the storeroom where she had been selecting food for the evening meal, a useless exercise since they most likely would be unable to eat anything. Neither of them had any appetite.

"Sit there," Tarik ordered, pointing to the second chair before the computer-communicator. "Can you see this screen? Good. I want you to be aware of the result of your foolish action the other day. Look at this."

It was scanning screen to which he pointed. Narisa noted the range and direction at which it was set. A small green dot moved with astonishing speed along a line that intercepted the planet.

"The Service rescue ship," Narisa whispered. How sorry she was to see it. Once they were aboard it, all chance of inducing Tarik to love her again was lost.

"Do you really think that's what it is?" Tarik worked the many buttons and dials with long, slender fingers. An image sprang up on the computer's second screen, a diagram of the ship approaching them and a list of its characteristics and probable armament. Narisa recognized it at once with a shock.

"No," she whispered in horror. "Please, no. Not that."

"You see what you have done, my dear," Tarik told her with grim humor. "You've brought the Cetans down on us."

Chapter Seven

"What are the Cetans doing in the Empty Sector?" Narisa cried. "They stay away from it for the same reason Jurisdiction ships do."

"Unless," Tarik told her coldly, "they intercept a weak rescue signal and imagine they smell easy plunder. They'd be greedy enough to risk it if they know there are no other ships in the immediate area."

"How can we defend ourselves against them? We have no weapons." Narisa had not really believed Cetans would find them. Now she was trying to suppress the panic that threatened to destroy her composure. She knew what Cetans were said to do to their captives. Male or female, human or other Race, it made no difference to them. The fortunate ones died promptly, as her family had done. The captives who survived the

brutal initiation were taken as slaves to Cetan
planets. There was no information on the
exact fate of those poor souls. No one had
ever escaped to tell of it. At the thought of
what might happen to her, and to Tarik,
Narisa's hands began to shake uncontrollably. She held them together in her lap to
hide the involuntary motion and tried to
speak calmly. "I would rather kill myself than
be captured by them."

For the first time in a day and a half, Tarik
looked at her without bitter anger in his eyes.
He reached toward her as if he would touch
her reassuringly, then withdrew his hand
before he made contact with her flesh.

"I," he said, "would rather die fighting
them. I do believe, Narisa, that I can trust you
against the Cetans, if in nothing else."

She bore the insult without comment,
loving him hopelessly and aching with pain
and guilt for what she had done to them both.
Then her practical nature asserted itself once
more, telling her there was no going back and
no use wishing she could. She took her usual
refuge in a professional attitude and in words
that sounded calmer than she really felt.

"Tarik, if you have a plan of some kind, tell
me what it is."

"There are weapons here, in a case in one of
the storerooms. They are listed on the inventory."

"One case of weapons can't be much, and
they will be very old. We need more than
small arms to fight off a Cetan ship."

"Perhaps not. The Cetans are answering a rescue call. They are likely to send a shuttle down to the planet's surface to investigate before they begin using major weapons. From what I know of them, they wouldn't want to destroy any valuable loot. When they arrive at the planet, they will come directly here, because this island is where the rescue call originated.

"And now, Narisa," he went on, "you will see the value of learning true history, the kind scorned in favor of the carefully censored version the Jurisdiction teaches. The kind of history written in a pile of rotting books I once found on a seldom-visited planet, far from the center of Jurisdiction authority, and took back to the Capitol to my old history teacher. It was he who taught me it is possible to learn from the experiences and the mistakes of ancient societies."

"I am aware that citizens of the Jurisdiction are not told everything they might want to know." Narisa spoke through stiff lips, determined to hide her barely leashed terror and impatience. She did not want to alienate Tarik any more than she had already done. If they were to have any hope against the Cetans, they had to work together. "What is it you know that might help us?"

"There is an ancient way of making war when you are few and your opponents are many. We will use that method now. We won't face the Cetans in the open as Service officers are taught to do. Instead, we will hide among the trees and kill them one by one. When we are done, we will have the shuttle, and a better chance of taking the main ship. If we find heavy weapons on the shuttle, we might even destroy the main ship. It must be well armed because the Cetans have no way of knowing what they will find when they descend to the surface of an unknown planet."

"I agree with the first part," Narisa said slowly. "I have never heard of fighting that way, but I think it might work. We are more familiar with the island than they will be. I have never had to use a weapon against any living being before, but these are Cetans. I'm sure I can do what you want me to. But, Tarik, are you really going to attack a spaceship with just a shuttle and whatever weapons you can find?"

"Why not? It's better than letting them take us prisoner, which they will if we don't fight back."

"I want you to promise me something."

"Promise?" His mouth twisted scornfully. "Promise what, lieutenant?"

"If the fight goes against us, or if I'm captured, I want you to kill me. I don't want them to do to me what Cetans do to their prisoners. Not after I've lain with you and learned what love is."

"Narisa." His hand touched her cheek briefly. "I promise."

"I'll do the same for you," she said softly, made hopeful by that display of tenderness.

"I'm sure you will," he replied dryly, "and

most likely when my back is turned. Don't
worry, Narisa, I won't let them take you. Now
I want you to listen carefully to me, memorize
everything I say, and do not deviate one iota
from my instructions."

Near sunset the amphibious space shuttle
from the Cetan ship landed on the lake and
swept smoothly up onto the sandy beach
where Narisa and Tarik had first reached the
island. Narisa watched it from her concealed
position high among the thick leaves of a tree.
She was wearing her Service uniform again,
and had two force-guns, one in her hand and a
spare slung over her shoulder. As she had
expected, the weapons they had found in the
storerooms were heavy and old-fashioned,
but she and Tarik had practiced with them,
and she was certain they would be effective.
They were set at kill force.

She studied the shuttle as it came to rest
near the tree where she crouched. It was
elliptical in shape, slightly pointed at one end,
a dull dark gray in color with a red stripe
down the side. As she nervously watched, a
door near the pointed end opened and a Cetan
appeared. He was tall and burly, with long,
matted yellow hair and a scraggly beard.
Narisa noted black Service boots with loose
green Demarian trousers tucked into them, a
garish red belt from some unknown place in
the galaxy, and a shiny black jacket of the
kind Assembly Members wore. This last garment was patched in several places with un-
matched fabric and was left open in front to

reveal a broad, hairy chest. She also saw that
the man appeared to be unarmed. He jumped
awkwardly to the ground, or perhaps he was
pushed. She could not tell for certain.

The first Cetan was followed by five others,
all as badly dressed as their companion, but
these were heavily armed with the ugly blunt
weapons that were a Cetan invention. What
was more, they had their weapons pointed at
the first man. Narisa watched them, wondering what was happening. She waited, as Tarik
had instructed her to do, until the Cetans
were all out of the shuttle and away from its
protection before using her force-guns.

Someone pushed the first Cetan, sending
him sprawling onto the ground, and another
kicked him hard. He doubled up, crying out in
pain. The Cetan who appeared to be the leader
kept his weapon aimed at the yellow-haired
one. He had to be guilty of some crime, Narisa
decided, though what a Cetan could possibly
do to offend his fellows she could not imagine.
At any rate, it looked as though the leader was
about to kill one of his own men, making her
task, and Tarik's, that much easier.

"Chon. Chon-chon. Chon." In a flurry of
blue and green wings a dozen birds swooped
down upon the Cetans. Narisa saw with
horror just how dangerous the birds' claws
and beaks could be as they tore at the men on
the beach, preventing them from using their
weapons. Within space-seconds, each of the
Cetans had been lifted off his feet by two
birds and was being carried far out across the

lake. Narisa could hear their despairing cries and curses growing fainter and fainter.

A pair of remaining birds circled the beach a few times, then flew off after their comrades, but not before Narisa had recognized them. The blue one had an old scratch across its beak, and she was certain the green one was the same bird who had given her the fruit.

The birds had carried away only five Cetans. In the confusion of that brief battle she had seen the yellow-haired Cetan scrambling about on his hands and knees. Now he had disappeared.

When the birds had gone, Narisa clung to the sturdy tree trunk, shaking with relief. She had not wanted to kill another living being. She had thought her hatred of Cetans would overcome her scruples, but it had not, and she was deeply grateful to the birds for having relieved her of the need to do something so abhorent.

Recalling that there was still work to be done, she slid down from her tree and ran toward the shuttle. Tarik had warned her there might be other crewmen left inside it as reinforcements or guards, so she eyed the entrance cautiously as she approached it. Tarik was there before her, racing across the sand from his own hiding place. He pulled the sliding door all the way back, thrusting his head and shoulders through the entrance, weapon poised and ready in his hand. He backed out quickly.

"There's no one in there," he said.

"Did you call the birds?" Narisa asked.

"No. I thought you might have done it."

"We were both thinking about the battle to come. Perhaps," Narisa speculated, "they sensed what would happen and they came to help us. They might retain some memory of what the Cetans did long ago on this planet. I wonder what they will do with those five men. And why would they leave one man behind?"

"I don't care what they've done with the ones they took away. We can discuss possibilities later," Tarik said shortly. "Right now, we are the ones who need to find the sixth Cetan."

"He was unarmed," Narisa reminded him. "They pushed him out of the shuttle before the others so that he would take the first shots if someone began firing at them right away."

"That might have been some kind of trick." Tarik was searching among the trees with sharp eyes. "I want him alive, Narisa. He will have information about the ship that we can use."

She nodded absently, her own attention on the sand, looking for the Cetan's tracks. She touched Tarik's arm and pointed. "He left the beach there. He must have been crawling. Perhaps they hurt him badly when they kicked him."

"That would be our good fortune. Hurt and unarmed he can't fight. I just hope he's able to talk and understand us."

It was not hard to track the Cetan through crushed weeds and broken small bushes, evidence that he had tried to walk and had fallen several times. They found him by the stone wall that surrounded the central clearing. He huddled on his side against the wall, clutching at his abdomen and moaning softly. Narisa trained her force-gun on him while Tarik made a hasty search for concealed weapons. The Cetan offered no resistance. He cried out when Tarik rolled him over, but it was clear he was trying to muffle the sound.

"Don't want them to hear," he ground out between clenched teeth. The Cetan accent was thick, but he spoke in the standard patois of all spacemen. Narisa had no trouble understanding him, nor did Tarik.

"You needn't worry about your friends. They have been disposed of most efficiently. I doubt we will ever see any of them again." Tarik produced a length of cord. "Sit up, Cetan, and put your hands behind your back."

"I am not certain I can," the Cetan said. "The pain is great."

"You'll have more pain if you don't do what I say," Tarik told him. "That's an old-fashioned force-gun my lieutenant is holding. I'm sure you know what such a weapon can do. If you don't obey me, she will start at your toes and work her way upward slowly."

The Cetan struggled to sit, his face white above the tangled yellow beard. When he tried to put both arms behind himself, he blanched even more.

"He really is hurt," Narisa said.

"All the better," Tarik responded. "He'll be more likely to do what we want."

When the Cetan's hands were tightly bound behind his back, Tarik ordered him to stand. He tried. He got to one knee, but wavered, trying to get his other leg under himself, and Tarik had to help him. Once he was on his feet, Tarik led him through a break in the wall and toward the building in the center of the clearing. Narisa stayed close behind them, her force-gun pointed squarely at the Cetan's back.

"What . . . strange place . . . is this?" The heavily accented words were spoken carefully, and Narisa heard the effort it cost him.

"Never mind," Tarik snapped. But he did offer a hand to help the Cetan up the three shallow steps and into the building. They took him to the central room.

"How beautiful," the Cetan said, looking around. "How peaceful."

"What do Cetans know of beauty and peace?" Narisa asked harshly. "They only know how to destroy both."

"My mother . . . my mother was . . ." The Cetan crashed to the floor and lay there, face up, unconscious, with his muscular legs sprawled wide and his arms twisted behind him.

"Is he dead?" Narisa asked, and found to her surprise that she hoped he was not. As much as she hated Cetans, she was curious about this one. She wondered why his companions had intended to kill him, and what he had meant to say about his mother.

"He's still breathing." Tarik squatted beside the Cetan and gently poked at his abdomen. A low moan came through parted lips. "He may be badly hurt. We need him conscious and able to speak."

"There is medical information stored in the computer," Narisa said, thinking quickly. "Let me see what I can find." When he moved between her and the computer, she looked him straight in the face. "I will not use the communicator," she said, fighting to keep her voice level. "There will be no more unauthorized messages sent from here. It would be the height of insanity to try it with a Cetan ship orbiting the planet."

Tarik nodded and stepped aside, letting her reach the computer. Her search took a remarkably short time.

"We should use the juice from the same fruit the birds gave us for you," she announced. "There are other remedies for non-humans, but the Cetans are human like us, and for unspecified internal injuries, that juice is the only medicine available on the planet."

"Would the birds bring it to us to cure a Cetan?" Tarik wondered.

"We won't need the birds." Narisa brought up another screen. "There is a small supply of the juice in the second storeroom, third cabinet on the left, second shelf from the top."

"After all this time will it still be potent enough to do any good?"

Tarik came to stand behind her. She was still feeling somewhat shaky after the strange

battle on the beach. She wanted to lean back
against him and feel his strong arms around
her. She believed if she did lean back, he
would reject her. They were working well together to carry out his plan, but he had not
forgiven her for what she had done. Perhaps
he never would. She had better concentrate
on their immediate problem and deal with
Tarik later. She ran a second check on the
Cetan's apparent injuries with Tarik watching
over her shoulder.

"There is nothing else we could possibly
use on him," she said.

"I'll get it." He headed for the storeroom.

The Cetan was conscious again. He had
golden eyes, and they looked at Narisa im-
ploringly.

"My arms ache," he said. "I cannot roll to
my side."

He did look very uncomfortable on his back
with both arms behind him. Narisa pulled a
pillow off the couch and stuffed it under his
head and shoulders.

"I thank you." He tried to smile at her. The
effort turned into a grimace of pain. "You are
kind."

"Kinder than you deserve, considering
what you and your friends have done to so
many planets. Like Belta. You showed no
kindness, nor any mercy, there."

"I have never been to Belta," the Cetan said.

"Is he awake? Good." Tarik was back with a
small glass vial in one hand. "This, Cetan, is
medicine, the only thing we have that could

cure your injuries. I will hold it to your mouth
and you will swallow it."

"Why do you want to cure me?" The man on
the floor seemed to have regained some
strength. "Is it so you may then torture me
longer before I die? I will not swallow your
medicine so you can make sport of me."

"We don't torture people," Narisa said
angrily. "We aren't Cetans."

"You are from the Jurisdiction. I know your
uniforms. There is little difference between
us." The Cetan tried to move his arms. He
winced from the pain the effort created. "If I
tell you something important, will you unbind
my arms and let me die in fair combat? I will
fight you with no weapons at all."

"I won't fight a wounded man." Tarik
regarded his prisoner with interest. "I will
make a bargain with you, however. I will give
you this medicine, and in return, you will tell
me the 'something important.' "

"And then you will torture me."

"No, then you will help me with my plan,"
Tarik said, his voice soft as he watched the
man's reactions. "What is your name?"

"Gaidar."

"Well, then, Gaidar, this medicine will
make you sleep while it works, so before you
take it you will tell me how soon the men on
the shuttle were to contact your parent ship
up there in orbit."

"One space-hour after landing," the Cetan
replied promptly.

"Space-hour? Do you use Jurisdiction

time?"

"It is simpler to do so. Easier to track and destroy Jurisdiction ships." Gaidar paused, breathing deeply as if to gather all his strength. "I will help you. I have no cause for loyalty to them. They would have killed me for a very stupid reason."

"What reason?" Narisa asked.

"I suggested we not kill whoever we found on this planet. I am tired of killing. I wanted to hold you for ransom. I thought it would be profitable."

"And for that they were going to kill you?"

"They do not like new ideas, except for new weapons. They are confirmed in all their old hatreds against the Races of the Jurisdiction. They want to continue killing and destroying. It gives them pleasure."

"You say, 'they,' " Narisa said. "You are a Cetan, too."

"Only half Cetan. My mother was Demarian. Another reason for my shipmates to dislike me. Help me to rise," Gaidar told them, "and I will send whatever message you want, and thus satisfy the Cetan crew."

"No," Narisa cried. "We know what Cetans are. You can't expect us to trust you."

"Nor should I trust you," Gaidar countered. "But I recognize when I have no choice. Perhaps you should do the same." He closed his eyes.

"Tarik," Narisa appealed to him, "don't let this creature near the communicator."

"I don't see how he can do more harm than you did," Tarik responded, causing Narisa to wince at the barb. "Don't forget, lieutenant, the birds left him behind when they took the other Cetans away. Suppose they did it deliberately?"

"Why would they do that?"

"The others had murderous thoughts in their minds. This one, unarmed and scheduled to be a victim, did not. Perhaps the birds thought he could be of use to us."

"It's possible," Narisa admitted, "based on what we know of the birds. But I still don't trust him."

"Neither do I, not completely, but I think we have to take the chance. We haven't much time before the captain of the Cetan ship expects a message."

Narisa did not agree with Tarik, but she did not want to alienate him any further.

"I withdraw my objection," she relented.

Tarik looked pleased. Gaidar opened his golden eyes and stared at her.

"I promise I will not disappoint you," he said.

"You won't have a chance," Tarik told him. He handed the vial of medicine to Narisa, then assisted Gaidar to the computer-communicator. The Cetan gave a short laugh when he saw it.

"This is an old machine. Very old. Cetans have better, even on that bad ship up there." Gaidar glanced upward.

"This one works well enough," Tarik remarked. Then he grew deadly serious. "Gaidar, you will say exactly what I tell you to say. Be aware of my lack of trust in you. You still need to prove yourself to me. If you deviate in any way, Lieutenant Narisa here will use her force-gun on your most sensitive parts. Do not expect her to show mercy. She has just cause for wishing all Cetans dead."

"What shall I say?" Gaidar slumped in one of the chairs at the console. Narisa could tell by his white face and clenched jaw that he was in considerable pain. She almost felt sorry for him.

"You will make your voice sound like the leader of the men who came in the shuttle," Tarik ordered. "You will report that Gaidar is dead, and you have killed two people you found on the island. You are now beginning to search this building for booty. Is there a specified time for a second message after this one?"

"Not until the shuttle is ready to return to the main ship. Communications are arranged that way to keep other Cetan ships from taking our loot if they should intercept a message, or possible rescue ships from interfering with a raid. An approximate length of time is agreed on for the men on the shuttle to finish the job and be ready to return, but sometimes the captain grows impatient and simply destroys the planet whether his own men are on it or not. He always fears a trick if his men are captured. I don't think he will do the usual thing this time, though. This is the only shuttle he has left. He wants it back."

"A charming man, your captain. Tell him it will take time down here because this is a large building with many locked rooms. Say you believe there are many valuable things stored here. That should hold him in orbit and keep him relatively patient."

Tarik dialed the frequency Gaidar had told him to use, and Gaidar spoke into the communicator. A harsh voice rasped back at him, and Gaidar nodded at Tarik to end the transmission.

"Now," Tarik said, "while you can still walk, we go into one of the personal rooms. You will lie down on the bed, and I will give you the medicine."

"Will you untie my arms?"

"No, but we will make you as comfortable as possible with pillows."

Gaidar stumbled as he walked, but he made it to the bed Tarik indicated. He opened his mouth and took the medicine from the vial, swallowing it without protest. He was asleep before Narisa and Tarik had finished piling pillows around him to support his back and shoulders.

"What next?" Narisa asked.

"I will inspect the shuttle, while you stand guard here. I don't think Gaidar has tried to trick us. It wouldn't be to his advantage to help people who want to kill him as his former shipmates do, but just in case I have misread his character, I want you to stay alert while I'm gone."

She did as he ordered. Tarik returned an hour later.

"We can fly the shuttle," he reported. "The

controls are nothing unusual. All we have to
do now is wait until Gaidar wakes up. I want
all the information he has about the crew and
the layout of the ship."

At his suggestion, Narisa tried to sleep, but
found she could not. She remained too appre-
hensive about the second part of Tarik's plan,
which was to try to capture or destroy the
Cetan spaceship, and thus put an end to the
danger they were in. Narisa feared they
would not succeed, but if they should, what
would happen then? If she did her part well,
would Tarik forgive her for what he called her
betrayal? She ached for his touch and wanted
desperately to know he still cared about her.
And what of Gaidar, what would they do with
him? Her mind was filled with so many
questions and possibilities that she hardly
knew what to hope for or expect, and tossed
restlessly on her narrow bed. She had just
begun to drift into a half sleep when Tarik
shook her.

"Gaidar is awake," Tarik said. "He's much
improved. Come and hear this important
information he claims to have."

"Will you believe what he says?" she asked,
swinging her feet to the floor.

"I'll know that after I've heard him. He has
good reason to side with us against his former
companions. They will kill him on sight, while
we at least will give him a chance to fight for
his life."

Tarik had moved the still-bound Gaidar to
one of the cushioned chairs in the central

room. There was food on the table, along with
a pitcher of the hot herbal brew Tarik liked.

"I have told Gaidar," Tarik said, indicating
that Narisa should take a seat on the couch,
"that we will untie him and let him eat, but I
will have a force-gun aimed at him every
second. Knowing how you hate Cetans, I'll do
the job so you won't have to touch him."

"I will not attack you," Gaidar promised.
"It would be foolish for me to do so."

Tarik gave his force-gun to Narisa to hold
while he untied Gaidar. Then he settled comfortably into the second cushioned chair and
took the gun from Narisa.

"Go ahead and eat," he said to her. "You,
too, Gaidar."

Narisa poured herself a cup of the herbal
brew and sat sipping it while Gaidar rubbed
his wrists and flexed his shoulders and
fingers. After a while he picked up one of the
round loaves of flat bread and began to eat it.

"I want information." The prod was verbal,
but the way Tarik held the force-gun con-
stituted a silent backup to his cool words.
"We had a bargain, Gaidar."

"So we had, and whatever you say about
Cetans, we keep our word. I regret making
you wait, but I was not fed for three space-
days before we landed here, and I am hungry.
The captain saw no sense in wasting valuable
food stores on one who would soon be dead."
Gaidar took the cup of steaming liquid, which
Narisa had filled and pushed across the table
toward him. He raised it, saluting her with it

before he drank. "I thank you again, lieutenant, for your kindness. Commander Tarik, I think perhaps I should first tell you a little about my life. It will help you to believe me."

"We don't have much time," Tarik objected.

"It will not take long." Gaidar picked up another loaf of bread. "As I told you before, I am only half Cetan. My mother was a Demarian slave. She lived long enough to teach me that there are other Races with more peaceful ways of living before my father killed her. I was nine Cetan years old when he broke her neck. I saw him do it. There was nothing I could do to help her. She had made me understand that to survive among the Cetans I must pretend to be like them in every way, so I did not attack my father for what he had done. I pretended I did not care. I went on to become a mighty warrior, and my father was proud of me.

"As I grew older, I began to hate myself, for I saw the damage Cetans do to innocent Races that have not harmed them in any way. I then tried to change my father's methods, to convince him to treat his captives better. For my efforts I was degraded and punished further by being made to serve on that pirate ship up there in orbit, whose crew are the scum of the Cetan worlds. My father thought it would break my pride to be subject to that captain. He underestimated my endurance. I was determined to survive and eventually to find a place where I could live in peace. Unfortunately, I made the mistake of suggesting we ransom you instead of killing you. You know the rest.''

Narisa never took her eyes off Gaidar during this recitation. She believed he was telling the truth. For the first time in her life she felt a stirring of sympathy for a Cetan. She glanced at Tarik when Gaidar had finished, to see if she could discern from his expression what he thought of Gaidar's story. She knew Tarik's family was from Demaria. He might feel some pity for a Demarian slave who had tried to teach her child peaceful ways, and thus be sympathetic to that child. Tarik's face revealed nothing of his feelings, nor, when he spoke, did his voice.

"This is not the important information you promised us," Tarik said.

"I come to that now," Gaidar told him. "The Cetans are massing to attack the Jurisdiction at its Capital. For once the Cetan leaders will work together. Their joint desire to destroy the Jurisdiction may keep the old hatreds among the various warlords under control long enough for them to succeed."

There was silence when Gaidar finished speaking. Narisa and Tarik both sat staring at him, each of them thinking what this information would mean.

"Where are they massing these ships?" Tarik demanded at last. "What type of ships? How many? When?"

"Even now," Gaidar said. "In the old Beltan Sector which was so decimated by Cetan attacks years ago that it is still underpopulated.

Much of it remains in Cetan control. It is a safe place for Cetans, with the advantage of being just within Jurisdiction borders. There are fifteen great warlords who have agreed to fight together. Each has at least ten large ships in addition to many smaller ones, and every ship will be equipped with a Cetan invention that will make interstellar travel both faster and safer than it has ever been before. With the new Starthruster device, it will take just three space-days to move the entire fleet from Belta to the Capital, moving so quickly that no Jurisdiction vessel will be able to see or stop them."

"That's impossible," Narisa cried. "I can think of a dozen problems such speed would cause to the ship's structure, to human bodies, to navigational instruments and communications. It can't be done."

"It has been done and tested," Gaidar said. "That is the other part of my information, and the reason I know so much about this new device. The ship above has been equipped with Starthruster. When we intercepted your rescue call, we were on a trial voyage. Like you, the captain was skeptical. He wanted to test Starthruster before joining his warlord at Belta."

"I still can't believe what you say. It's too incredible," Narisa insisted.

"This planet is located far inside the Empty Sector, lieutenant. How do you think we reached you so quickly after your rescue call went out, if Starthruster does not work? And, incidentally, we were not travelling at full speed."

"It would explain the remarkable speed registered while we were tracking your ship," Narisa admitted.

"How does it work?" Tarik interjected.

"That," Gaidar said with a smile, "will remain my secret. I will tell your Assembly, after I have been given my freedom, and my life."

"You are very clever," Narisa breathed. "Tarik—"

"Yes," Tarik said. "I know my duty. We must capture the Cetan ship without destroying it, or damaging this Starthruster device, and then we have to take it to the Capital. The Assembly must be warned, and Starthruster turned over to Jurisdiction scientists. We have no choice. We have to return to the Jurisdiction at once."

Narisa should have been pleased to hear him say so. Instead, she was suddenly uncertain she wanted to return to her old life.

"You need fear no punishment from the Assembly since you are the one who warned us of the coming attack," she said to Gaidar, but she said it as much to reassure herself as to placate his concern. She regarded him with deep and increasing interest. He had a wide, pleasant face, with a square jaw evident beneath his unkempt beard, and a nose that looked as though it had been broken once or twice and never reset properly. She looked at his large square hands, now holding his cup while he drank. The last joint of his left little finger was missing. Gaidar saw the direction of her glance.

"It was a punishment," he told her. "Cetans begin by removing the fingers, one joint at a time. Then they progress to the toes, later to more sensitive parts. Most Cetans have at least a few fingers missing. I was fortunate. My mother was not. When she died, she had no fingers on her left hand."

"No wonder you feel no loyalty to them."

"I do not, lieutenant, but I must confess I do not completely trust in your Assembly, either. I would like some further guarantee that they will not take Starthruster, and all the information I can provide about it, and then take my life, too. I want to see more of our galaxy before I die, and I want to die honorably in battle, not as a broken prisoner."

"I give you my word," Tarik swore, "my most solemn promise, Gaidar. The Assembly will not harm you after you have told your story."

"You have my word also, Gaidar," Narisa added. "I will stand with Tarik on this." She was rewarded by a warm look from Tarik, but it was not only for his approval that she had spoken. Despite her earlier reservations, she believed Gaidar's story completely. Her doubts had disappeared as she had listened to his straightforward speech. Because of Tarik's searching questions put to her about Jurisdiction law, she had some serious concern about how honorably the Assembly would deal with a Cetan, even one who brought them information of such monumental importance. But Gaidar's story must be told, and for his sake, and Tarik's, she would stand with them both no matter what happened when they faced the Assembly.

"I believe it is ordained," Gaidar said, "that I should travel to your Capital. My mother used to tell me her people believed in going boldly out to meet one's fate. I will begin to think of myself as Demarian, and follow that creed."

"The Demarians are my people, too," Tarik said.

"Are they? Then we should be friends. I believe you are an honest man. I will trust you, and your lieutenant, if not your Assembly." Gaider put out one huge hand. After a few seconds' hesitation Tarik put out his own, and to her astonishment, Narisa watched Commander Tarik Gibal of the Jurisdiction Service shake hands with a Cetan.

Chapter Eight

Narisa left the building in the gray early morning light, leaving Tarik and Gaidar discussing the final details of their plan to capture the Cetan ship. They would not miss her for the little while she would be gone, and there were things she wanted to do before the coming day's dangerous events.

She went to Dulan's grave first, to whisper a farewell to that last, valiant spirit of the ancient settlement. Then she went down to the lake shore on the opposite side of the island from the Cetan shuttle. Here the beach was narrower, the sand smooth and undisturbed by violence. Tiny waves lapped along the water's edge.

Narisa stood still, absorbing the peace and beauty while the sky turned brighter. She thought back to the first sunrise over the lake, which she had watched from the mainland. Everything that had happened since that morning had changed her a little more, compounding the changes that had begun the moment she and Tarik had landed on this planet. Now she did not want to leave it, and that was the biggest change of all. She felt that she and Tarik belonged here. This world was their home, the place each of them had been seeking; Tarik deliberately, herself unknowing until he showed it to her.

She watched the brilliant sunrise streak the sky with a dazzling array of colors, saw the snow atop the single distant mountain begin to glow with the golden sunlight, and knew she wanted to climb that mountain and to explore whatever lay on the other side. There was a salty sea far beyond the horizon; she knew that much from the computer. Next to the sea lay the original settlement. Narisa wanted to see it, and she wanted Tarik beside her when she did.

"Chon." Blue-feathered wings fluttered, then folded against a lustrous blue body. It was the first bird she had ever seen here, the same one that had saved her from the snake. Narisa recognized the scar on its beak. Each bird was different from all the others. If she had had time, she could have learned to know them all. It was her own fault her time on this planet was ending, and in that quiet dawn moment Narisa fully recognized all she was losing by leaving it.

She approached the bird. It waited for her,

cocking its head as she moved nearer. She
reached out and stroked the bird's wing, as
she had done once before, feeling the stiff
flight feathers beneath her fingers. Then,
daringly, she touched the softer feathers of
the bird's chest. It did not move away. Narisa
took another step, coming nearer to stroke
the bird from its throat down along its rich
blue body. As she did so, the bird's wing
came around her, enfolding her against itself.
Narisa rested there, her cheek and one hand
against its soft chest. She could see out of the
corner of her eye the bird's three primitive
fingers at the last joint of the wing, and the
long, toothed beak, just slightly open. She felt
no fear at all, only a great sadness at having to
leave creatures she had come to think of as
friends, and this friend in particular. And
with her mind open to the bird, she sensed an
understanding, a comprehension on the bird's
part that she must go and was sad about it.

Return one day. The thought lay deep in her
mind, and she did not know absolutely if it
was herself or the bird that had put it there.

She heard Tarik calling her. The bird
refolded its wing.

"Good-bye," Narisa said, her voice breaking
on a sob, and ran back to the building in the
center of the island.

Gaidar knew everything about the Cetan
ship. It was large, with plenty of cargo space
for the booty the Cetans loved so much, but it
could easily be piloted with a small crew. The

captain remained aboard with three crew members.

"The smaller the crew," Gaidar told them, "the greater the profits for each crew member. That will be to our advantage. We will not have so many Cetans to overcome. But be warned, the artificial gravity aboard the ship is somewhat greater than you have been used to on this planet. You will have to adjust yourselves to it as quickly as possible."

Tarik, Narisa and Gaidar were well armed when they went aboard the shuttle. Narisa had felt a thrill of fear at the sight of an armed Cetan, but had agreed with Tarik that Gaidar would need to defend himself against his former crew mates.

With Narisa navigating, Tarik piloting and Gaidar handling communications with the main ship by pretending to be the lost leader of the shuttle crew, they docked the vessel with the larger Cetan ship. According to the plan, Gaidar stepped out first, force-gun in hand. Before the single crew member posted at the docking deck to monitor the return of the shuttle could recognize him and give any alarm, he was stunned into unconsciousness.

"Only three left," Tarik said, helping Gaidar to bind the Cetan securely. "Let's lower that to two."

Gaidar stepped to a communications panel in the nearest bulkhead and, still mimicking the voice of the shuttle commander, called for another crew member to help unload he shuttle, mentioning a great deal of heavy and

very valuable plunder. The man appeared a
few space-minutes later, and promptly joined
the first Cetan, unconscious and tightly
bound.

They all paused on the docking deck for a
while so Tarik and Narisa could begin to
adjust to the heavier gravity. They allowed as
little time as possible, for they did not want
the delay to cost them the element of surprise
they still enjoyed. Gaidar had drawn them a
diagram of the interior of the ship, and Tarik
and Narisa had memorized it. They located
the bridge with no trouble, while Gaidar made
a quick check of the rest of the ship to make
certain they would have no unexpected
problems.

At the entrance to the bridge, by their pre-
arranged plan, Narisa silently handed her
force-gun to Tarik and went in alone. The first
officer was there, lolling idly in the captain's
chair. Narisa recognized him from Gaidar's
description. He came to immediate attention
at the unusual sight of a woman on the bridge.
He stood up, one hand reaching for the communicator button, but he crumpled before his
fingers made contact with it, stunned into unconsciousness when Tarik used Narisa's
force-gun.

"There is only the captain left now," Gaidar
announced as he joined them. He watched
Tarik tie up the officer while Narisa retrieved
her force-gun. "He is mine to take."

"This is too easy." Her original distrust of
all Cetans returning, Narisa wondered if they
were being caught in a trap. Her concern was

dispelled a moment later, as well as her lingering doubts about Gaidar, when the captain himself arrived on the bridge. He was a short, dark man, with huge shoulders. The rank smell of his unwashed body filled the small bridge of his ship. He carried a huge Cetan hand weapon.

"So," the captain snarled, "you still live, do you, Gaidar? Not for long. Stand away from those instruments. I don't want to damage them when I kill you. Where are my other men from the shuttle? I've been calling the docking deck and getting no answer."

"They are gone forever," Gaidar told him, clutching his force-gun and edging farther away from the menacing captain. "You will be, too, if you cause me any trouble. I would enjoy repaying you for all the indignities you brought on me."

"I am only sorry," the captain said, "that I did not kill you the first day you came on board."

As Gaidar slid along the panel of instruments, Narisa realized what he was trying to do. Tarik was hidden behind the captain's chair, where he was down on his knees while tying up the first officer. Narisa was to the right of the hatch the captain had used, pressed flat against the metal bulkhead. The captain had come in the hatch, seen Gaidar, and focused all his attention on him. He had not noticed Tarik or Narisa. Gaidar kept moving away so that the captain, following him, had his back to the other two.

Narisa lifted her force-gun. It was a dif-

ficult shot. If she missed, she would almost
certainly hit Gaidar. But she had to take the
chance; the captain was going to kill him, and
would do it at any second. Narisa fired.

Something was wrong with her weapon.
The button clicked loudly as she pressed it,
and she felt a slight recoil, but the captain did
not fall. Instead, he turned on her, his huge
weapon poised.

"A female!" The captain leered at her. "And
armed. Too bad. I would have enjoyed raping
you, but now I'll have to kill you instead."

Then everything happened at once. Gaidar
fired his own force-gun at the captain, but it
worked no better than Narisa's had, and in
frustration he brought the barrel down on the
back of the captain's head. At the same time
Tarik fired from his position behind the captain's chair. The captain's weapon went off,
ploughing a hole in the inside bulkhead just
above Narisa's left shoulder. She was
knocked to the deck by the force of the impact
and by the pull of the ship's gravity.

Narisa shook her head, trying to clear her
senses. Gaidar was sitting on the captain's
back holding the man's arms together while
Tarik bound them. On Gaidar's face was the
broadest grin Narisa had ever seen.

"Narisa, are you all right?" Tarik asked,
pulling the cord tighter around the captain's
wrists.

"I think so." She rubbed her left shoulder.
"The force-guns didn't work."

"I noticed. We must have done something
wrong with them. Perhaps they need re-

charging, or it could be the change in gravity. We'll tend to them later. Gaidar, get off his back. You may have the honor of carrying him to the brig."

"They call it the hole," Gaidar said, still grinning. "It is self-contained, and no one can escape from it. Prisoners are one to a cell, each with its own piped-in supply of moldy food and bad water. It is constructed so that if anyone tries to escape, his cell is automatically ejected from the ship with no air supply. No one tries. I spent a few space-days in one of those cells early in the voyage. It's the most efficient section of the ship."

"It sounds ideal." Tarik gave a harsh laugh. "I suggest we deposit each of our four friends in his own cell. Narisa, can you help us?"

"Yes." She was on her feet again, a little shaky, but unhurt.

It was difficult to drag the unconscious men to the brig. Gaidar, being used to the ship's gravity, tossed the captain over his shoulder and stalked through the ship with him, but it took both Tarik and Narisa to carry the first officer. Once they had reached the brig, it required little time to seal the captain and his three crew members into their cells. When that was done, Narisa, Tarik and Gaidar returned to the bridge and prepared to leave orbit.

"The equipment is easy enough to understand," Narisa reported from her seat at the navigator's station, "except for this panel. Do you know what it is, Gaidar?"

"Starthruster," Gaidar replied promptly.

"You will have to tell Narisa how to use it," Tarik said. "Otherwise, we won't reach the Capital in time to warn the Assembly."

"I understand." Gaidar made no protest about revealing information he had planned to keep secret a while longer. Perhaps he had concluded by now that his two companions were trustworthy, Narisa thought as he leaned over her shoulder. While Tarik stood on her other side, watching, Gaidar quickly explained all he knew of Starthruster's function. "I have never used it myself, but before I fell afoul of the captain, I was often on the bridge, and I watched the navigator carefully."

"Is he among the men in the brig?" Tarik asked. "We might be able to convince him to supply more information."

"He's gone," Gaidar told them. "He was the leader of the shuttle crew."

"Well, then." Tarik drew a deep breath. "We will take our chances on Narisa's skills, which are brilliant."

Narisa warmed at the compliment. She felt remarkably calm as she plotted their course away from the Empty Sector and on to the Capital. Although she knew that nothing in the Empty Sector ever stayed the same for long, she committed to memory the exact coordinates of the planet they had just left in case, she told herself, she ever had a chance to return. She blinked away unexpected moisture that suddenly filled her eyes, and took the Cetan ship out of orbit. Then, following Gaidar's instructions, she activated Starthruster. He had told her that the speed made possible by the device would overcome most of the navigational eccentricities of the Empty Sector. In that he was correct. They were out of the Empty Sector in two space-hours.

"Incredible," Tarik said. "When do you estimate our arrival at the Capital?"

"In one point three six space-days." Narisa was as amazed as Tarik. "There is no apparent effect on us or the ship, though I would assume these speeds will play havoc with time. We will probably arrive at the Capital younger by a few hours than we were when we left the planet."

"There is another effect of this speed we haven't thought of," Tarik mused. "We can't contact anyone until we drop back to orbital speed when we approach the Capital. We had better prepare a message to send out the instant we arrive, or the Service guards will blast this Cetan ship into atoms as soon as we appear."

"I can cut the speed a little ahead of time to give us a few extra seconds," Narisa suggested.

"Good idea. You've done well, Narisa." Tarik rested his hand on her shoulder a moment before he turned to Gaidar and began asking detailed questions about Cetan warships.

Only Tarik and Narisa took turns piloting the ship. Gaidar made a single joke about their lack of confidence in him, then let the matter drop and busied himself with living arrangements. In contrast to most spaceships, where order was considered a matter of safety, the Cetan ship was unbelievably dirty. It was littered with cast-off clothing, open food packets and bits of malodorous garbage. Gaidar cleaned out two small cabins just off the bridge, one where Narisa and Tarik could take turns sleeping, and one for himself.

Narisa was loathe to lie down upon a Cetan bunk, although Gaidar assured her the covers were the cleanest he could find, but she found she was tired. She slept deeply, dreaming about the birds and sunrise over the lake until Tarik called her for her watch.

Her second sleep period was more restless, for the bunk was still warm from Tarik's body and the covers smelled of him. When she finally slept, she dreamed he had begun to make love to her and then left her. She awakened with her body aching from an odd combination of wanting him and the effects of the heavy gravity. She lay with her eyes closed, listening to the unfamiliar sounds of the ship, and of Gaidar talking to Tarik before he went into his own cabin and closed the door. She heard Tarik enter her cabin, and felt him bend over her.

"Narisa, wake up, it's your watch."

She raised her arms, locked them around his neck and pulled him down to her. She had moved quickly, and the heavy gravity helped her purpose. Tarik fell on top of her, his face buried in her neck. She clung to him, kissing his cheek, running her hand through his hair. He moaned just before his mouth found hers and they gave themselves up to a deep, passionate kiss. He moved on her, and she knew he wanted her, too, but when the kiss ended, he pulled away and stood up.

"Tarik," she whispered, reaching for his hand.

"No," he said, "not here. It's too dangerous. One of us should be out there on the bridge every space-minute."

"Then just kiss me once more."

"I can't." But she saw the longing on his face, and her heart began to sing.

"Have you forgiven me?" It was the wrong question. His face closed into a tight, sharp mask. "Tarik, please. I've said I'm sorry."

"This is not the time, or the place, to discuss our personal relations. I honestly don't know what I feel about you, Narisa. I only know we both have a duty to get Gaidar safely to the Capital so he can tell his story. After that, we can talk. We will have to wait until then. Now, please get up. It's time for your watch, and I'm tired. I want to sleep."

"It's the gravity. I tire easily, too." She stood up, accidentally bumping against him and wanting to put her arms around him. But she couldn't. She knew he was right; this was no time for dalliance. They would both have to wait, though it took all the discipline and self-control she could muster. Still, she had gained something from this brief encounter. She knew now that he still wanted her. That would have to be enough for the present.

They left the Cetan ship in formal Service

procession, escorted by four Service guards, and with Narisa walking the correct three paces behind Tarik. They had docked at the spaceport, which orbited above the Capital. The Cetan prisoners had been removed and taken below to be confined on the planet's surface. Gaidar had been taken away, too, despite Tarik's strong protest that the man was under his personal protection.

Narisa knew Tarik was already chafing under Service regulations. The most disquieting thing about their arrival was that Narisa herself was irritated at the refusal of Service personnel to listen to either Tarik or her until all the formalities had been carried out. It was not so long ago that she would have insisted on every step of their arrival being done by strict protocol, but at the moment she felt like screaming at everyone in Service uniform.

"While we are being forced through correct procedures," she muttered, "the Cetans could attack and destroy the Capital."

"If we protest, the Assembly will refuse to hear us," Tarik warned over his shoulder. "Be patient. From what I see ahead, we may be fortunate after all."

They had reached the official reception room. The little procession came to a stop before a tall, thin man in the black jacket and trousers of a Member of the Assembly. That he was a high-ranking Member was evident from the rows of silver braid at his collar and wide cuffs and the silver sash draped from right shoulder to left waist. Nor did Narisa need the formal introduction Tarik was making. She knew him at once. This was Tarik as he would be in forty years, still lithe and slim, his sharp features traced with lines, his dark hair threaded with silver. Only his eyes were different, a paler blue than Tarik's, and piercing, searching, never resting.

"My father, Assembly Member Almaric," Tarik said, and Narisa gave a smart regulation salute.

"I am sent to escort you both to the Assembly," Almaric announced without any personal greeting to his son. "It is in session, and you will be heard at once, since you have insisted you have news of desperate importance. I must tell you that most Members would have preferred to wait until the next session to hear you. Your appearance will disrupt the order of our business."

"This can't wait," Tarik replied.

"You always were impatient," Almaric said with a hint of distressed tolerance. "Come to the transporter then, and on the way down to the Capital perhaps you will tell me what is so urgent."

"We must talk in private," Tarik said. "Please send these guards away. And I want Gaidar released at once. I gave him my word he would be unharmed."

"I assure you he is unharmed. Do calm yourself, Tarik. These are not guards, they are an honor escort. This Gaidar you want protected is waiting outside the Assembly chambers under correct guard. You didn't really expect us to let a Cetan wander freely about the Capital, did you? Even unarmed, Cetans are dangerous."

"He's half Demarian," Narisa spoke up.

"What did you say?" Almaric fixed an icy blue eye upon her.

"His mother was Demarian," Narisa replied.

"Oh. A slave then." Almaric dismissed Gaidar's mother with a shrug. The gesture set something burning in Narisa's mind and heart.

"Gaidar has dealt honestly with Tarik and me," she declared. "He is an honorable man. Both he and his mother were badly treated by the Cetans. He wants to help the Jurisdiction."

"I will remember your recommendation," Almaric responded cooly. "Of course, once the Cetans take a Demarian woman, she is dead to us. No one could be expected to consider accepting such a woman back into our society after the Cetans have had her."

"You don't have to worry," Narisa told him, feeling her anger with this cold, controlled man beginning to boil, and wanting to make him feel something, if only outrage. "The woman really is dead. Gaidar's father broke her neck right in front of their young son."

"And there you see," Almaric said smoothly, apparently unruffled by this revelation, "just why we could not let this Gaidar roam loose through the Capital. Such violent people, the Cetans."

Narisa had her mouth open to say something more, but they had reached the transporter car, and Tarik took her arm, squeezing it rather hard.

"Be quiet," he whispered, putting his mouth near her ear. "Don't argue with him."

Tarik's face was as solemn as his father's, but in his dark eyes Narisa saw both laughter and warm approval of her sudden outspokenness. Once they were seated in the cream and gray molded metal car, and the transporter was under way, Tarik began to speak.

"Perhaps it's just as well our guards—forgive me, sir—our *escort*, should hear me. The more people who know what is going to happen, the more likely the Assembly is to be moved to do something about it. I know how little they care for emergencies that disrupt their carefully arranged schedule of debate on unimportant matters." Tarik raised one hand to stop his father's protest against this impolite view of the august Assembly. He then began to recount in sketchy detail the destruction of the *Reliance*, the crash landing on an unknown planet, the sending of the rescue signal, which he told as though he and Narisa had done it together, and finally, the arrival of the Cetans and Gaidar's story. He never mentioned the birds at all, merely saying the Cetans had been overcome. While he spoke, Narisa noticed that every member of their escort, ostensibly at formal attention, was actually listening intently to each word Tarik said.

"Do you believe this Gaidar?" Almaric asked when Tarik had finished.

"I do, and we have a Starthruster to prove his story."

"Then we must order the Service to test it, to see if it works as you claim it does."

"You can't do that. Gaidar and I disconnected it before we left the ship, and we have hidden an essential part. You see, we wanted to be certain the Assembly really would listen to us. Knowing how that body functions, I feared it would discount our story and order the Cetan ship destroyed, lest any new ideas cause alarming changes in Service procedures. If anyone tries to move the ship without the part we've taken, it will blow up and take the spaceport with it. That's how powerful a machine Starthruster is."

"Is this true?" Almaric demanded of Narisa.

"Yes, sir, it is."

"Where is the hidden part?"

"I don't know, sir. Commander Tarik and Gaidar would not tell me." They had said she would be safer not knowing, and now she realized they had been right. She could not be made to tell what she did not know.

"Well, Tarik," Almaric said, "you will report all of this to the Assembly at once."

"You will stand with me?"

"I have no choice. You are my son. If what you say is true, we will have to do something to stop the Cetans."

"It is true," Tarik said calmly.

The Assembly did not believe Tarik. The Members were so shocked that a Cetan had been admitted to their hallowed chambers that they could think of nothing else. They sat on cushioned chairs in row upon tiered row, looking down with haughty disapproval upon their unwelcome guests. On the red-floored open space in the center of the square meeting room, Tarik and Gaidar stood together, looking back at the Members with calm confidence.

Narisa had been awed by her first view of the fabled Red Room, and of all the Members assembled there. Almaric had allowed her and Tarik only a brief pause to ascertain that Gaidar was unharmed and had been treated well. Then he had led the three of them into the Red Room through a small door at the lowest level, so that as they crossed the empty square, they had to look up to meet the eyes and frowning faces of the very annoyed Members. Narisa recognized Tyre, the famous Leader of the Assembly, sitting bolt upright in his ornate chair at the first level. The Leader was a big man, much overweight, with flushed face and the deepest frown of all.

Narisa had quickly been given a seat in a corner at the end of one of the bottom rows, in case her testimony should be required. She had scarcely reached it before Tarik was ordered to speak.

It had been hard for her to sit still in her place upon soft red cushions through the hours of tedious argument that followed Tarik's speech, without coming to his defense. She was growing more and more upset by the attitude of the Members. Tarik's assertions about the Assembly, which she had once rejected as treasonous, now returned to haunt her. She felt as though her eyes had at last been opened to a great and frightening truth.

She had always trusted the Assembly, without thinking very much about it. These were the representatives of the civilized Races, who had been specifically chosen to guide and protect the citizens of the Jurisdiction, and they were supposed to have the safety and well-being of those citizens as a first concern. Yet for the most part, the Members who had spoken thus far appeared to be lazily secure in their exaulted lifetime positions, interested only in their scheduled esoteric debates on obscure legal niceties. They were remarkably uninterested in revelations that could mean life or death for them and the people they were empowered to protect. She began to understand why Tarik had been so scornful of Jurisdiction laws and Service regulations. The Service, after all, was completely controlled by this Assembly. The stupidity of the debate over Tarik's and Gaidar's claims of an approaching Cetan war fleet brought Narisa to a state of acute frustration. She began to wonder how much longer she could observe regulations and remain silent.

"Do you expect us to believe," asked a portly Member, whose black jacket shone tightly across his ample belly, "actually believe, that you ventured into the Empty Sector and survived to leave it?"

"I have told you the truth," Tarik replied patiently, too polite to remind the Member that he had previously answered the same question several times.

"There can be no such planet as you describe," the Member proclaimed.

"How do you explain our story then?" Tarik asked. "Or the fact that we returned in a Cetan ship?"

"You were obviously captured by the Cetans," another Member called out. "They have used mind-changing devices against you. It was all in your imaginations. You are wasting this Assembly's valuable time."

"No! Listen to him!" Narisa was on her feet, pulling away from the hands that tried to hold her back, striding to the center of the floor to stand with Tarik and Gaidar and proclaim the veracity of their story. "It wasn't imagination. I didn't believe it, either, not at first, even though it was happening to me, too. But Commander Tarik is telling the truth. You must listen to him. Your lives depend on it. Why won't you believe him?"

"Lieutenant, you are out of order!" Leader Tyre pounded on the rail in front of his chair, hitting it again and again with his fists, while the jeers and laughter of many Members rang in Narisa's ears. "Everyone knows the Cetans are pirates and that they quarrel among themselves constantly. They would never have the self-control required to work together in the way you describe. Therefore, your story cannot be true."

"They have agreed to stop fighting each other," Narisa cried, "because they have a new and deadly weapon. They are willing to forget their rivalries for just a while. It will be long enough for them to destroy us. Please, listen to us. The survival of the entire Jurisdiction is at stake."

"I insist that you be silent, lieutenant, or you will be removed." The look the Leader of the Assembly cast upon her recalled Narisa to Service discipline.

Silence fell in the great square chamber. Leader Tyre had put on his silver cap, which meant he was about to make an official pronouncement. Narisa stood between Tarik and Gaidar and watched the ranks of the Members. There were few friendly faces gazing down at them. Almaric was frowning deeply.

"I command," Leader Tyre intoned, "that Commander Tarik Gibal, Lieutenant Navigator Narisa raDon and the Cetan known as Gaidar all be kept in confinement until appropriate sentence is passed upon them."

"What sentence?" Narisa whispered to Tarik. "We haven't done anything wrong."

"I further command," Tyre went on, "that the Empty Sector is to be sealed off completely to all traffic from the civilized Races. All who enter there do so on pain of death."

"Is he mad?" Narisa asked. "The Empty Sector has nothing to do with the present danger."

"Be quiet!" Tarik's whisper sounded like a shout to her. "Don't make him any more angry or we'll never be released."

"In truth," Gaidar's low voice rumbled on her other side, "these folk are as mad, and every bit as stupid, as the Cetans."

"Leader Tyre." Almaric had risen from his

seat, and now bowed gracefully to the man in the silver cap. "May I make a request of the Assembly?"

"Of course." The Leader's cold official tones had changed to a smooth, friendly voice that sounded false to Narisa's ears. "What is it, my dear Almaric?"

"As all here know, this confused young man is my son. I ask that he, and his subordinate, Lieutenant Narisa raDon, be released to me. My home here in the Capital is entirely secure. They will be safe there until the Assembly can decide what to do with them."

"Ahh." With a sigh of relief, Leader Tyre appeared to be considering Almaric's request. Several Members near him tugged at his sleeve or nodded. "Because of your high rank and excellent reputation, the Assembly agrees to your suggestion. Commander Tarik, Lieutenant Narisa, you are remanded to Member Almaric's custody." With another sigh, Leader Tyre pulled off his silver cap and sank back in his chair as if he were exhausted.

"Gaidar, too," Narisa said to Tarik.

"They won't let me go," Gaidar told her. "To them I am a Cetan pirate, nothing more."

"We gave you our word." Narisa could not recall ever having been so angry or frustrated.

"Go quietly, Gaidar," Tarik said. "Give them no cause to harm you. I will talk to my father and try to get him to use his influence to have you released to him."

"I understand." Gaidar smiled at Narisa. "I knew this would happen, in spite of your word. I'm not a complete fool about groups like this. They are little better than the Cetans. Cetans usually kill each other when they disagree in assembly. These just sit here and debate, then do nothing. That is why the Cetans will conquer them."

Two Service guards appeared at Gaidar's side.

"Till we meet once more, my friends," he said, and went away with them.

Chapter Nine

Narisa was still seething when their closely guarded party reached Almaric's house. Her mood was not improved by the undisguised laughter she saw in Tarik's eyes each time they met hers. Considering the situation in which they found themselves, his humor was infuriating to her. When Almaric had formally ushered them into a large reception room, Narisa could be quiet no longer.

"I just want to say," she began, but stopped, surprised when Tarik laid two fingers firmly across her lips.

"Not one word," he said softly and intensely. "For your life's sake, and mine, be silent, Narisa."

She saw something in his eyes besides laughter. A warning, a plea, she could not be certain which. She held her tongue and waited.

"After so long an absence, you will of course want to greet your mother at once," Almaric was saying smoothly. "Do you wish to present your subordinate officer to her?"

"With your kind permission," Tarik answered with equal smoothness.

"Then I see no reason why your guards should not relax in this comfortable room with whatever refreshments my servants can provide for them. Is that agreeable to you, sir?" Almaric smiled benignly upon the youthful leader of the half-dozen guards who had accompanied them from the Assembly chambers. The young man, charmed at finding himself in the company of one of the Assembly's most renowned Members, acknowledged the improbability of Tarik wanting to escape from his own father's home, and made no objection to Almaric's suggestion.

Thus it was that Almaric, Tarik and Narisa went without servants or guards to the second floor of the house and walked in silence along a richly decorated corridor to a door that Almaric opened without knocking. They entered a square hall, which had a door in each wall. The one to their right opened, and a woman appeared. Without speaking, she opened the door directly in front of Almaric and went through it. The others followed, and the door closed behind them. The woman slid a second door over the first and sealed it shut, so tightly that Narisa could barely see the crack in the wall around its edges. Only then did the woman turn to Tarik with a bright smile on her face. She opened her arms. Tarik went into them, hugging her tightly, while Almaric watched them with the first unguarded expression Narisa had seen on his face since they had met. After a while Tarik disengaged himself from the woman's arms.

"This is my mother, Kalina," he told Narisa.

Kalina was not a pretty woman. She was tall and rather stout, with strong, regular features. Her thick bronze hair might once have given her a claim to beauty, but it was now streaked with gray and tamed into a knot at the back of her head. It was her sparkling blue eyes and warm smile that made her attractive. A quick glance at Tarik and an even faster look at Almaric convinced Narisa that both men adored her.

"You must be wondering," Kalina said in a rich, musical voice, "why we meet in such a secret room."

"It is a most unusual room," Narisa responded, looking around at the pale gray walls and ceiling, and the floor covered by Demarian carpets in patterns of red, blue, green, and gold. There was little furniture— three wide arm chairs and a simple bed, all covered in pale gray. The room was lit by clear glass oil lamps set on plain cube tables. There were no windows, and only the one sealed door.

"It is a secure room," Kalina explained. "Smooth and unornamented surfaces are easily checked for eavesdropping equipment.

Most Assembly Members have such rooms for
private conversations. I am certain high-ranking Service officers must have them, too, not
to mention rich merchants. How else would
they stay rich, save by keeping their trading
secrets private? Please be seated, lieutenant."

Narisa sank into one of the wide chairs.
Almaric and Kalina took the remaining chairs
while Tarik prowled about the room.

"I want to know," Almaric said, craning his
neck to see Tarik, "exactly how much of your
story is true."

"All of it!" Narisa would keep silent no
longer. "Every word, and more besides."

"Be careful, my sweet." Tarik laughed from
behind his father's chair, and Narisa flushed
at the endearment. "You are growing dangerously independent in thought and word."

"I am not," Narisa insisted. "We aren't
lying, and I wish someone would believe us."

"I asked the question of my son," Almaric
stated flatly.

"Narisa saved my life twice during our sup-
posedly imaginary adventures," Tarik told his
parents. "She deserves a medal and a citation
from the Assembly, not disbelief and censure.
She has earned the right to speak freely here,
and to discuss this situation with us."

"As you wish." Almaric nodded at Narisa
with little obvious change in his reserved
attitude. "I thank you for my son's life."

"And so do I." Kalina, warmer and more
openly emotional than her husband, reached
forward to take Narisa's hands in hers.

"Tarik is precious to me. You have my life-long gratitude, Lieutenant Narisa. But what is this story my husband thought to be untrue? How did you save Tarik's life?"

"I had better tell you that." Tarik spoke quickly before Narisa could open her mouth. She could not tell from his next words if he was angry with her or only teasing her. "Narisa would insist she was only following regulations. She is an exemplary officer."

"I am glad to hear someone follows the rules," Almaric observed dryly, "since you so seldom do."

Narisa had the distinct impression that Tarik was about to make some heated response to this, but Kalina gave both her husband and her son an unmistakable look, which effectively quelled any incipient quarrel.

"If Narisa agrees, Tarik shall tell the story," Kalina decreed.

"I have no objection." Narisa tried hard to control her amusement at the ease with which Kalina managed her two strong men. She remembered Tarik telling her once that he always made his father angry. That there was tension between the two Narisa could easily discern, but she thought there was affection, too, a proud, reserved love, which neither man could admit. She sat thinking about this while Tarik quickly recounted for his mother everything he had previously told Almaric and the Assembly.

"I don't suppose," Almaric said when Tarik had finished, "that you would consider leaving the Capital at once? That would calm the Assembly. It could be arranged."

"I'm sure it could," Tarik replied. "They would like that. They could forget we ever appeared before them, and get on with their endless foolish debates. I can't go. The Cetan threat is real."

"I think," Narisa said, "that we ought to try talking to some of the top Service officers. They always enjoy fighting Cetans, and they would certainly like to have Starthruster. They might listen to us."

"Not while you have a Cetan for a friend," Almaric told her.

"Gaidar is not a friend." Narisa still could not accept that idea. "But he is an honest person who has dealt fairly with us, and both Tarik and I gave him our word he would not be harmed by anyone at the Capital. We are therefore obligated to keep him safe, no matter what it takes, no matter who does not believe us."

"I want you to know I do believe you." Almaric looked upon Narisa with growing respect. "I admire your honesty, and the faithfulness with which you are determined to carry out your word. Please believe that not all Members of the Assembly are as foolish as our Leader and his friends."

"Tell her all of it, Father," Tarik urged. "You know as well as I do that Tyre and his adherents are something more than foolish. Corrupt and incompetent would be a better description."

"I wish you would choose your words more

carefully." Almaric was silent for a moment. Then, seeming to make some inner decision, he continued, speaking directly to Narisa. "Unfortunately, you and Tarik and Gaidar have been caught in my political conflicts with Leader Tyre. He and his friends were predisposed to disbelieve your story because my son told it."

"Surely you have your own adherents among the Members," Narisa said.

"I have. Most of them wisely kept silent today, not wanting to rouse Tyre to some hasty action that would be unfavorable to any of you, or to me. When the question of your punishment for defying the Assembly is raised, they will vote with me. Tyre is well aware of my growing power. That is why he released you and Tarik to me, to pacify me and my friends, and perhaps also to put us off guard.

"Tonight and tomorrow," Almaric continued, "I will meet privately with several close friends who I feel certain will be as alarmed as I am by your story. We can gather a group of like-minded Members together, and through protracted debate we will eventually force the entire Assembly to agree that something must be done."

"We don't have time for political maneuvering," Tarik said impatiently. "The Cetans are gathering near Belta right now to refit their ships."

"Belta is many light-years away from the Capital," said Kalina, who had been listening silently yet intently to the discussion.

"Haven't you understood, Mother? With Starthruster installed on each Cetan ship, Belta is only *two days* away from the Capital."

"Then," said Kalina calmly, "there is only one thing to do. Send for Halvo."

"I tell my fellow Members that Kalina is the secret of my success in the Assembly." Almaric actually laughed, much pleased with his wife. "They think I am being modest, yet you have just heard the proof of my assertion. Were this room not completely secure, had anyone recordings of our conversations in here over the last forty years, I would stand unmasked. Halvo is exactly the person to help us."

"I should have thought of him myself, Father, and so should you," Tarik said ruefully. "Where is he?"

"One space-day from here," Kalina replied. "What more natural than for a mother to want both her sons home at the same time, especially when they have been away for so long? I will transmit a message to him at once. I will use the secret words we agreed upon to let him know it is an urgent call. He will come." She rose and headed for the door.

"Do you mean Admiral Halvo?" Narisa asked, impressed. Tarik had never mentioned his brother's name to her. "He is your son?"

"He is," Kalina replied proudly. "Is there anything else you wish to say before I open the door? Almaric? Tarik?"

"I will go to find my friends from the Assembly." Almaric rose, too. "If they are alerted, there may be something we can do when Halvo arrives."

"Father, a request. Will you ask Jon to visit me?"

"Your old teacher? Yes, certainly." Almaric paused by the door. "Is there anything else you need?"

"A few minutes here, to speak freely with Narisa."

"Seal the door after we leave," Kalina told him. "When you have finished, Narisa, there will be a servant in the corridor to take you to your guest chamber. Tarik, your old room is being prepared for you." She came back to kiss her son again before leaving him alone with Narisa.

She had stood up when Tarik's parents did. She watched him seal the door, uncertain what he would say or do. He looked so serious.

"The most important thing to remember, Narisa, is that every room in the house, except this one, probably has at least one eavesdropping device hidden somewhere in it. That is why this room is essential. You cannot speak freely outside it, not even in the garden. Somewhere in the Assembly chambers, some adherent of Leader Tyre is listening to every word he can hear, hoping we will say something to prove our story a lie, or discredit my father."

"I will remember. Tarik, I am sorry I sent out that rescue call. You would not be in danger from the Assembly if I hadn't done it, and it's clear to me our coming here won't make any difference to the Jurisdiction's defenses." She wanted to tell him she now knew he had been right in everything he had said about the Assembly, and probably about the Service, too, but Tarik stopped her with words and actions.

"I am not sorry." He caught her face between his hands. "You did the correct thing, Narisa. If you hadn't, no one would know about the Cetan plan until it was too late. I was angry because you had sent out a message without my express permission as your superior officer, and because I wanted, very foolishly, to stay on that peaceful planet, alone with you. But you were right, and I was wrong and selfish. Difficult as our situation is, we belong here, trying to convince the Assembly we are telling the truth, doing everything we can to save the Races who live within the Jurisdiction. We will find a way to do that. I know it."

"I miss the planet," Narisa said, "and the birds. Especially the birds. At the end, I wanted to stay there, too."

"I know," he whispered. "Just you and I, alone together. At least we are together now. We have this short time, if nothing else, my love. Until the Cetans come."

She was hypnotized by his purple-blue eyes, by his wide, tender mouth so close to her own. She wrapped her arms around his waist as he brought her face, still clasped between his hands, forward until their lips touched lightly, separated, then met again more firmly.

They were shaken by a gust of passion so intense neither of them could resist it. They clung to each other, swaying, until Tarik caught her beneath her knees to lift her off her feet, and they sank together upon the soft Demarian carpets. Tarik pulled open the clasps of her jacket, searching for her breasts, while Narisa tore at his uniform, and then her own, wanting his hot flesh on hers. All the time their mouths touched as both were unwilling to lose that sweet contact for an instant. Finally they were naked. Narisa's hands roved over his beautiful, tightly muscled body, while he caressed and probed gently with his fingertips, driving her wild with ever-rising desire. They came together, fitting so perfectly they might have been two halves of one body, and Narisa cried out in joyful release, hearing Tarik's answering cry, and then his murmured words telling her he loved her, loved her, loved her. . . .

"And I love you," she whispered back, and felt his arms encircling her even more tightly, felt his mouth on her throat and cheeks, and then her lips, and they ended their lovemaking as they had begun it, with their lips touching lightly again and yet again.

Narisa was conducted to the guest chamber that would be hers by a tiny Demarian maidservant, a creature scarcely out of childhood, who said, between giggles, that her name was

Chatta. Narisa's room, like the rest of the
house except the secure room, was ornately
decorated in typical Jurisdiction style, with
dark green and deep red covering walls and
floors and oversized carved furniture. The
windows were long and narrow and heavily
draped in red and green fabric so that little
natural light could enter. This lack was offset
by black metal torchieres placed at intervals
along each wall. The upward flaring light from
these lamps cast strange patterns on the
carved molding where the walls met the
ceiling, and made dark shadows around
draperies and furniture. The bed was huge,
covered with a dark green fabric that seemed
to absorb most of the artificial light. Narisa
had never thought much about decor or
furniture, but she suddenly felt oppressed by
her surroundings. She found herself longing
for the serene simplicity of Dulan's glistening
white island retreat.

"The bathing room is here," Chatta announced, giggling again. "My mistress Kalina
has ordered fresh clothing to be brought to
you, so you may wear something other than
your uniform for the evening meal."

Narisa, who had followed Chatta through
the pointed archway into the next room,
nodded without listening very closely to what
the maid was saying. She could not take her
eyes off the tub. It was big enough to hold at
least six people. In contrast to the gloomy
dark red walls of the bathing room, the tub
was of deepest green stone, with lighter green

streaks swirling through it. The openings for water were gold, shaped like the heads of Demarian leopard-wolves, and there was a twisted gold railing along one side of the three steps that led down into the tub.

"I would rather swim in the lake," she said, sighing.

"There is no lake here," Chatta said with a giggle, turning a lever to start the water flowing. She opened a green glass bottle, letting a heavy odor fill the room. "Do you wish scent?"

"No," Narisa said hastily, wrinkling her nose. "Nothing. Just plain water and plain cleanser." She should not have mentioned the lake. She had to remember Tarik's warning about eavesdroppers, and little Chatta might report anything she said.

Chatta added cleanser to the bubbling water. Narisa pulled off her uniform and underclothes, folded them neatly on a carved black and red bench, and then stepped into the tub. She sat on the lowest step and let the warm water foam up about her shoulders. She felt pleasantly relaxed after her love-making with Tarik. She did not want to think about what might happen to both of them, and to Gaidar. Just for a little while she wanted to revel in being a woman in love. She slipped dreamily backward into the water, wetting her hair. As she lifted her arms to begin washing it, Chatta started giggling again. Narisa wished the silly girl would stop. She was beginning to break Narisa's peaceful, romantic mood.

"Oh, Mistress Narisa," Chatta said, laughing and pointing one small finger. "You are hairy."

"Hairy?" Narisa stopped scrubbing her head and stared at the maid.

"Your arms," Chatta said between giggles. "And your legs, too. I noticed them when you undressed. How very funny. I have never seen a woman so hairy."

"It's not funny at all," Narisa said patiently. "Commander Tarik and I were marooned without supplies. We haven't been able to take our pills for more than eight space-days. Of course I have hair on my body, and he has a beard." It had started growing once again after they had left the island, for the Cetans favored beards and did not stock the pills aboard their ships. Tarik looked as rough-faced now as he had when they had reached Dulan's island.

"I saw him." Chatta continued her giggling. "Commander Tarik looks almost as fierce as a Cetan warrior. Isn't it fortunate the pills are only for body hair? It's not like the ancient days. Now we have an injection each year for the other, and we don't have to worry about forgetting and breaking the law."

"You are too young to talk about such things," Narisa said, starting to wash her hair again. But Chatta would not be silenced.

"Next year I will have my first injection," she announced proudly.

Narisa recalled her own excitement when

the time had come for her first annual injection. It was an important turning point in
life for every boy and girl. The law Chatta had
mentioned dated from the days, space-centuries before, when a series of medical advances
had made overpopulation a problem on all
but the most inhospitable planets. The
Assembly had passed a law requiring every
citizen of the Jurisdiction, of whatever Race,
to have an annual antifertility injection. The
same law made it necessary to apply for permission before reproducing. The law had
worked well. Jurisdiction population had
stabilized. In some places it had actually
dropped off in the last century or two with
Cetan raids destroying large numbers of the
Races, but the Assembly had never bothered
to repeal the law. The Assembly, Narisa reminded herself sourly, disliked any kind of
change. The Reproduction Law had been in
effect for so long that most people accepted it
without question. But Narisa had lately begun
to question a great many things. She floated
in the warm, soapy water, wondering what it
would be like to have Tarik's child, to hold a
tiny body in her arms and know the two of
them had created it with their love.

"Mistress Narisa?" Chatta's giggly voice
broke into her dreamy thoughts. "What shall
we do about your body hair? It is not fashion-
able, you know."

"I do look awful, don't I?" Narisa found her
own laughter matching Chatta's. "You had
better find me some shaving equipment so I'll

be presentable tonight. Remind me tomorrow
to ask the Service for another supply of pills."

The gown Chatta brought her to wear was
of heavy dark green fabric, intricately draped
and folded and gathered on the left shoulder
with a huge red stone clasp. Every possible
edge of the dress had a wide band of dark red
embroidery.

As she followed Chatta through gloomy
deep green corridors and down wide red
stone staircases, Narisa felt dragged down
and encumbered by the weight and
complexity of the garment. At least her right
arm and shoulder were bare. She had refused
to wear any of the heavy jewelry Chatta had
offered to her, but she had given in and
allowed the little maidservant to draw her
hair into a thin gold band, which held the
golden brown tresses away from her face,
pulling them up onto the back of her head.

Chatta had also insisted on painting
Narisa's face, lining her eyes with with wide
streaks of gray powder until they looked deep
and mysterious, the gold flecks in the gray
irises showing clearly. Then Chatta had tinted
Narisa's cheeks and lips with coral polish,
and buffed all her nails with a matching coral
powder. High-heeled slippers in a shade to
match the dress completed her costume.
Narisa, accustomed to flat Service boots,
found it necessary to negotiate each steep,
polished stone stairway with great care.

Along their way they were joined by two of

the guards who had accompanied Almaric's party from the Assembly chambers to his house. The men said nothing; they simply fell into step with the two women, one ahead of Narisa and to her left, the other a little behind her and to her right. Their positions served to remind Narisa she was a prisoner. She could not, for instance, walk through the main entrance, which she saw just ahead, and stand on the top outside step breathing fresh air, which was what she wanted to do. She felt as though the dark colors and heavy decor of Almaric's home were stiffling her.

Chatta looked frightened when the men appeared. She was pale as she turned to the left, away from the entrance, and beckoned Narisa to follow her down a corridor. She showed Narisa to a wide double door of black carved wood, then stopped.

"I was told to bring you here," Chatta said nervously. "I will return to your bedchamber to wait for you there."

The maidservant fled, and one of the guards opened the doors for Narisa. She walked past him, into the room where they were to eat. It had shiny black floors, deep red walls and a series of black and gold lamps hanging from the ceiling over a long table of polished red stone. But this room was not as oppressive as the others she had seen, because one long wall was a series of pointed arches opening onto a wide terrace. Beyond the terrace lay a garden, with a fountain splashing into a tiny pool. It was a carefully tended garden, and artificially heated in this cold season on the Capital planet, but over-cultivated or not, it contained the fresh growing plants and trees for which her spirit longed. She went through an arch onto the terrace, her guards following at a discreet distance.

Tarik was there in Service uniform, shaved and with his hair freshly trimmed. He was so handsome her breath caught in her throat at the sight of him. He came to her at once and took her hand.

"You look," he said, "like a wealthy and very elegant Demarian woman."

"I feel most unnatural."

"I remember a simple silver-gray robe." His night-blue eyes twinkled. "A robe you did not keep on for very long."

"This one would be more difficult for you to remove." Her heart was thudding hard in her chest. How she wished he could unclasp the red stone brooch at her left shoulder, unfold the fabric and unfasten all the clips and clasps and loops of her gown to free her from its weight, and then take her hand again and lead her out there into the garden, under the trees, amongst the low-growing flowers and the sweet-scented leaves. When he smiled at her, she knew he felt the same way.

He touched her lips with his fingertips. The gesture was as gentle as a kiss, yet silenced anything else she might have said, recalling her to the present, to the elderly man who stood behind him, and to the guards waiting in the shadows of a nearby archway. Then she

remembered with a start just where they
stood, and that it was unsafe to speak too
freely.

"This is Jon Tanon," Tarik said, "my old
teacher and a dear friend. It was Jon who first
awakened me to the uses of history."

Narisa held her breath. She hoped Tarik
would say nothing to betray his opinions
about the Jurisdiction version of history. Not
with the guards standing so near. She and
Tarik and Gaidar were in enough trouble already. They didn't need anything else for the
Assembly to blame on them. To her relief,
Tarik launched into a funny story about his
school days, during which Narisa was able to
study the elderly man.

The teacher was short, plump, with white
hair thinning on top, blue eyes and a round
pink face presently wreathed in an infectious
smile as he listened to Tarik's account of his
student days.

"He never stopped asking questions. He
was my most difficult pupil," Jon told Narisa,
"and my most brilliant. I had hoped he would
become a teacher himself, but Almaric
wanted him to enter the Service."

"And see what has become of me," Tarik
said too softly for the guards to hear.

"Never mind." Jon Tanon laid a blue-veined
hand on Tarik's arm. "With Almaric behind
you, this trouble will not last long. Ah, here
are your parents."

Kalina wore a black gown trimmed with silver, similar in style to Narisa's. On her tall,

dignified figure it was most impressive and
stately. Almaric, in his black and silver
Assembly Member's uniform, complimented
his wife's dignity.

"We are eating a little early," Kalina said to
Narisa, "because Almaric and I are required
at an official function this evening."

"It will offer a marvelous opportunity,"
Almaric added, "for me to speak with many of
my friends. Assembly business is so pressing,
we do not often have time for informal conversations."

Narisa understood from this that Almaric
would spend the better part of the evening
trying to convince his fellow Assembly
Members that Tarik was telling the truth.
Kalina would probably do the same with her
friends. Narisa began to feel more hopeful
about Tarik's and her own prospects.

When they sat down at the red stone table,
all six of their guards sat with them, a guard
at every second place. Narisa was deeply
offended at this invasion of a private meal,
but Almaric and Kalina treated the guards as
though they were invited guests, and Tarik
was a model of politeness, successfully hiding
the irritation Narisa knew he must feel.

"I know you will excuse us," Almaric said
to the leader of the guards when the meal had
ended. "Please stay here and have all the
wines and sweets you want. My servants are
available to you at any time."

"Where are you going, sir?" inquired the
guards' leader.

"A brief family conference before my wife and I leave for the Assembly chambers," Almaric told him.

"And the old man? Master Teacher, you are no family member." In contrast to his deferential attitude toward Almaric, the guard looked threateningly at Jon.

"A dear friend and advisor." Almaric took the teacher's arm and helped him to rise. "His knowledge of Jurisdiction law and history will be helpful in resolving my son's difficulties. Jon is spending the night with us."

"Go, then." The leader of the guards, perhaps thinking he had previously been too lenient with his charges, now seemed to feel a need to assert himself. "You, Member Almaric, and your wife, may leave the house, since it is on Assembly business, but these other three must remain above the second floor once they go up those stairs. No evening strolls in the garden, no wandering around the lower levels where the outside doors are."

"For myself," Narisa declared, glad to rise from the table and end the strain of sitting between two guards, "I will be happy to stay in my room. It has been a long and tiring day."

They made their way back to the secure room in Kalina's quarters. After a quick discussion of how much Almaric should tell his friends when meeting them at a public and official function, Tarik's parents left.

"And now," Jon said, rubbing his hands together, his pink face shining with eager anticipation, "tell me about this new planet you have discovered. I want to know every-thing."

It was long hours later before Jon sought his room, leaving Tarik and Narisa near exhaustion from all his questions.

Narisa stretched in her chair. "Do you think it was wise to tell him about the birds? I would rather have kept their existence a secret. Talking about telepathy, even a primitive kind like theirs, is dangerous."

"Not when we are talking to Jon." Tarik sat on the carpets by Narisa's chair. He laid one arm across her knees in a familiar gesture that warmed her heart. "I would trust Jon with my life."

"You just did, my love." He smiled at her use of that phrase, and moved his hand along her thigh, warming her body's most secret places. "Do you know, Tarik, there was a time when I thought I would never see you smile?"

"That was before I knew you could love me." He slid his hand higher. Narisa felt her-self begin to tremble. Her need for Tarik was like a disease, growing stronger each time he touched her, until she would be completely consumed by it. It might kill her before they were done with upcoming dangers. She did not care. The joy of loving him, and knowing he loved her, was compensation for any punishment the Assembly could have in store for them. Tarik had filled the empty places in her heart, healed the wounds left by the death of her family, and most important, he had opened her mind, so she was capable of seeing and understanding facts she had ignored or been blind to before.

"I love you, Tarik."

"Come here." He pulled her down into his arms. "Lie with me again."

She pressed herself against him where he still sat. "Tarik, I don't know how you are going to get me out of this dress. I can't do it by myself. I have never seen any garment with so many closures and so much material."

"I could always just pull up your skirt." He reached for the hem of the dress and tugged at it. Narisa tried to stop him, laughing and slapping at his hands. He pulled again, catching more of the fabric this time. She tipped over, rolling onto the floor, tangled in her dark green draperies. With her bare right arm she caught him, and he landed on top of her, laughing as hard as she was, and buried his face in her well-covered bosom. There he stayed for a time, caressing her through all the thick folds of her gown while she stroked his thick hair, weaving her fingers through heavy strands. Their laughter gradually dissipated as the tension between them grew.

"You may be content with this," he whispered after a while, "but I am not." He unfastened the brooch at her left shoulder and pulled the dress down rather roughly to expose her breasts, further entrapping her left arm in twisted material.

"I can't move," she complained.

"You don't need to. I'll do it all." He proceeded to plunder her throat and shoulders and breasts, holding her right hand prisoner while his strong legs straddled her, giving her no choice but to submit to the delicious torture his lips were inflicting on her. He began pushing the dress farther down her body, reaching beneath it to caress her abdomen. With his mouth he burned a path of fire upon her skin.

"Tarik, stop," she moaned. "I heard something tear."

"My trousers, I'm sure." Although his voice was muffled against her skin, she could hear renewed laughter. But when he spoke again, it was with anguish. "If I don't get this ridiculous dress off you soon, I'll explode."

"I know, I feel the same way," she gasped. "Let my hand go, my love, and I'll help. Let me go."

He freed her right hand, and together they pushed and pulled at the dress until it was down around her ankles and she could kick it away. Her shoes had been lost long before, and now the gold band in her hair fell off, too. She wore no undergarments, the dress being constructed so she would not need them.

Narisa felt gloriously free, as though she had been released from chains. She stretched luxuriously, feeling the silky pile of the thick Demarian carpets against her back. They made a wonderful bed, soft and firm at the same time. She stretched again and preened, deliberately inciting Tarik to greater passion.

The moment her dress had come off, he had begun tearing at his uniform jacket. She reached for the waist of his trousers and saw he had not been far wrong when he had said he would explode. His desire for her was obviously desperate, and knowledge of his need increased her own desire. She slid her hands along his flanks as she slipped his trousers lower. With a deep, rumbling growl he finished the job himself, removing trousers and boots with one rapid motion. When he turned toward her, she caught at him, pulling him down on top of her again, his body hot and hard and brimming with barely contained passion.

Narisa, laughing aloud from the pleasure of his touch, raised one knee and hip and pushed hard. She was strong, and he had not expected the sudden movement. She managed to tumble both of them over until she was on top of him. His shout of surprised laughter changed to a moan of sensuous delight as he achieved what he wanted most. She straddled him, and he became part of her, filling her completely while he caressed her breasts until she screamed, and screamed again in ecstacy as her moment came upon her. He pulled her down hard to stop her mouth with his tongue, and she lay quivering and shaking on his chest while he poured himself into her.

Something filled Narisa's heart as she lay in Tarik's loving arms, an ancient, atavistic desire that shook her to her very roots and cut the last bonds of unquestioning loyalty to Jurisdiction and Service.

"I love you," Tarik whispered, kissing her

brow.

"Tarik," she said, "I want your child."

He tightened his arms around her and lay without speaking for a moment. Narisa, her face hidden against his chest, held her breath, fearing rejection. His response, when it came, was a harsh whisper.

"Are you sure?"

"I am absolutely certain."

"So am I."

She raised her head to find his night-dark eyes suspiciously moist. She kissed him quickly before her own emotions could overcome her. It was more than a kiss they shared then; it was a pledge.

"Until this morning," he said after they had both gotten their feelings in hand again, "you might have had a chance for approval of an application to reproduce. You are the last surviving member of your family. The Reproductive Agency would have favored you for that. I might even have had a chance of being approved as the father. But I doubt the Agency will be so amenable to either of us now."

"No," she agreed. "After my outburst in the Assembly chambers, my application would never be accepted for consideration, much less approved. Jurisdiction law is wrong in this matter, Tarik."

"I never thought I'd hear you say that." There was no laughter in him now. He smoothed back her ruffled hair with great tenderness. "What do you suggest we do, my love? I have a few ideas of my own, but what do you say?"

"There are two possibilities," she told him. "We can leave the Capital as your father suggested earlier and return to the Empty Sector. Jurisdiction law does not apply there, and we could live as outcasts. Or, we can change the law."

"Dangerous words. Have I done this to you?" he wondered aloud. "Have I made you into a rebel?"

"I have never before wanted to do anything important that was against Jurisdiction law or Service regulations," she replied. "Perhaps I would have come to this myself in time, but you opened my mind, Tarik. You and the birds and that strange, beautiful planet. There, I was forced to think in different ways. I want your child, and if you want it, too, we will find a way."

"Before we can do that," he reminded her, "we must deal with the Cetan threat. If we survive that, and if my father and his friends can convince the Assembly to be lenient . . ." His voice slowed and stopped.

"The Cetans." Narisa took a deep breath. "All else must wait until they are defeated. And if they are not, if the Jurisdiction loses the battle with them, our plans will remain hopeless dreams."

"Then," Tarik told her, "we must see to it that the Jurisdiction does not lose the battle."

Chapter Ten

She could not get back into the green dress alone. Tarik had to help her, with time out for much tender laughter and many kisses and sweet, mischievous caresses, which ignited new fires between them. At one point he pulled the dress off her again so they could make love one more time before parting. They never did get it adjusted so it would hang as it should.

Narisa was glad the corridors were deserted when she made her way back to her own chamber, and very grateful to find Chatta asleep on a low couch. It was just as well that Chatta could not see the rumpled dress. Narisa liked the little maid, but she did not want Chatta gossiping about her relationship with Tarik. Any information about Narisa and Tarik that leaked back to the Assembly and its

Leader could be used against them, or against
Almaric.

Narisa pulled off the hated dress, dropping
it carelessly over a chair, and crawled into the
huge, heavily-draped bed. She was not sleepy,
which was just as well. She had a great deal to
think about.

When she and Tarik had made love, they
had shared more than physical intimacy.
Each had touched the other's innermost
being, and their agreement to have a child
bound them together in love and trust. They
belonged to each other for the rest of their
lives. Tarik was the man for whom her heart
and soul had longed. She could never take
another into her heart or into her arms, and
she believed he felt the same way about her.

She knew their love for each other would
not keep them safe. They might be separated
by a ruling of the Assembly when their
punishment was decided. But before that
could happen, one or both of them would very
likely be killed when the Cetans attacked, unless they could convince someone in power to
prepare a defense. Never before had Narisa
had such hopes for the future, and never had
the future seemed so elusive.

She sighed, turning over in the too-soft bed.
How complicated everything had become.
How simple life had been before she had
learned to love Tarik. Simple and easy, she
told herself scornfully, to be oblivious to
reality. She was fully aware now, and she had
no desire to retreat into her former state of

blind obedience. Because of Tarik she was happy, and she was terrified at the same time. And most important, she was determined to fight for what she wanted, if need be until there was neither breath nor blood left in her body. She knew Tarik would be at her side to the end.

Drifting toward sleep at last, Narisa's thoughts turned to Dulan's planet, to the simplicity and freedom it offered. She could almost see the birds behind her closed lids, and their calls echoed in her heart.

Chon. Chon-chon. Return one day. Return. Return.

Chatta greeted the new morning with the announcement that Mistress Kalina would like to see Narisa as soon as she had dressed and eaten.

Narisa decided to wear her Service uniform. She would not, she told Chatta firmly, be fastened into another complicated gown like the one she had worn the night before.

"You will not have to," Chatta replied with her usual series of giggles. "Mistress Kalina ordered Beltan dress prepared for you. She thought you would find it more comfortable."

Chatta held up a cream-colored garment. Narisa snatched it from her fingers with a delighted cry. She had not worn the dress of her youth since she had put on the Service uniform. It slipped easily over her head, the rounded neck circling the base of her throat, the long narrow sleeves wrist length. Chatta fastened the small silver clasps along the left shoulder. The ankle-length uncinched garment was narrowly cut so it clung to her figure, yet it was loose enough for easy movement. The footwear Kalina had sent was Beltan, too—flat sandals with silver strips winding between her toes and around her ankles. On Belta, Narisa would have worn a wide silver bracelet on each wrist. There were none to be had, but she did not care.

"This," she said happily, "is much more comfortable than the clothing you wear here at the Capital."

"It looks like an undergarment for the cold season." Chatta sniffed, offended. She brightened, however, when Narisa said she was needed for an important errand, and sent her off to Service Headquarters to get a supply of the pills that prevented growth of body hair.

"My Mistress Kalina has some," Chatta exclaimed. "I'm sure she would share them with you."

"I'm certain she would," Narisa agreed, "but the Service provides them free to all its personnel. There is no need to take Kalina's pills." She had an ulterior motive for sending Chatta. She hoped the talkative, friendly girl would pick up any gossip that was circulating about the Cetan threat, and some hint of what, if anything, the Service proposed to do about it. Almaric undoubtedly had more orthodox sources of information, but Narisa wanted to hear what ordinary Servicepeople were saying. With Chatta on her way, Narisa hurried to meet Kalina in the little square hall just outside the secure room.

"There is someone I want you to meet," Kalina said after Narisa had finished thanking her for the new Beltan clothes. "This may be difficult for you, Narisa, but please listen to what she says and believe her as I do. It is extremely important that you do. How I wish Almaric and Tarik were here."

"Where are they?"

"They left early this morning with Jon. I can't say more here." Kalina opened the door and motioned to Narisa to enter before her.

There, in the center of the secure room, stood a woman who was a few inches shorter than Narisa, who had flame red hair, large green eyes and a voluptuous figure.

"Suria, what are you doing here?" It was Tarik's former lover, who had been navigator of the *Reliance* before Narisa, the sensuous, throaty-voiced creature of whom Narisa had been so jealous.

"Greetings, Narisa." Suria put out her hand, and under Kalina's expressive look, Narisa felt compelled to take it. "I came here to warn you."

"Of what?" Narisa wanted to shout that Tarik was hers, and that Suria had no right to come back into his life. She could not keep the hostility out of her voice. "What do you want, Suria?"

"Narisa, please." Kalina moved between the two younger women. "I asked you to listen to Suria. I have known her for years, and I am certain she is telling the truth. Let us sit down and speak rationally."

Narisa sat, perching on the edge of a chair, never taking her eyes off Suria, who sank gracefully into another chair, while Kalina took the third one. Narisa had noticed something about Suria, and could not contain her curiosity. Suria wore the simple wrapped garment over trousers that was the costume of her home planet. Her waist was tiny, and though her hips curved in a way that must be inviting to men, her abdomen was flat.

"I understood," Narisa said in a slightly more pleasant tone than before, "that you had left the *Reliance* in order to reproduce. It has been more than six space-months since that time, yet your figure is unchanged. Has no genetically suitable father been found?"

"No." Suria laughed bitterly, and her next words sent a chill through Narisa. "I have been refused permission to have a child."

"But I thought with your important family, there was no question of refusal." Narisa looked more closely at Suria. With a new understanding born of her own intense desire for Tarik's child, she saw the sadness on that beautiful face, the tiny lines around eyes and mouth, and the shadows beneath the green eyes. How would she, Narisa, feel if told she would never be allowed to have a child? A sense of comradeship began to erase her initially hostile feelings toward the woman facing her. "Suria, I am sorry. You were willing to postpone your career in the service . . . you must have wanted very badly to reproduce."

"And now I have neither child nor Service career," Suria responded. "I was too insistent. I even taught myself midwifery and child care. I wanted to raise it myself. That was one of the reasons I was refused. I was told my eagerness was a sign of emotional instability."

"But there are many planets within the Jurisdiction where people raise their own children," Narisa objected. "Belta, for example, or Demaria, and on those planets some people are even permitted to have more than one child. I don't understand why you should be refused for such a wish."

"As you know, Narisa, all planets living under the Jurisdiction are permitted their own laws only at the discretion of the Assembly. The various planets tolerate this arrangement because the Assembly has succeeded in keeping peace within the Jurisdiction for many centuries. We are all taught in childhood just how terrible were the wars that preceded the Great Agreement, which led to the formation of the Jurisdiction and establishment of the Assembly to rule it. I don't have to remind you how all the Races were nearly destroyed by those long-ago wars, and how grateful we all should be for the peace we have now.

"But," Suria went on, "The various agencies of the Assembly can be capricious in their judgments for individuals, and they are not required to explain their decisions. I pressed the Reproductive Agency for an explanation of their denial of my application. As a result of my determined persistence, I am no longer permitted to leave the Capital. I have been told I am free here, but it has become a prison for me. I can't even return to my home planet. My own family refused to take me in. I disgraced them by failing to get permission to reproduce, and they want nothing more to to do with me."

"You have been a loyal officer of the Service," Narisa cried. "To treat you this way is outrageous."

"No more outrageous than the Assembly refusing to believe Tarik and placing him under arrest," Suria replied. "I believe his story, Narisa. I know him well enough to know he is completely honest, well enough to be aware of his doubts about the Assembly and the Service, his fears that both have become so powerful and irresponsible they make a mockery of the original Jurisdiction Agreement. There were times when I thought Tarik was an overly romantic fool. Now I realize he was right."

"I thought he was foolish, too," Narisa murmured.

"You love him." It was a simple statement. It required no answer, but Narisa bowed her head in acknowledgment of Suria's perception. Unexpectedly, she felt Kalina's hand on hers.

"I came here to give vitally important information to Tarik, not to seduce him. I have no desire to become Tarik's lover again,"

Suria said bluntly. "It was a convenience between us, and a certain fondness, but no more. We were always honest with each other. We treated each other well. We remain friends. I will be your friend, too, if you will allow it. Tarik found me trustworthy, and Kalina will vouch for me." She faced Narisa, half challenging, half fearful.

Narisa could find no spark of anger or jealousy in her heart toward the unhappy woman. Suria had deserved better from the Jurisdiction she had served so well. More importantly, it was obvious Kalina believed her. If Kalina trusted Suria, then Narisa would trust her, too, though friendship was another matter. Still, Narisa would give what she could.

"I see no reason why we should be enemies," she said, and felt a reassuring pressure from Kalina's hand, which was still holding her own.

"Suria, tell Narisa what you have learned," Kalina urged. "Tell her what you would have told Tarik had he been here."

"To earn my daily food supply, I have taken a menial position in the household of the Leader of the Assembly," Suria told Narisa.

"But you are an expert navigator. How can you let all that training go to waste?"

"I have no choice. I had to resign from the Service before applying for permission to have a child, and now they won't let me rejoin. If I could leave the Capital, I might find a place with a private merchant's fleet, but no one wants a navigator who is forbidden to go into deep space. If Leader Tyre hadn't taken me in, I might well have starved. There are those who would say I should have done that instead of accepting his proposal." Something in Suria's voice told Narisa exactly what those last words meant.

"He uses you?" Narisa whispered in horror, and heard Kalina's soft cry of distress. When Suria nodded, Narisa continued, "Against your will? The Leader of the Assembly, that unpleasant man, forces you to lie down with him?"

"He lies down. I'm not allowed to," Suria responded wryly. "It's not very often. He would rather eat and drink."

"My poor child!" Kalina cried. "I did not know about this. We are old friends—why did you not come to me?"

"I was too ashamed." Suria sat up straighter, lifting her chin. "I'm not ashamed any longer. I think it is a good thing I remained in that dreadful man's household and have admittance to his most private room. Kalina, that is how I heard of the plot to kill you."

"Leader Tyre wants to kill Kalina?" Narisa was in a state of confusion. She wasn't certain she had understood this last charge.

"Not just Kalina," Suria responded. "He wants all of you dead—Almaric, Tarik, you, and the Cetan who came to the Capital with you."

"Gaidar." Narisa was still trying to take in all Suria was telling her.

"Gaidar, that's the one. You see, Narisa,

Leader Tyre fears the prestige Almaric has
attained by being honest and devoted to the
welfare of the Jurisdiction rather than to his
own personal advancement. He believes
Almaric is plotting to overthrow him. That is
what Tyre would do in Almaric's position, so
he wants to strike first and eliminate Almaric.
Tarik's appearance before the Assembly has
provided Tyre with the perfect opportunity.''

"The Assembly has to be told what their
Leader is planning," Narisa said. "The
Members aren't all corrupt. Surely they
would never allow such violence."

"Why not? They have allowed violence
before when it suited their purposes. The
Jugarian Civil War, for example. The
Assembly could have prevented that, but they
let it happen. The Jugarians are an unpleasant
Race, so the majority in the Assembly voted to
allow them to kill each other until there were
few left. The Assembly will now have Jugaria
resettled with colonists of Leader Tyre's own
choice. I know Almaric voted against that
decision. It's one of the reasons Tyre hates
him so much.

"Then there was the Cetan destruction of
Belta ten space-years ago. The Assembly knew
Cetan ships were headed there, and yet the
Beltans were given no warning." Suria
paused only a moment at Narisa's strangled
gasp at disclosure of this information. "The
Beltan people were too free, or so Tyre
thought, and they needed scourging. The
Assembly let the Cetans do the job. It is a very
different planet now from the one you once

knew, Narisa. It is not so open a society. It's much more like the Capital.

"No," Suria went on, "to be fair, you are right. Not all Members of the Assembly are corrupt. There are decent ones, like Almaric and a few others, but too often they are shouted down or their decisions are subverted by Leader Tyre and his cronies. It's a wonder to me that the good ones haven't all left the Capital long ago."

"My family died for the convenience of the Assembly? They could have warned Belta or sent help and did not? I was here at the Capital when it happened. How could I have been so blind to all of this?" Narisa cried. She did not doubt what Suria had said. It fit too well with what she had come to understand on her own. She felt bleak, helpless despair over any chance of ever changing an Assembly that could allow such things. "It seems my life since the day I entered the Service has been based on lies. How could I have been so stupid?"

"Don't blame yourself," Suria replied. "Few people know the truth about the Assembly. We only know what we have been taught. Those of us in the Service are so sheltered during training, and later spend so much of our time in space, that we are separated from the restrictions and difficulties of ordinary life. When we are inconvenienced, we charge it to Service regulations and take pride in doing our duty. Or we disregard what our own minds and hearts tell us because we can't bear to accept the evidence before our eyes. I was like that until I was refused a child and took service with Leader Tyre. It was only in his household that I was finally forced to accept the truth."

"And so," Kalina said, returning with remarkable calmness to the principal reason for Suria's visit, "I, my family and Narisa are all to be destroyed."

"And Gaidar," Narisa added, "to whom Tarik and I have both given our word that he will be safe."

"About this Gaidar," Suria said tensely. "The Cetan has been removed from confinement in the Assembly chambers and taken to Leader Tyre's own house. He is now sealed into a room on the lowest level. It will be more convenient for Tyre to have him killed there."

"I can't let that happen," Narisa cried.

"Then you and I will have to remove him at once." Suria's green eyes gleamed, and her lovely face took on a purposeful look. "After we have freed Gaidar, will you accept him here, Kalina?"

"I will have no laws broken. Almaric's position is precarious enough if Tyre thinks he can have us killed and not be brought down himself. I thank you for the warning, Suria, and we will do our best to prevent his plan from succeeding, but if one broken law or the absence of Tarik or Narisa from our house can be laid to us, we will be unable to help them in any way when they come before the Assembly again."

"Tarik is absent now," Narisa pointed out.

"In his father's direct custody on legal

business," Kalina said sternly. "That does not violate Almaric's agreement with the Assembly. They have gone openly, and three of the guards have gone with them. It is a very different thing for you to slip out with Suria and secretly enter Tyre's house. Narisa, if you were found there, you would be killed at once, and Tyre would have an excuse he could use to justify killing the rest of us."

"Narisa has to go with me. Gaidar knows her. I doubt he would trust me," Suria said. "She can enter with me, dressed as a servant. I'll say she's an acquaintance of mine from another house who offered to help me carry packages home from the Market. That is where I am supposed to be. Leader Tyre is planning a feast tonight for some of his closest friends. I suspect from what I have overheard that Gaidar's death is going to be the entertainment, which is why we have to release him promptly. Narisa and I can enter by the servant's way, loaded down with the freshest fruits and vegetables. No one will look at our faces if we are carrying outlandish parcels. Kalina, could you find a servant's dress for Narisa, and then make up a small bundle of clothing we could take with us, something a serving man would wear, perhaps an old Demarian coat with a hood? Narisa can tell you how big Gaidar is."

"And shaving equipment and scissors," Narisa added. "Gaidar has a beard and long hair. He will be better disguised without them."

"I cannot take the risk without consulting

Almaric." Kalina remained opposed to the plan.

"How long will Tarik and his father be gone?" Narisa asked her.

"Until the evening," Kalina replied. "We are all to gather in this room before the evening meal. Halvo will be here by then, too."

"We can't afford to wait that long to help Gaidar," Narisa insisted.

"I am glad to hear Admiral Halvo is returning to the Capital," Suria said. "Officers of the Service will follow him, even in opposition to Leader Tyre, should there be a direct confrontation. You and Almaric are safer with Halvo here, Kalina."

"Gaidar should be in this room when Halvo arrives." Narisa was thoughtful, speaking slowly as she worked through the problem of releasing the Cetan. She believed Suria had just given her the argument that would convince Kalina to go along with their hasty plan. "It will save time if Gaidar is here and can provide detailed information to Halvo about Starthruster, much more than Tarik and I know. Suria is right, Kalina; we have to rescue Gaidar at once."

"We will come directly back here," Suria persisted. "Kalina, you can't let Gaidar be killed if Tarik has promised his safety. Narisa and I will be careful, and no one ever looks very closely at servants."

"Please," Narisa begged. "Kalina, please help us."

There was a silence that seemed inter-

minable to Narisa as Kalina studied the two
younger women.

"Very well," she said at last. "I may as well
help you, since I doubt I could stop you. Wait
here. I won't be long."

Kalina left the room, and Narisa and Suria
sat looking at each other rather uncertainly.

"Thank you for believing me," Suria said.
"Let me tell you how I think we should
proceed. Since you know Gaidar, you may
have some suggestions to add to my plan."
They were still talking when Kalina reappeared.

"Put this on." Kalina handed Narisa a plain
gray gown of rough material and a pair of
shapeless old boots. "There is a short jacket
with a scarf you can wind around your head.
This bundle has a man's shirt and trousers
and a hooded coat. Also a pair of old scissors.
I didn't dare take any shaving equipment. No
one uses it except for very old men. I didn't
want to ask the servants for it."

"I hadn't thought of that." Narisa recalled
the shaving equipment in her own bathing
room, but she was afraid to go and get it lest
she meet someone who might question her.
"We will just have to trim Gaidar's beard as
short as we can with the scissors and hope no
one notices the stubble after he pulls up the
hood."

"At least the weather has turned colder,"
Kalina said. "There will be a lot of people on
the streets with their heads covered against
the wind."

When Narisa had changed into the servant's dress, she and Suria followed Kalina along the back corridors. They met an occasional servant along the way, but since Kalina was mistress of the house, no questions were asked.

"I'm not taking you out through the kitchen and the servants' way," Kalina said, turning a corner. "There is an old entrance in the wall around the garden. It has been unused for so long it is almost forgotten. There are no guards near it, so it will be safe for you to leave through. When you return, come back to the secure room by these same corridors." She opened a door, and they found themselves at one side of the garden. A hidden path wound between the high outer wall and a tall hedge growing a few feet away from the wall. Kalina led them along it.

"The gardeners use this way," she said, "though they don't use the door anymore. Here is the security panel. Memorize the numbers, Narisa. You will need them on the other side to get back in. I'll see to it the door into the house is left unsealed." The door in the garden wall slid open at her touch.

"Be careful," she whispered as she shut it behind them. "Come back safely."

Narisa and Suria found themselves in a narrow ally between two large houses. Suria touched her arm, and Narisa went in the direction she indicated. They came out of the ally into the street behind Almaric's house and began walking in the direction where Suria said the Market was.

Narisa had never wandered about the Capital very much. Trainees for the Service were expected to remain in their own compound, and she had been too busy with her studies to join the forays some of the braver cadets occasionally made to drinking houses. She was surprised at how crowded the streets were, and at the diversity of people she saw.

"All the Races come here," Suria explained. "This is not only the Capital of the Jurisdiction, it is an important trading post. You can buy almost anything in the Capital."

It was difficult to make their way through the crowds into the Market, but Suria managed with an expertise that told Narisa she had been doing it for some time. Suria also knew the best shops and stalls. Both of them soon had their arms loaded with produce brought to the Capital from many planets.

"It's always like this when the Assembly is in session," Suria said. "All the Members want their native foods."

"Surely there is an easier way to stock up on fresh provisions," Narisa grumbled, trying to keep a branch of heavy purple fruits from falling off the pile she held. She did not like the fetid smell of those fruits at all, and wrinkled her nose. "Couldn't these be ordered by computer?"

"They could, but they wouldn't be as fresh after being packaged and shipped. Leader Tyre fancies himself as an Epicure. Nothing but the best and freshest for him. Besides, I never complain about this chore because it gives me a certain amount of freedom. I can come and go from the Leader's house almost whenever I want."

Narisa thought her arms would break from the weight of all the strange fruits and vegetables she was holding. Suria's arms were loaded, too, her collection topped by an enormous Jugarian crab whose legs, fortunately, were tied together, but whose red eyes kept rolling wildly. Finally, unable to carry one item more, they left the Market and started toward Leader Tyre's house.

It was more like a palace, Narisa thought when she first saw it. The facade of heavily carved red stone went on and on. They came to the end at last, turned a corner and walked halfway along the side of the building to the servants' entrance. There they were briefly stopped by a guard. Suria identified herself. When the guard began to ask her who her helpful friend was, Suria tilted the bundles in her arms while she looked up at him, letting the Jugarian crab begin to slide off the top.

"Ho, don't let that thing loose near me," the guard warned, stepping away from them. "Go on, take it to the kitchen where someone will know what to do with it. You, there, have you got anything as dangerous as the crab? What is that terrible smell?"

"I'm not sure," Narisa answered breathlessly. "Possibly these fruits, or the Demarian cheese. I only offered to help Suria, and she began giving me all these heavy packages to hold. I just want to put them down."

"Then follow Suria to the kitchen, right at

the end of that hallway."

A moment or two later they were in the cavernous kitchen, where they unloaded their parcels and all the loose produce. The Jugarian crab was taken off to a cooling room to await the evening meal. Suria spoke to one of the cooks, then picked up a tray laden with dishes and nodded to Narisa to follow her. Together they went through a pantry to a narrow corridor, hurrying along it until they reached a steep flight of steps going down to the lower level of the house. It was gloomy and poorly lit. Narisa stayed close to Suria, taking the bundle of clothes intended for Gaidar under one arm and holding on to the stone wall with her free hand. The stairs curved toward the bottom and then ended in a square gray stone room. There a guard lounged in a chair with his feet up on a table.

"Well, Mistress Suria." The guard was openly insolent. "What has our Leader's latest woman got for me today? Some new delight?" He leered at her.

"Be careful," Suria said sweetly, "or I'll report you to Leader Tyre at a moment when he cannot refuse me anything. Here is your meal." She plopped the tray on the table next to the guard's feet, then removed a covered bowl. "This is for the prisoner."

"Who is she?" The guard stared at Narisa.

"A friend of mine," Suria answered. "She wants to see what a Cetan looks like."

"You'd do better to stay with me, friend of Suria. I'm more entertaining than that surly fellow."

"Is he as ugly as they say Cetans are?" Narisa asked with every appearance of goulish interest.

"See for yourself." The guard waved them on and picked up a plate of stew from his tray. "Here, take the key if you want to go inside the cell. Just don't scream for me if he attacks you."

"This is poor security," Narisa whispered to Suria as they made their way to Gaidar's cell.

"They are overconfident and lazy like their Leader," Suria replied. "It's a good thing for us they are."

They found Gaidar in the fourth cell on the left, an airless hole lit only by a smoking oil lamp, and without the furniture, the running water or the sanitary facilities required for all Jurisdiction prisoners. The stench in the corridor outside the cell was sickening.

"The guards say all Cetans smell like this," Suria said, wrestling with the ancient lock and key.

"That's not true. Gaidar is fairly clean. Suria, I am appalled by the lax security. There is no sign at all of an observation system, either at the guard's post or here in this hall. Why isn't Gaidar being monitored the way prisoners usually are?"

"I told you, they are lazy."

"Either that, or they want him to escape."

"Why would they want that?" Suria had just succeeded in turning the key in the lock, but she made no move to open the door.

"Think, Suria, as I have learned to do,

thanks to Tarik. If Gaidar escapes, where can he go? On this world, where he is considered a deadly enemy, to whom can he flee? There is only one place. Almaric's house, where Tarik and I are lodged."

"You think I am tricking you, that I'm involved in the plot to destroy Almaric and his family? Narisa, I swear to you, I would do nothing to help Leader Tyre, not after the things he has made me do for him. He is the most disgusting creature. I risked my life to go to Almaric's house and warn you what Tyre is planning, and I'm risking it again to help with this escape. I admit I like taking risks and I enjoy danger, but I'm not completely mad. I can easily imagine what Tyre will do to me if I am discovered with you and Gaidar."

"I believe you, Suria. That doesn't mean Tyre isn't hoping Gaidar will try to escape, either on his own or with Tarik's help, and perhaps Almaric's."

"We can't just leave him here," Suria argued. "If Gaidar doesn't escape, Tyre certainly has some particularly nasty end planned for him tonight. I know what I heard Tyre say."

"Then let us release him," Narisa agreed, "but be on guard and warn him what may happen so he can be prepared."

The door swung open without the creaking of rusty hinges Narisa had half expected, then clicked shut behind them as Suria pulled on it. Gaidar crouched in one corner of the cell. His hair and beard were matted and dirty.

The single oil lamp gave enough light for
Narisa to see him, the bowl of rotting food on
the floor beside him, and the pile of excrement
in the opposite corner. She gagged and
thought she would be sick, until Gaidar
looked up at her and she saw hope leap into
his golden eyes.

"Narisa?" His voice was rough, as though
his throat hurt.

"Hush, don't say a word, just listen." She
went to her knees on the filthy floor in front of
him. "This is Suria, a friend of mine. We are
going to try to smuggle you out of here. The
first thing we have to do is cut your hair and
beard."

"Cut it? No, never."

"Gaidar, it's for a disguise. A Cetan is
supposed to be bearded." Narisa pulled open
the bundle she had been carrying and brought
out the scissors. "Hold still, now, I have to
work quickly."

"Don't cut it!" He whipped out his hand and
caught her wrist. "Leave me alone."

"Wouldn't you like to be free, Gaidar?"
Suria asked, her throaty voice pitched to its
most enthralling tones. She had picked up the
oil lamp from the floor and was holding it so
her beautiful face was illuminated. Narisa,
glancing over her shoulder, saw Suria smile
and heard Gaidar's indrawn breath. "Let
Narisa do what she wants with your hair. It
will grow back soon. With or without it, you
are still a man. A strong man, one who should
live to fight and love for many more space-
years. Leader Tyre plans to kill you this night.

Let us help you before it's too late."

As the hypnotic voice went on and on, Gaidar loosened his restraining hold on Narisa's wrist.

"Cut it, then," he said hoarsely. "Be quick about it, before I change my mind."

"Have they given you no water?" Suria inquired, still in that seductive tone of voice. "Is that why your voice is rough?"

"No water, no wine, only one bowl of salty food, deliberately given to make me thirsty. I see you've brought another bowl. I would not eat the first, I will not eat that one, either." Gaidar's golden eyes were fixed on Suria's face. He made no further objection when Narisa began to cut his hair just below his ears.

"There will be food and drink for you once you are safe," Suria continued.

"Safe?" Gaidar managed a coarse laugh. "Does that mean you are taking me off-planet?"

"Trust us, Gaidar," Narisa whispered. "There may be eavesdropping devices in here that we cannot see, so don't ask us questions. Please, just do as we tell you."

"I have no one else to trust. Not my beard, too?"

"All the men in the Capital are clean shaven," Narisa pointed out. "I wish I could shave you, but a close trim will have to do for now."

Once Narisa had finished with him, Gaidar stood up and stripped off his ragged and dirt-encrusted Cetan clothes.

"Keep your boots," Narisa advised, handing

him the servant's trousers Kalina had provided. "Lots of people wear cast-off Service boots. Yours won't be noticeable." She was not at all affected by the sight of a naked Cetan. His tall figure with bulky muscles at arms and shoulders did not stir her in the way that Tarik's sleeker body could. She gave him the shirt, which he began to pull over his head.

Suria was still holding the oil lamp, watching the gleam of its light on Gaidar's shoulders and torso. Gaidar pulled the shirt down, leaving it outside the trousers, and reached for the coat Narisa held out to him.

"Pull up the hood to hide your face," she cautioned. "And Gaidar, be warned, we may be stopped. I cannot promise this escape will succeed."

"I understand. Have you a weapon for me?"

"No."

"Then I'll use my hands." Gaidar flexed his large, strong fingers.

"There is a guard just down the hall," Narisa said.

"I'll start with him." He looked at Suria and grinned. "Put down that lamp, woman, and let us be on our way. I'll gladly strip and let you stare at me as long as you want once we are out of here."

"I wasn't staring." Suria set the lamp on the floor. "I'll go first and distract the guard."

"It won't be difficult for you." Gaidar chuckled, and Narisa looked at him in surprise.

Suria opened the cell door and went into the hall, the other two following her. The guard had finished eating and was standing beside the table, stretching, his back to them. When Suria would have approached him, Gaidar shouldered her out of the way and crept up behind the man. Narisa did not know exactly what Gaidar did. The guard's hands were still stretched well over his head when the Cetan wrapped his own arms around the man's middle and pressed hard. Within a second, without a sound, the guard hung limply from Gaidar's arms.

"Is he dead?" Suria asked softly as the guard was lowered to the floor.

"Unconscious, and will stay that way for several space-hours," Gaider replied. "He won't give any alarm. Where do we go now, Narisa?"

"To the steps. Follow Suria." They approached the bottom of the steep staircase that led to the kitchen. "Stoop a little, Gaidar. Try to look more like a servant and less like a proud warrior."

Gaidar went into a crouch and began walking with a limp, a performance that under other circumstances would have made Narisa laugh aloud. Just now she was too busy listening and looking for danger, and too frightened to be amused.

It was the curve at the bottom of the stairs that saved them. They could hear footsteps coming downward and a man's low voice, but because of the curve, they could neither see nor be seen.

Without a word, all three of them turned and fled back across the square room, past the unconscious guard, toward Gaidar's cell.

Chapter Eleven

As Narisa hurried down the corridor she heard a noise behind her. Glancing backward, she saw Gaidar had picked up the unconscious guard and was carrying him. He stopped at his own cell long enough to dump the guard into it and shut the door. He turned the key in the lock and pulled it out.

"Looking for him should delay them a little before they discover I've gone," he said in a hoarse whisper. "What's at the end of this hall?"

"I have no idea." Narisa began to run, Gaidar close behind her.

Suria had not paused with them. She was far down the hall, racing toward an unlighted area that offered at least a little shelter. The other two went in the same direction, trying to move as quietly as possible.

"This way." Suria beckoned from a cross

corridor. "They won't be able to see us around this corner."

They entered a smaller hall with no doors and a downward sloping floor. Dampness dripped from the walls, the air was dank and chill and the only light was the dim glow from the corridor they had just left. Gaidar reached around Narisa to capture Suria's shoulder in one large paw and stop her forward motion.

"Where are you taking us?" he rumbled.

"I honestly don't know. That stairway is supposed to be the only way out. We would have had a chance if we could have gotten up it and into the kitchen."

"So you are taking us deeper into this pit of a prison?"

"What else can we do, Gaidar? Perhaps if we wait here a while, whoever was coming down the stairs will go away and we can escape as planned."

"Or perhaps they'll come back for us here," Gaidar said.

There was a shout from the direction of the stairway, then another.

"It seems we have no choice." Gaidar looked grim. "That sounds like the beginning of a search to me. We have nowhere to go now except along this hall. It must end somewhere, and there should be a door, otherwise why have a hall here at all? You go first, Suria. I'll watch our rear. I'll be watching you, too."

"Don't you trust me?"

Gaidar's answer was a mirthless grin, barely discernable in the gloom.

"Start walking, woman. We'll argue about trust later."

The hall seemed to go on for miles, slanting ever lower and growing darker and damper and more vile-smelling as they went. By the time they reached the end, they would have been in complete darkness were it not for a small blue light glimmering above an ancient wooden door.

"It's locked," Suria reported, trying the handle.

"It's also half-rotted." Gaidar listened a moment. "I can still hear them up there. They will be coming down this hall any minute. Let me see if I can lift this door off its hinges." He reached for the rickety middle hinge at one side of the door.

"Let me help." Narisa knelt, working at the pin in the lowest hinge. It would not come out, but the hinge itself came free from the door frame, as did the hinge Gaidar was assaulting with greater strength, and slowly the lower half of the door began to bend out of the frame while the third, uppermost hinge held fast.

"Squeeze through, Suria," Narisa grunted, "and push from the other side."

As Suria wriggled her way around the edge of the door, the noises behind them grew louder. Narisa felt the door begin to move further from Suria's weight against it.

"Go through, Narisa," Gaidar ordered.

"No, you go first, Gaidar. You are bigger. It will take someone on each side of the door to hold it open enough for you. I can pull it shut again as I go through. Hurry!"

Gaidar did not argue. He forced his bulk into the narrow space between door and frame, puffing and groaning and trying to smother a few unpleasant words when the middle hinge scraped the back of his head. The last Narisa saw of him was his arm reaching around the door to drag her after him.

She ducked below the hinge and let him pull her through. The voices coming down the hall were much closer, and Narisa silently blessed the darkness that would make it difficult for their pursuers to notice the activity at the hall's end.

Gaidar was doing his best to reset the door from the inside so the tampering would be unnoticed. He needed no help, so Narisa looked around. Her heart sank. They were on a muddy stone ledge that ran around a huge underground cavern illuminated by lurid red lightglobes. In the center of the cavern was a lake. No, not a lake, more like a gigantic pit. It was thick, heavy and bubbling, and she knew by the smell what it was before Gaidar spoke.

"We are in the sewer," he said. "Our good luck. There will be a way out of here. All we have to do is find it."

"We won't have time." Suria was listening at the door. "They are going to open this to see if we are in here, and if the hinges don't hold, they will know where we are."

"Then there is only one place for us to go so they don't find us." Gaidar was at the edge of the stone ledge, reaching down toward the

ooze with one hand to search along the stone.
"There is space between sewage and the
ledge, enough for our heads so we can
breathe. We go under the edge and stay
hidden there until they leave. Our footprints
won't be noticed. This ledge is well trodden.
Garbage must be dumped here every day."

"Go into that slime?" Suria looked as if she
was going to be sick. "I can't do that."

"If you won't go," Gaidar told her, "I'll kill
you and throw you in so they won't find your
body. I don't plan to be retaken by Leader
Tyre's men. I'd rather die."

"I said that about the Cetans once." Narisa
sat down on the ledge next to Gaidar. She was
every bit as reluctant as Suria. Just the
thought of that disgusting mess in the pit
touching her skin made her feel ill, but she
would not let Gaidar see her revulsion. From
the sounds on the other side of the door she
knew there wasn't much time. "Will you hold
my hands, Gaidar, and let me down slowly so
my face doesn't go under?"

Gaidar was sitting on the edge, his feet
already in the muck. He took both Narisa's
wrists in his. She took a deep breath and slid
off the edge, feeling his great strength as he
lowered her into the oozing pit until she could
run her fingers along the slippery underside
of the ledge and he carefully let her go. A
moment later Suria, her disgust at the pit's
contents overcome by Gaidar's threat to kill
her, slipped slowly down beside Narisa.
Gaidar followed, hanging on to the ledge long

enough to smooth out any visible finger marks along its edge.

"Turn your face away from me," he whispered. "There will be a splash when I come down."

A moment later Narisa felt moistness wash up the back of her head into her hair. The pit was warm and thick, and solid objects kept bumping against her legs and feet. The smell was so bad she thought she would faint from it.

The three of them moved as far back beneath the ledge as they could possibly go, and waited while the door above them was unlocked. Footsteps squished on the muddy surface just above their heads. Lights flashed across the pit and onto the ledge that surrounded it.

"If they came in here, they are in the pit," said a voice, "and drowned in it. There is no sign of them."

"They must have taken the other corridor," came a second voice. "Let's hope the group searching it finds them. I don't want to tell Leader Tyre his prisoner is gone."

"He's more likely to be upset about his latest woman being gone. Imagine sharing your wench with a Cetan. That is a serious indignity. I wonder what he'll do to her when he finds her?"

One of the men above them made a nasty noise and spat into the lake and they both laughed. The footsteps moved away. The door slammed shut.

"Don't move yet," Gaidar cautioned almost soundlessly. "There's an old Cetan trick."

For a long time there was no sound but the bubbling of the pit. Then the door opened again.

"Anything?" It was the first voice they had heard.

"Not a sound. No movement." That was the second man, and Narisa realized he had been standing just above them all the time. "I thought that trick might draw them out, if they believed we had both gone. If they were here, they are dead. We may as well go see what the other search party has found. Remind me to order those hinges fixed."

The door closed again, and again Gaidar made them wait for what seemed to Narisa an eternity. At last he paddled out from under the stone ledge and looked around.

"They've gone," he whispered, "but be quiet. They might have left a guard outside the door. That's a Cetan trick—to pretend you've gone and then come back again, but Cetans do it twice. These men are lazy."

"Perhaps it's the smell that drove them away," Suria suggested sourly.

Gaidar did not answer. He was heaving himself up onto the ledge. Once there he pulled the two women out.

"Look at me." Suria held out her slime-covered hands, then tried to wring out her clothing. "I'll never get clean again. I can't walk in these clothes."

"Would you rather be dead?" Gaidar asked rudely.

"She has a point, Gaidar," Narisa interrupted. "Our clothes are so weighted down
with dirt from the pit that it will be hard to
move quickly. And they're dripping, so if you
plan to walk along this ledge to the opposite
side of the cave, we will leave a clear trail for
anyone to follow."

"What do you suggest? A bath and clean
clothes?"

"I know what I'm going to do." Suria unfastened the top of her garment and let it
drop, then pulled down her trousers. She
kicked both into the pit. She was still very
dirty, but in her underclothes she could move
more easily.

Narisa followed suit, tossing jacket, scarf,
and dress into the lake, but like Suria, retaining her boots and undergarments. Gaidar
looked at them, his golden eyes lingering a
little longer over Suria's luscious curves than
Narisa's slimmer figure.

"How are you going to walk through the
Capital unnoticed once we get out of here?"
he asked.

"I'll worry about that when we do get out,"
Suria told him pertly. "I suggest we hurry. All
exits from Leader Tyre's house must have
been covered by now, and it probably won't be
too much longer before someone thinks of the
sewer outlets."

Gaidar nodded approvingly and pulled off
the servant's garments Kalina had sent for
him, retaining only his boots and a loincloth
that barely covered him.

Even coated with grime, his tall figure with

the massive shoulders was impressive. Narisa
noticed Suria looking at him. Well, why not?
Poor Suria had had only Leader Tyre to look
at for a long time. Gaidar was a good deal
more manly and attractive, and the way he
looked at Suria suggested something more
than mere admiration. Narisa shook her head
in amazement at her own thoughts. A few
space-weeks ago she would never have
dreamed of approving the pairing of a woman
of the Jurisdiction with a Cetan.

Narisa left them to follow her and led the
way along the ledge, heading toward the far
side of the pit. They had to walk carefully
because at intervals along the ledge there
were gaps in the stone, inlets where more
sewage entered the pit.

"I think this cave serves more than one
building," Gaidar said, "so we may be outside
the Leader's house already. It may be that his
men are prevented by law from following this
system beyond his own house. Let us hope
so."

Just opposite the door where they had
entered the cave was another door, this one of
smooth, heavy metal, which spanned the
outlet channel from the pit.

"There is no way we can open that," Suria
said.

"No, but we can swim under it." Narisa
pointed to the space between the surface of
the sewage and the bottom of the door. "I
wonder what we will find on the other side?"

Suria shrank back. "I don't want to go into
that vile mess again."

"Then stay here and rot." Gaidar was into the pit and edging his way along the side of the outlet channel. "It isn't very deep. I can stand here. It doesn't matter what is on the other side, Narisa. I'm going on."

Narisa did not want to re-enter that lake of sewage any more than Suria did, but she could see no other choice. Sooner or later Leader Tyre's guards would come back to the cave in search of the fugitives they had not found. She would rather drown in sewage than be caught by them. She got into the outlet channel beside Gaidar. Suria joined them.

"It's nicer here than in Leader Tyre's bed," she explained. "Don't look at me so scornfully, Gaidar. I never went to him willingly, but if I hadn't pleased him, I would not have been able to get into your cell and free you. Nor would I have known that he planned to have you killed tonight, and Tarik and his family, too."

Gaidar did not respond, though Narisa thought the hard expression on his face had softened a little. He went to the metal door and felt along its edge with one hand, then ducked under it. A moment later his arm appeared beneath the door, motioning for them to follow him. Narisa and Suria went under the door together.

They came out into a brightly lit, white-walled room. The sewage from the cave flowed through the channel where the three of them stood, then downward into a round pool in the center of the room where gleaming silvery metal machinery poured chemicals into it. A series of open metal walkways crossed the room at several levels. There was a man standing on one of the walkways, apparently checking the processing sequence. His back was to them; they were as yet unseen.

Gaidar pointed to a metal ladder set into the wall of the channel beside them. The ladder extended upward out of the channel and along the chamber wall to meet each of the walkways high above them.

"The only door I can see," Gaidar said in a low voice, "is that one, just past the man on the walkway. There is no way out at our level. We have to climb up there."

"We can't cross on that level without being seen," Narisa objected. "The man will see us and give an alarm."

"We could do it," Suria whispered, "if we climb all the way to the top of the ladder and cross on the walkway above him. Then we could drop down on top of him."

"Or fall into the vat of chemicals and sewage below. Still," Gaidar said, considering, "it's a good idea. We should go up the ladder one at a time. You first, Narisa."

She began to climb, finding it a slippery business with her hands and feet wet from the pit. She went up slowly and carefully, not daring to look toward the man on the walkway, just setting one hand and one foot at a time on the ladder, up and up and up until she began to think the ladder would never end and she must be spotted soon.

At the top she pulled herself onto the open

walkway and crawled behind the railing, trying to make herself smaller. She moved along the metal grid that was the floor of the walkway to let Suria crouch beside her. Gaidar came last, and at his nod, Narisa began to run, still crouching, toward the center of the processing room. It was there that the walkway they were on crossed the lower one. At that spot they would have to drop to the lower walk, overcome the man still standing on it and then get to the door they could see at the far end of that second walkway.

Narisa stopped thinking about whether they could do it or not. She cleared her mind of fear and worry and concentrated on the steps she would need to take to get the job done. It was Service training that had taught her to function this way, and she sensed that Suria, directly behind her, was doing the same thing. They came to the middle of the walkway.

"Suria, you find the exit from the plant," Gaidar whispered. "Narisa, keep the way clear for her."

He disappeared over the side of the walkway. Narisa went to the other side of the walkway and dropped over the edge, holding on tightly to the metal grid on which she had been standing, her legs dangling into empty air. She heard a shout, and glancing downward saw Gaidar wrestling with the man who had been standing below them. She let herself fall to the lower level, landing hard on another metal grid floor. She had bruised her knee, and it hurt badly, but she had to get out of Suria's way so she could jump, too. She pulled herself upright, hanging on to the railing. Suria hit the floor of the walkway beside her and rolled nearly to the edge.

Someone had heard the noise. Another man was coming toward them from the doorway they had to use. Narisa forgot her sore knee.

"I'll stop him," she told Suria. "You get past us and find that exit."

She stood up before the oncoming man, her arms spread wide. He stopped for an instant, shocked at the sight of a filthy, nearly naked woman standing on a walkway high up in the processing room. During that brief hesitation Suria brushed past him and ran for the door at the far end of the walkway.

"Wait!" The man turned, uncertain whether to go after Suria or confront Narisa.

Narisa solved the problem for him. She gave him a hard push that bent him backward over the railing, and she kept on pushing. The man let out a cry and tumbled from the walkway, his fingers grabbing at the grid floor as Narisa herself had done a few minutes before.

"Help me!" he cried, his eyes wide with fear. Below him the processing vat bubbled softly.

"Help yourself," Narisa told him. "Work your way along the grid a few feet and drop down to the walkway at the next level. You can save your own life if you want."

"Stamp on his fingers," Gaidar advised, breathing hard behind her. He had left his own opponent unconscious on the walkway and he bore a few scrapes and bruises.

"I won't kill him," Narisa said. "He hasn't hurt us. It's not his fault we are here."

"If that's what you want, I won't disagree, but let's not stand here arguing." Gaidar gave her a none-too-gentle shove in the direction of the door, and Narisa began to run toward it. They came off the walkway into a small white room just in time to see Suria punch a short, heavy-set woman in the jaw, knocking her unconscious.

"You fight like a Cetan," Gaidar complimented her.

"I had to do it,—she had a weapon and was going to call for help." Suria rubbed at her sore knuckles. "I found some coats in the next room. We can at least cover ourselves with them."

The coats must have belonged to the three workers they had met. Suria took the short one, which was much bigger around the body than she was. Gaidar tried to squeeze his bulk into the largest one and split it down the back. Narisa's wrists stuck well out of the sleeves of her coat.

"We look like the beggars from the outskirts who come into the city each day to find food or work," Suria said. "And we smell terrible. No one will look at us for more than a glance. It's a perfect disguise."

"Have you discovered how to get out of here?" Gaidar asked.

"I have. I checked the computer. The only personnel here were the three workers we met. I have cut off the communicator and rearranged the program for the doors so once we go out and seal one, they will all stay closed until tomorrow morning."

"Good." Gaidar beamed at her, then glanced at the woman on the floor. "I'm glad you are not my enemy, Suria."

After their desperate flight, they expected to be stopped on their way out of the sewage processing plant. Instead they simply walked through the main gate and made their way along the back streets of the Capital.

It was growing dark, and a chill wind blew dust and loose refuse into the air. Narisa, her undergarments still damp, drew the coat more closely across her chest and shivered. No one bothered them. They looked too poor for anyone to rob them, and they stayed well away from the main streets, which were brightly lit. Once or twice they thought they were lost, but Suria's knowledge of the Capital was extensive, and she had a good sense of direction and soon found their way again. They came without incident to Almaric's house and walked along the wall to find the garden entrance.

"Did you notice? There are a lot of extra Service guards around the main entrance," Narisa said. "Perhaps Admiral Halvo has arrived early."

Gaidar stopped walking.

"Admiral Halvo is here?"

"He is coming to meet with Tarik and his father," Suria explained.

"And you are taking me to the same house? Halvo is the Cetans' greatest enemy. He'll cut me into little pieces on sight. I'll have no time to tell him about Starthruster. I won't go in there."

"Gaidar, if we wanted you dead," Suria snapped, "we could have left you in Leader Tyre's prison cell and saved ourselves a lot of trouble, not to mention a most unpleasant bath."

"Ah, well." Gaidar heaved a great sigh. "I really haven't any other place to go, have I? I'll have to depend on Tarik to protect me."

"You don't need protection," Suria told him. "The people around you do. Narisa, why are you waiting? Have you forgotten the seal numbers?"

"I remember them." Narisa had found the garden entrance. "I was just wondering again about those extra guards."

She pushed the correct numbers into the security panel, and the garden door slid silently open. After they had slipped inside, it closed behind them just as silently. The garden lay in evening shadow, deserted and almost completely dark. They made their way along the path between wall and shrubbery until they found the door to the house. Kalina had said she would leave it unsealed, so Narisa pushed on it. It slid back, opening upon an unlighted corridor.

Narisa's nerves were tense as she sensed something was not right within the house. She jumped at a movement in the darkness. As her eyes adjusted, she recognized Kalina, who stood with her fingers raised to her lips to caution them to silence. Kalina stepped outside onto the path and drew Narisa and Suria close to her so she could speak softly.

"We will be safe here for a little while. We can't be seen from the house, and there is no one in the garden. I made certain of that. I have been so worried about you. There has been some kind of secret alarm given. Leader Tyre has ordered extra guards posted here, both inside and out. I thought it must have been because you had succeeded in releasing the Cetan. The new guards demanded to see you, Narisa. I told them you were overtired from your recent ordeal and needed a long sleep. I had to invoke all the privilege accorded to the household of an Assembly Member to keep them away from the second floor, but they are everywhere on the first floor, so we must be careful. Are you the Cetan?" Gaidar had pushed between Narisa and Suria to hear what Kalina was saying.

"I am," he said, "and no enemy to the family of Tarik Gibal."

"I am Tarik's mother."

"I honor you, mistress." Gaidar made an odd, formal bow. Narisa saw through the gathering darkness the expression of surprise on Kalina's face, for Gaidar had just used the form of address Demarians reserved for highly ranked dignitaries.

"Tarik has told me your mother was a Demarian," Kalina responded politely. "I see she taught her son good manners. You are welcome in my house, Gaidar, for her sake and your own."

Now it was Gaidar's turn to be surprised.

"My mother often told me she was dead to her own people once she had been raped by her Cetan master, and I, as the child of that rape, would never be accepted by Demarians."

"I am afraid she spoke the truth, Gaidar. But there are women, on Demaria and elsewhere, who consider that custom too harsh and who understand a helpless captive cannot prevent what is done to her. In any case I would welcome you because you have dealt fairly with my son and have risked your life to warn us of the coming Cetan attack." Kalina paused, sniffing delicately. "Forgive me the rude question, my friends, but is that smell coming from you? I cannot avoid noticing it."

"We had to hide in the sewage pit," Narisa explained, and almost laughed out loud at Kalina's horrified reaction. "We will tell all of you the entire story later. Have Tarik and the others returned yet?"

"No, and I think you three had better be cleaned before they do. Come with me."

Kalina did not take them to the secure room on the second floor where Narisa had expected they would go, but to Narisa's chambers. They went by way of the back corridors they had used before. They met no one at all.

"I'm keeping the servants on the first level, and I have sent Chatta to work in the kitchen," Kalina told them, ushering all three directly from the back corridor into Narisa's bedroom. "I have managed to deactivate the eavesdropping system here and in the corridor immediately outside your door, so the guards could not detect your absence. I gave them my word you were asleep, and they accepted it. If my lie is discovered, no one will ever believe me again."

Narisa knew how precious the reliability of a Demarian's word was and how much it must have cost Kalina to lie while swearing she was speaking the truth. She would have embraced Kalina in thanks for that lie, but she had become uncomfortably conscious of her unkempt state.

"Is the bathing room safe, too?" she asked, and at Kalina's nod led her companions into that room. "We will need some clothing for Gaidar and Suria."

"I'll find something, and some food, too, and try to think of a way to dispose of those disreputable garments you are wearing without creating suspicion. Narisa, your Beltan clothes are on your bed."

Kalina left them. Without a word or any sense of false modesty all three of them immediately removed every piece of their clothing. At Suria's suggestion they bundled all of it into a large towel and tied it up so Kalina could take it away more easily.

"First," Narisa said, producing the razor, "Gaidar must be shaved. Make no objection, Gaidar. If it becomes necessary for you to try to escape again, a clean face and a Service haircut are your best disguise."

Gaidar did not argue. It took only a few minutes. Afterward they made him sit on the lowest step in the bathing tub while Suria trimmed his hair into a neat style compatible with Service regulations. Lastly, they filled the tub with hot water and cleanser. The women scrubbed Gaidar thoroughly and then washed themselves. There was no time for playfulness while they did this, for they did not know when the door to Narisa's chambers might burst open and Service guards appear in spite of Kalina's attempts to keep them away. They worked quickly and efficiently. The tub was drained and filled again for a second scrub before they were satisfied that the last traces of sewage had been removed. By then they all looked like ordinary people instead of fugitives, and they began to relax a little.

"It seems strange," Suria said as they soaked in the fresh suds, "to treat a Cetan as a friend after all the centuries of fighting them. It's difficult to disregard all I've been taught and accept that idea."

"On the Cetan planets," Gaidar told her, "warriors owe allegiance only to their war-lords, who quarrel and make peace as they please. It is common for a Cetan to fight side by side today with yesterday's enemies, against yesterday's friends. So it is not a strange thing to me."

"We stopped that kind of treacherous warfare centuries ago when the Jurisdiction came into being." Suria's voice was full of pride.

"Which left you only Cetans to fight." Gaidar grinned wickedly. "And now you have to fight your own leaders to regain your freedom from them. That is what you will have to do in the end, you know, because you have been lazy and let the Assembly grow too powerful and do whatever it wanted. It would never have happened to Cetans."

"Hush, don't talk like that here," Suria admonished. "We can't be completely certain Kalina was able to stop all the eavesdropping equipment."

"I will remain silent," Gaidar promised, "if you will use that green sponge on my back again."

Narisa was only partially listening to this conversation. Her mind was on Tarik. She hoped he was safe. She thought he had to be, since Kalina had expressed no concern for either husband or son. However, Narisa was not so distracted she did not notice that Suria seemed to enjoy washing Gaidar's broad shoulders and arms, with special attention given to the scrapes and cuts he had sustained, before beginning a second sudsing of his hair. Nor did she miss the appreciative gleam in the Cetan's eyes whenever he looked at Suria. She watched in some amusement how he stepped quickly out of the tub when Suria had finished with him and hastily wrapped a thick towel around himself. It was not hard to imagine what he might have done had he been alone with the voluptuous redhead.

Narisa herself was distressed by the many bruises on Suria's lushly curved body. They could not have come from the day's adventures. They were old bruises, and they were in the wrong places. No one today had grabbed Suria's breasts, or pummelled her inner thighs and upper arms.

"Leader Tyre did it." Suria answered Narisa's timid question calmly. "It excites him to hurt women."

"Oh, Suria, I am so sorry."

"It won't happen again," Suria said. "My actions today have freed me of him. Tyre and I are enemies now. When he learns what I have done, he will want me dead, not least of all because I might speak of the terrible things he does in private."

"Cetans do that sort of thing to their women." Gaidar turned to face them with his towel firmly fastened about his middle. "My mother complained of it. She said women prefer their men to be gentle and not hurt them. But when I tried to be gentle with a Cetan woman, she called me unmanly."

"It depends upon the woman," Suria said, looking into his golden eyes. "Perhaps you should ask first."

"Perhaps I will," Gaidar answered softly, and Narisa felt as though she was intruding upon some private ceremony.

To her relief, the mood was broken by Kalina's return. She had brought a tray of food and a Service uniform for Gaidar to wear.

"It was my son's," she told him. "It's the only thing I have that could possibly fit over those shoulders of yours. You are much the same size."

"Not Tarik, he's not this big." Gaidar held up the uniform jacket. "Have you another son, Mistress Kalina?"

"Halvo, my older boy. It's the first uniform he wore after he became a Service officer."

"Admiral Halvo is your son? These foolish women didn't tell me that." Gaidar swallowed hard and tried to give the jacket back to Kalina. "Don't you think he will object to my wearing his clothes?"

"He'd object much more strenuously to your appearance in a towel," she said tartly. "Put it on, young man. And comb your hair."

"Only my mother ever spoke to me in that tone and lived," Gaidar growled. A sudden grin split his face, making him look younger and less hard. "That was the first bath I've had since she died."

"Don't try to shock me, Gaidar. It can't be done. I raised two sons of my own, remember. Narisa, Suria, into the other room and dress there. Allow the poor man some privacy."

They ate while they dried themselves and dressed. Kalina had brought them heated bowls of vegetable stew, bread, cheese and wine.

"It's a feast," Gaidar called from the bathing room, and Kalina smiled at his delighted voice.

Narisa was happy to put her Beltan clothes on again. Comfortable in the simple garment and refreshed by her bath, she brushed her clean golden brown hair until it swung in a short, straight veil about her face. The only thing she lacked now was Tarik's presence. She hoped he would return soon. She had so much to tell him.

There was a dark green dress for Suria, in a

similar style to Narisa's. It was too long, but she bloused it over a tightly cinched belt. In the months since her disgrace her red hair had grown longer than Service regulations stipulated, and now it curled almost to her shoulders. The green of her dress made her eyes appear larger and greener. Her skin was creamy pale, and the bruises were hidden by her clothing.

Narisa felt a stab of jealousy looking at her, then brushed it away. Suria's recent life had been nothing to envy, and she could not want Tarik and still look at Gaidar the way she did. There was nothing to fear from Suria.

When Gaidar walked out of the bathing room, Narisa would not have known him had it not been for his eyes. In the dark blue uniform jacket and trousers, he might have been a young Service officer. His yellow hair was neatly combed, his wide, square-jawed face was handsome. Even the once-broken nose did not mar his appearance, but only made him look more interesting. Yet the golden eyes were pure Cetan, fierce and searching. Narisa reminded herself he was not a member of the civilized Races. He might be almost a friend, and trustworthy, but he was still *different.* She wished Suria would remember that. From the expression on her face, Narisa did not think she would.

"You look quite presentable," Kalina told Gaidar. "My husband and Tarik have returned. Come with me, please."

Chapter Twelve

Had she not been trying so hard to keep from flinging herself into Tarik's arms in front of his parents, Narisa might have laughed at the expression on his face when he looked from her to Suria and back again. She saw plainly the uneasiness he must have felt at finding his former lover and his present love entering the secure room together with no sign of strain between them.

Almaric seemed unaware of the tension in Tarik's carefully composed face and stance, for he had focused at once on Gaidar.

"By what means," he demanded, "has a junior Service officer gained admission to my wife's most private chamber?"

"He is not a Service officer at all." Kalina had finished sealing the innermost of the two doors and now approached her irate husband. "I gave him those clothes."

"By all the stars," Tarik swore, "it's Gaidar.

I know those eyes. What are you doing out of prison, and with a clean face? And you, too, Suria, why are you here? Mother, is this one of your famous arrangements? Have you prevailed on Leader Tyre to let Gaidar go free?"

"I will not have my wife begging that insolent, incompetent blot on the Assembly's honor for anything," Almaric sputtered.

"Don't blame Kalina. It was my idea," Suria announced.

"And I helped her," Narisa added. "We realized we had to rescue Gaidar before Tyre had him killed. You and Tarik weren't here, so we did it ourselves."

"*You did what?*" Almaric looked like a volcano about to erupt. "You left here after I gave my word to the Assembly that you would not, and then you removed a prisoner from Jurisdiction custody? Is that what you did?"

"What does it matter?" Gaidar put in. "If Tyre is incompetent as well as perverted, you ought to simply kill him and be done with it."

"Silence, you Cetan animal!" Almaric roared. "How dare you come here? Lieutenant Narisa deserves to be court-martialed for what she has done. As for you, Suria, a rehabilitation planet will be your fate if I have anything to say about it."

"You can't do that," Narisa cried. "Suria has suffered enough already from the Assembly's stupid laws and from Tyre himself. I won't let you do anything more to her."

"Watch your words, young woman!"

"Don't talk to Narisa that way." There was

fire in Tarik's eyes, and he actually took a single threatening step toward his father.

"Stop it, all of you." Kalina did not need to raise her voice to restore order. "Almaric, I ask you to control your anger until you have heard what these young people have to say. I not only gave Narisa my permission to leave our house, I helped her. My dear, you know I would do nothing to jeopardize our position. Only let us explain and you will understand we could not wait for your return."

"You brought a Cetan here!" Almaric's voice was a little milder when he spoke to his wife. "A Cetan who is a prisoner of the Jurisdiction."

"A man to whom Narisa and I have given our word that he would be safe if he would help us," Tarik told his father angrily. "Narisa would not act foolishly. She is always as scrupulous in her obedience to the law as is my mother. Therefore, there must be a good reason for Gaidar's presence here."

Narisa flashed him a grateful look. She was deeply touched by his faith in her. She took advantage of a moment of silence.

"Gaidar was no longer a Jurisdiction prisoner," she said, looking from Tarik to his father to observe their reactions. "He had been moved to one of Tyre's private cells below his own house. It was a terrible place, with neither water nor ventilation."

"Such an action would be against the law," Almaric admitted grudgingly. "Tyre would not dare to do such a thing."

"But he did," Suria declared, "and planned

to kill Gaidar tonight, and you, too, Almaric, and all your family with you."

Almaric looked as if he would loose another barrage of angry words at Suria. His mouth was opened to begin, but he stopped, hearing a sound at the door.

Kalina rushed to the entrance, checked the security panel, cleared it and waited while the two sealed doors opened.

Narisa had never met the man who entered, but she would have known him without Kalina's glad greeting. Where Tarik, the younger son, closely resembled his father, Halvo, the elder by seven space-years, was very like his mother. He was tall and heavily built, with the beginning of a paunch. His uniform jacket gleamed with gold and silver braid, and on the left arm it bore the sixteen-pointed star of a full admiral. Only one Service insignia conferred more authority, the twenty-four-pointed star of Admiral of the Fleet. Halvo's face was a masculine version of Kalina's strong features. His dark hair was lightly silvered at the temples, his gray eyes cool and intelligent. They swept the group in the secure room while he patiently endured his mother's emotional embrace.

"Welcome home, my son." Almaric's embrace was somewhat more restrained than Kalina's had been, but was no less loving or proud.

When Tarik's turn came, both men hesitated as though something kept them apart, until Tarik grabbed his brother's shoulders and the two came briefly together.

Narisa, watching them, remembered then
that Tarik and Halvo had quarreled at their
last meeting and had parted in anger.

"It has been too long, Tarik," Halvo said
with slightly forced politeness. "Too many
space-years. I am pleased to see you again."

"My navigator," Tarik said, presenting
Narisa.

"You are out of uniform, lieutenant," Halvo
charged cooly.

"It's my doing, Halvo," Kalina interjected
before Narisa could defend herself. "Since
she is not on active duty just now, I thought
private clothes would be a nice change for
her."

Halvo was plainly not pacified by this
explanation, but his attention was diverted by
the sight of Gaidar.

"I see by your eyes that you are a Cetan. In
my old uniform. You needn't explain, I can
guess who gave it to you. Will you reform the
entire Service, Mother? Shall we add recruits
from outside the civilized Races?"

"I have no desire to join your Service,"
Gaidar stated firmly.

"Now, Halvo," his mother said, "I want you
to sit down and listen to the story Tarik and
Narisa have to tell. It is why I called you home
so urgently. They will tell you the truth, and
so will Gaidar. Then Narisa and Suria will tell
us how they freed Gaidar from Leader Tyre's
house."

Narisa barely repressed a giggle as the
great Admiral Halvo overcame his
amazement at this speech, sank obediently

into the chair his mother had indicated, and prepared to listen.

He seemed to believe them as she and Tarik spoke. He asked shrewd, penetrating questions of Gaidar concerning Starthruster and the Cetans' plan of attack, and expressed outrage at the way Gaidar had been removed from the official Assembly prison to Tyre's cell. And he sat hiding a smile behind clasped hands when Tarik, having finally learned what Narisa and Suria had been doing during his absence, began to scold Narisa.

"How could you risk your life like that?" Tarik began. "Narisa, you could have been killed. If you had been caught, if you had fallen into Tyre's clutches, I can't bear to think what might have been done to you, or what a terrible weapon he would have had against us."

"I didn't think of that," Narisa admitted. "Gaidar's life was in danger, we had given him our word for his safety, and you weren't here, so I did what had to be done. I don't regret it."

"Where were you," Halvo asked Tarik, "that you could not go to Gaidar's aid yourself?"

"Do you mean you approve of Narisa's and Suria's mad expedition?" Almaric looked stunned.

"I regret to say I do, Father. Something must be done about Tyre's corrupt rule, and soon. Most of the other Service officers feel the same way."

"What, the renowned Admiral Halvo fomenting treason with his cronies?" Tarik laughed. "I'm glad to hear it. It's about time you understood the situation, brother. If you mean what you've just said, perhaps we can forget our old quarrel and be friends again."

"You haven't answered me, Tarik." Halvo's tone was frosty, but he let the implication of treason pass. "Where were you today?"

"Father and I and my old teacher, Jon Tanon, went aboard the Cetan ship. It's docked at spaceport and under Service guard."

"I saw it when I brought my own ship into port. What were you doing there?"

"I was afraid Tyre might order the ship destroyed, and I wanted to gather as much information from it as possible before he could do that. Father agreed to go with me because as a Member of the Assembly he's empowered to go wherever he wants and thus could get us onto the ship. Jon and I made diagrams of Starthruster, and also sketched the design of the ship and all its armaments. It's a cargo vessel, a pirate ship really, not one of their newer warships, but still the information should be useful to us." Tarik pulled a sheaf of papers out of his uniform jacket. "Recordings might have been detected when we came through security after leaving spaceport, so we used these. Ancient methods sometimes work better than our own."

"Still studying history, are you?" Halvo took the papers. "For once I'm glad of it."

"Tarik, where is Jon now?" Kalina asked.

"He stayed aboard to examine the ship further. He was fascinated by it."

"I hope he'll have no trouble leaving spaceport."

"I gave him a pass," Almaric assured her. "There will be no difficulty. Now, Halvo, what are we to do? As I see the situation, we have three problems. The most immediate is the threat of a concerted Cetan attack, which could come at any time. The second problem is how to deal with whatever punishment is meted out to Tarik and his lieutenant navigator for their defiance of the Assembly. Whatever is done to them will affect the status of our family and thus our ability to act as a rational balance against Leader Tyre and his friends. Our third problem is what to do with this Cetan warrior who, I am forced to admit, deserves some consideration for warning us of his fellows' plans."

"I agree with your assessment of the first problem, but not the others," Halvo said. "It seems to me our second problem is how to remove Leader Tyre and his accomplices from power. That would solve the other problems by nullifying the case against Tarik and Narisa, and by making Gaidar a hero when we defeat the Cetans."

"Halvo is right." Tarik stood behind his brother's chair, with one hand on Halvo's shoulder. "We are finally in agreement. The Assembly must be reformed, and the sooner the better for the Jurisdiction and all the Races."

"Aren't you forgetting," Narisa asked, a distinct edge to her voice, "that while you sit here and calmly set forth problems and reasonable solutions, Leader Tyre plans to

kill all of us tonight? He should be delighted,
Admiral Halvo, to catch you in his net as well
as us. You must have seen all the guards at
the door when you came into the house. Tyre
will have been told by now that you are here.
What with trying to locate his missing
prisoner, wondering where Suria has gone,
worrying if you and your father are plotting
against him, and deciding how to dispose of
this family without destroying his own
position, Tyre may be ready for the worst
kind of violence, and upon a great many
people, not just us. There is no time to lose.
Tyre has to be stopped now, and every world
belonging to the Jurisdiction should be
warned about the Cetans."

Halvo regarded her with cool gray eyes.
Once Narisa would have been frightened by
his scrutiny and worried about her own
position in the Service. No longer. The Service
was not the primary force in her life anymore.
She was free. She might die at Cetan hands or
at Tyre's. If she survived those perils, she
might still be severely punished by the
Assembly for daring to defy its Members. But
nothing anyone did to her could ever again
imprison her mind and heart, or stop her
from loving Tarik. Or stop Tarik from loving
her. He was looking at her now, tenderness
flooding his purple-blue eyes. She could
almost feel his arms around her, though he
was on the opposite side of the room.

"We will stop Tyre," Halvo promised, rising
from his chair, "and the Cetans, too. Mother, I
need to use your transmitting equipment. The

first thing to do is notify the Service, and as Narisa has rightly suggested, warn all the worlds, especially those sectors lying between Belta and the Capital. After that, I'll demand an emergency meeting of the Assembly."

"Won't Admiral of the Fleet Momuri have to be told?" Tarik asked. "He is Tyre's man."

"Momuri is desperately sick, has been for some time, and will likely retire soon. He won't be a factor in this. Most of the other senior officers feel as I do about Leader Tyre. With them behind me, I believe we can oust him and select a new Leader."

"I would nominate Almaric of Demaria," Tarik said.

"So would I, but it's against the law to nominate family members," Halvo responded. With a sudden smile he added, "We will just have to get someone else to do it for us. Lieutenant Narisa, I'm returning you to active duty. Go put on your uniform."

"What about me?" Suria asked. "I want to help, too. I have my own reasons for wanting Tyre removed from office."

"You are no longer an officer of the Service." Halvo regarded her shrewdly. "However, I will assign you to private security duty. Almaric will provide you with a regulation weapon. You are to remain in this room with my father, my mother and Gaidar and guard them all with your life until I return or send Narisa to get you."

"Arm me, too," Gaidar said, and after a tense moment of deliberation with himself, Halvo nodded.

Narisa felt a curious distaste for donning the uniform she had once worn so proudly. It had come to symbolize for her all that was wrong with the Jurisdiction, all the unnecessary restrictions the Assembly placed on the lives of ordinary people. It took a considerable amount of self-discipline for her to fasten the jacket clasps and pull on her boots when she would rather have worn her Beltan costume. In a strange gesture of defiance, she folded the robe and sandals together and took them back to the secure room where she gave them to Kalina to hold for her.

"Till I return," she said, and Kalina nodded understandingly. "Where are Tarik and Halvo?" she then asked.

"One of Halvo's men called from the first level," Kalina replied. "I could tell by their voices that something has happened, but I don't know what it is. Halvo said for us to stay here until they are ready to leave for the Assembly chambers."

"Did he mention me? No? Then I had better go see what it is they are doing. I am on duty now." Narisa left the secure room and made her way along the oppressive red corridors and wide stone stairways to the main hall at the first level. There she met several guards, none of them men she had seen before. These were from the new contingent Leader Tyre had sent to guard Almaric's house.

"I am Admiral Halvo's aide," Narisa said boldly. "Where is he?"

"Through that door." There was respect in

the guard's response. Even Tyre's men felt a certain deference toward the hero of so many battles against enemies of the Jurisdiction. Narisa turned smartly and marched to the door the guard had indicated. She knocked, then entered without waiting for a reply from within.

"I said, no one comes in here!" Halvo whirled upon her, furious at any disobedience.

"I understood you required my presence at once, sir," Narisa said for the benefit of the guard outside the door. Once she had closed and sealed the door, she advanced a step or two into the room. "I apologize for interrupting, Admiral Halvo. Your parents are very concerned. I thought I could find out what is happening down here and reassure them. Why, it's Jon Tanon." She moved toward the figure lying on a couch.

"It was Jon." Tarik was supporting his elderly former teacher by the shoulders, trying to make him drink from a cup filled with distilled spirits. "There's not much of him left."

"He looks all right to me." Narisa knelt next to Tarik. "I thought he had stayed aboard the Cetan ship."

"Apparently he left it." Halvo's angry voice sounded just behind her. "Somewhere between the ship and my father's door, Tyre's men took him."

"Took him?" Narisa saw the perfectly blank face resting at Tarik's shoulder, and the staring, unfocused eyes. "What's wrong with him? Can't he speak?"

"With great effort," Tarik said, "he can
make sounds, but no sense. His mind has been
drained, Narisa."

"Drained? Do you mean like the Jugarians
used to do space-centuries ago, with their
dreadful machines? Mind-draining was outlawed, and all the machines were destroyed
when Jugaria joined the Jurisdiction."

"I would not be at all surprised," Halvo told
her, "to learn that Leader Tyre has such a
machine, or possibly the equivalent drugs,
which are also illegal. Whatever method was
used, Jon has all the symptoms of a man
whose mind has been emptied. How much did
he know, Tarik?"

"Everything." Tarik gave up his efforts to
encourage Jon to drink. He laid the elderly
man down on the couch, then stood to face his
brother. "More than we told you, Halvo. The
ancient settlers we mentioned were telepaths,
exiled by the Act of Banishment."

"Telepaths." Halvo stared at Tarik with the
strangest expression, as though he did not
want to believe what he was hearing. "You
star-blasted, romantic idiot, always pushing
the laws you don't like to their outermost
limits. Telepaths! And what else? I'm sure
there is more to this story." Halvo's gray eyes
were fixed on his brother's face.

"There were intelligent, semi-telepathic
birds on the planet. I thought Jon should
know about them for his historical research."

Halvo swore a long and colorful Demarian
oath that made Narisa want to cover her ears.

"You can understand," Tarik said calmly, "why we did not inform the Assembly of this."

"I do understand." Halvo was trying hard to control his temper. "I only wish you had not told Jon, because now Leader Tyre knows. With a weapon like that to use against us, our attempt to depose him will be infinitely more difficult. You two, along with your two friends upstairs, must have broken almost every Jurisdiction law there is."

"Except the one about not keeping a Demarian leopard-wolf for a pet," Narisa said, hoping to break his furious mood. Halvo glared at her, then gave a sharp laugh.

"You may have broken that law, too, lieutenant, when you tamed my brother. I do admire a person who can see humor in a bleak situation." He sobered as he looked at the man on the couch. "Tyre had Jon's mind drained and then had him delivered to my father's door. That action was intended as a direct threat. We won't have long to wait before he makes his next move against us." He spun around at a loud banging on the door. With a jerk of his head he indicated that Narisa should answer it. When she did, an irritated Almaric strode into the room.

"Kalina insisted on leaving the secure room to check on her communications equipment. I warned her not to, that you had told us to stay where we were, but she wouldn't listen to me. She said she would be safe with Gaidar for protection. Well, she was, I have to admit that. She intercepted an urgent message for you, Halvo. I would not let her come below

stairs—I said I would bring you the message
myself. Sometimes I wonder who is the head
of my family, that woman or me." The torrent
of aggrieved words stopped as Almaric saw
Jon. "What's wrong with him?"

"Mind-drained, at Tyre's command," Halvo
said shortly.

"That's illegal," Almaric protested. "All
these broken laws. It's disgraceful. I won't
tolerate it, I tell you, and neither will the
other Members. Something must be done."

"What's the message, Father?"

"Oh, yes, the message. Kalina says the
Cetan attack has begun, concentrated in the
Beltan sector. Belta is completely destroyed."

Narisa closed her eyes. The Belta she had
once known had been gone for long space-
years, yet still it hurt to hear those words.
Tarik put his arm around her, and she leaned
against him, drawing strength from his sensitive understanding.

"Projected Cetan movement?" Halvo
snapped.

"A direct line for the Capital," Almaric
replied. "The first ships vanished from the
Beltan Sector two space-hours ago."

"Lieutenant Narsia," Halvo barked. Narisa
made herself stop thinking about ruined Belta
and respond to his clipped phrases. "You are
the navigator here. Projected arrival time?"

"At Starthruster speeds," she replied after
a quick mental calculation, "they can arrive
here by late tomorrow, assuming they don't
stop to destroy any more planets along the
way."

"Why should they?" Tarik asked. "It would only be a waste of time. Once they have taken the Capital, the Jurisdiction will fall apart. After that happens, they can plunder and kill on any planet they choose."

"That, I suppose, is a lesson learned from your ancient history studies," Halvo observed dryly. "We will have to postpone our plans to deal immediately with the Assembly. This is more important, and for the moment we need the Assembly whole and functioning. Lieutenant Narisa, my private guards have been quartered in the eating room. I assume you know where that is. Send half of them here to me. Take the other half to the secure room to escort the people there to this room. Remember the eavesdropping devices and do not expect an explanation. Stay well away from the other guards—those posted in the main hall and at the entrance."

"I'll go, too," Tarik offered.

"I need you here." Halvo's tone brooked no objections. "We are going to clear out those unwanted guards."

It took only a few minutes for Narisa to obey Halvo's orders. His guards surrounded Kalina, Suria and Gaidar with a protective cordon as Narisa led them down the stairway to the main hall. There they found the second half of Halvo's men holding back Leader Tyre's guards and forcing them toward the door.

"Outside the entrance, all of you except my own men," Halvo ordered. A moment later the door slammed on the last of Leader Tyre's people. At the same instant Narisa heard the throbbing sound of a transporter coming from the garden.

"Halvo, what is going on?" Kalina demanded.

"We are leaving before Leader Tyre can capture the entire family," Halvo responded. "Once you and Father are safe, I'll deal with the Cetans."

"I can't leave with no notice. What about the servants? What will Tyre do to them, out of spite, if he can't reach us?"

"Call the servants on the communicator. Tell them the men I leave behind will take them to a safe place until this danger is over. They are to assemble here in the hall at once. Do it quickly, Mother. You are going to be on that transporter in less than three space-minutes, if I have to carry you myself." To Narisa, Halvo added, "We have a little more time than that, I think. Tyre will have the message about the Cetans from his eavesdropping devices in this house, and I don't doubt he's too busy looking for a safe place to hide to bother himself with us just now." He left her to give more orders to his men.

Kalina had gone to the nearest communicator to call the servants' quarters, and Narisa went looking for Tarik. She found him bending over Jon, while two of Halvo's men looked on.

"Surely we aren't going to leave him here, Tarik?"

"These men are going to carry him aboard the transporter. I am trying to get some response from him, but there is nothing, no sign of recognition." He motioned to the men, who came forward and gently lifted the frail body, carrying it out of the room. "It's my fault he's in that condition, Narisa. If only I hadn't told him so much."

"If you hadn't confided in him, Leader Tyre still would have had him captured and his mind drained, just on the chance you had said something to him. It isn't your fault, Tarik, it's Tyre's." She put her arms around him, holding him close, trying to comfort him. "I love you."

He crushed her to him in a fierce embrace, and his lips met hers in a hasty, desperate kiss.

"No matter what happens," he whispered into her ear, "I love you, Narisa, and I always will. I'm only sorry you have been put into so much danger." His mouth was on hers again before she could tell him there was no danger she would not dare if he were by her side. She forgot what she was going to say in the glory of his kiss. They both knew it might be their last. It was as though a lifetime of love and joy and passion and laughter was being exchanged, savored, and then slowly relinquished in that kiss, and when it was over, there were tears in both their eyes.

"Tarik, Narisa, we're leaving." That was Halvo, tactfully remaining outside the door. Tarik's hand lingered on Narisa's cheek, touching her with one last lover's caress before they joined him.

* * *

Narisa was astonished at Halvo's arrangements for his family's safety. He had judged Gaidar's character during their short meeting and never doubted his assessment. He sent Almaric and Kalina, along with the still-catatonic Jon, aboard the Cetan ship docked at spaceport. He put Gaidar in command, with Suria and two of his personal guards for crew.

"I know something of Cetan customs about hospitality and gratitude," he said to Gaidar. "I am making you responsible for my parents' lives. I have given you an experienced first officer and an engineer in my men, and an excellent navigator in Suria. Replace that missing part and use Starthruster to remove your ship to a safer sector of the galaxy. Return in three space-days. If the Capital has been destroyed and you are unable to contact me or Tarik, take my parents away from here, find a peaceful planet, if such a thing exists, and let them settle there."

"I know just the place," Gaidar said. "It's in the Empty Sector, where nothing is where it should be, but if I need to, I will find it somehow. You may depend on me, Halvo. I won't fail your trust."

Tarik and Narisa were ordered aboard Halvo's ship, Narisa as assistant navigator, Tarik as personal aide to Halvo. Both were instructed to make available to Halvo's crew all the information they had about Starthruster. Then the admiral's flagship left spaceport to take up a defensive position among the other ships Halvo had called together to prevent the Cetans from reaching the Capital.

The waiting was a tension-filled time. Narisa tried hard to keep busy with work. She talked with the Chief Navigator, explaining how the Cetan ships might function using Starthruster and suggesting alternative maneuvers for the Service ships. All messages between the ships were being sent in code, so she spent a good amount of time with the cryptographer, helping to draft the information about Starthruster into precise terms. When she had a few moments free, she thought about Tarik. He was with Halvo all the time, and his feelings for her, like her own for him, had to be put aside until the Cetans were defeated. And the Cetans had to be defeated. She could not think of any other possibility. In the meantime, during occasional flashes of fear or loneliness, she ached to feel Tarik's arms around her, longed for the two of them to be safe on their lost planet.

The Cetans arrived on schedule. So quickly were they able to travel that they were invisible until they slowed to less than Starthruster speeds and suddenly appeared in battle formation before the sparse grouping of Service ships. They took full advantage of their situation, blasting at the nearest Service ships before they were fully visible. Those first shots went awry, allowing Service ships to fire and disable a few of the smaller Cetan vessels before the largest Cetan ships recovered enough to retrain their armament and begin anew.

At Halvo's command defensive shields had been raised, but still his ship rocked as every Cetan salvo found its target. Narisa had been called to the bridge. She found it difficult to get there. She was buffeted about in the passageway until she stumbled onto the bridge, bruised and with her previously injured knee hurting again.

Halvo was not in the command chair, but stalking about the bridge, reading computer screens over his officers' shoulders and periodically calling orders into the speakers. He motioned for Narisa to join Tarik, who was monitoring the battle on the wide-field screen. As she stepped toward him, another blast shook the ship. She staggered backward until Tarik, holding on to the safety railing, reached out and grabbed her wrist to steady her. A second later he pulled her to his side with one arm around her waist.

"I don't want you hurt," he murmured before releasing her. He glanced quickly around the bridge. All the officers were busy at their own posts. No one had noticed the furtive embrace.

"How is the battle going?" Narisa felt foolishly cheered by that brief evidence of his concern and affection. While standing beside him, she was not afraid of anything at all.

"Not well." His face was grim. "I had no idea the Cetans could mass so many ships, and they are determined to take the Capital."

"Have they any chance of succeeding?" It was horrible to contemplate such an outcome. "Tarik, we can't let them win."

"Our greatest advantage," he said, pointing to the monitor screen, "is our discipline under fire. In spite of the Assembly's nearly total lack of military knowledge and the conflicting demands it makes upon the Service, Halvo and the other admirals have put together a remarkable fleet. We have been joined by Civilian Guard ships from several nearby planets, which have put themselves under Service orders. We are still badly outnumbered, but the Cetans have a habit of doing what they want instead of following their commanders' orders. Watch there." Pointing to the screen, he showed her a series of markers that symbolized a group of Cetans about to attack a line of Jurisdiction ships. Three of the Cetans left their formation to intercept two smaller vessels some distance away.

"Those are poorly armed merchant ships," Tarik said, shaking his head in disgust. "They've come to offer us what support they can. Their cargoes are too tempting for Cetan greed to withstand, so those three Cetan captains have left the attack to loot and pillage a weaker enemy. Watch the result." The markers that represented the line of attacking Cetan ships, weakened in strength by the departure of their comrades, now disappeared from the screen one by one, and the Service ships moved on to destroy the three Cetans who were attacking the merchants. "They seem unable to learn the first principles of warfare, or to obey anything but their own greedy impulses when plunder is available. That is our one hope, Narisa."

"Tarik, look." Narisa pointed to a line of ships just assembling on the screen. "That seems to be a disciplined group. They are coming directly toward us."

Tarik called out a report to Halvo, his words echoing those of another alert officer. Narisa heard Halvo shout an order to take evasive action. She felt the ship shudder a little, and she saw on the screen the conjoined wave of force that blasted from the Cetan ships and moved at incredible speed, coming closer.

"Hang on," Tarik yelled, grabbing the railing.

Narisa reached for the same rail. Her hands were almost on it when the force wave hit them. She thought their ship was turning up-side down. It shouldn't have made any difference—the ship had its own gravity so the decks were always down—but something was wrong. She was falling *upward*, then sideways. She saw Tarik's horrified face, watched him reach for her and miss as she fell past him.

The ship's gravity had corrected itself. Narisa's head hit the floor hard. A thousand stars exploded inside her brain, all the stars of a lost planet, red and gold and silver, scattering across a black sky. There was pain, worse pain than she had ever known before, and there was blackness closing in on her. It was her only hope of release from the growing agony. Wanting anything that would stop the pain, she welcomed the blackness, gave herself up to it and knew nothing more.

Chapter Thirteen

"Lieutenant Narisa, open your eyes."

She tried hard to obey the sharply voiced command. After a while she succeeded, but the bright lights above her made her headache worse, so she had to close her eyes again.

"I know you are fully conscious, Lieutenant Narisa. Do as I tell you."

A hand took her chin, holding her head steady, making her face directly into the light. Narisa winced.

"That's better. Keep your eyes wide open. I'm going to shine a light into them. Ah, good. No, don't close them. Just a little longer."

The piercing light went away. After blinking several times to remove the afterimages, Narisa found she could tolerate the overhead lamps, and she was able to see without brilliant pain lancing her throbbing head. The nausea began to recede. She looked around, being careful not to move her head too quickly.

She was in sick bay. She recognized it at once. They were all alike on any Service ship—white, with too-bright lighting and a falsely reassuring, overly friendly doctor. Except this one wasn't friendly. She was sour faced, with an unpleasant, gratingly nasal voice. The hostility emanating from a person who ought to have been comforting and encouraging to all her patients was disturbing and profoundly disorienting to Narisa in her present condition.

"You should be shackled to that bed," the doctor said. "If I weren't certain you would faint if you tried to get up, I would have you tied down. But then, I don't want to call any particular attention to you just yet. Not until I have talked to Admiral Halvo. The reward for locating you is rightfully mine alone."

"Why?" Narisa raised her head a little. The pounding began again so forcefully that she wanted to return to the painless blackness. Forming the simplest sentence took great concentration. She lay back on the pillow and tried once more, needing to have the answer. "Why shackle me?"

"You know perfectly well why, you shameless creature. You are a disgrace to the Service. We will be at the Capital soon, and I can't wait to get you out of my ward. It will be a pleasure to turn you over to the guards at spaceport."

"I fell, I hit my head. That's all I can remember. Why should you turn me over to the guards for that?"

"You will remember a great deal more than a fall by the time Leader Tyre has finished with you. Your sentence will be passed in accordance with Jurisdiction law, and I hope I am there to see it carried out."

Narisa could not understand what the woman was talking about. She wanted to ask where Tarik was and if he was safe, but some inner caution warned her not to mention his name until her own situation was clearer. Confused though she was, she had sense enough to try to make this gloating ship's doctor tell her what was wrong before she revealed anything more.

"I really can't remember what I've done," she said meekly. "Please tell me." With that simple request she unleashed a verbal flood.

"They called me to the bridge, where I found you unconscious." The doctor recounted the story with malicious relish. "I immediately diagnosed a concussion. In spite of what you laymen believe about the wonders of modern medicine, the only cure for a simple concussion is time and rest. But Admiral Halvo and Commander Tarik would not let you be carried to your cabin and put to bed and left alone while my staff and I paid more attention to seriously injured crew members. Oh, no, they couldn't accept my diagnosis, as though I haven't had thirty space-years' experience with shipboard medicine and surgery. They said I had made the diagnosis too quickly to be certain you weren't badly hurt, and that I hadn't used a diagnostic rod. Nothing would satisfy them except a complete examination.

"What a waste of time when I'm so busy, I thought. There is nothing wrong with this woman except a bump on the head. I was right, too. That is all that's wrong with you, as I promptly confirmed once I had you here in sick bay. Still, knowing how fussy Admiral Halvo can be about details, I checked with Central Service Information to see if you had any record of previous medical problems that might complicate your recovery. And there it was—a command overriding all other data in your file. Leader Tyre has issued a personal arrest warrant for you, Lieutenant Narisa."

"For me?" she repeated weakly. To gain a little more time and information, she added, "I don't understand. Why would he do that?"

"Did you think your treasonous activities wouldn't be discovered? Leader Tyre has ways of learning what he needs to know. You are accused of breaking your parole to a Member of the Assembly in order to effect the escape of a violent Cetan criminal. Since the Cetans have attacked the Capitol, that means you were helping an official enemy. There is a large reward offered to whoever turns you in. A very large reward indeed." The doctor was clearly looking forward to collecting the promised bounty. Her next questions caught Narisa by surprise. "Do Admiral Halvo and his brother know what you have done? Have they been protecting you? Is that why Halvo was so concerned about you?"

"No." Narisa responded as firmly as she

could, hoping the doctor had gleaned no other information from her search of Narisa's records. Her thoughts were more ordered now as the mist of pain-induced confusion began to dissipate. She realized that whatever happened to her, it was imperative that she reveal to the doctor no connection between herself and Tarik or Halvo. They must remain free to carry out their plan to remove Tyre and reform the Assembly. In that plan lay the only real hope of safety, not only for herself, but for Almaric's entire family, and Gaidar as well. The doctor had not mentioned Almaric by name. Perhaps she did not know he was involved. Narisa steeled herself to lie as convincingly as possible. "I don't know why Admiral Halvo or Commander Tarik would worry about me, except they seem to be good officers who are concerned about the people serving under them. I saw that during the battle. But I only met them yesterday. I think it was yesterday. The day before the battle."

"Not yesterday," the doctor told her impatiently. "That would be two space-days ago. You have been unconscious for a while. A good thing for both their careers if what you say is true." She paused a moment, as if considering something, then added, "It would be nice if I could tell the spaceport guards where to find the Cetan, and the woman named Suria, too. With the reward Tyre is offering for each of them added to the one I'll get for you, I could retire. Come on, my girl, you will be forced to tell Leader Tyre when you are taken before him, so you may as well tell me

now. Where is Suria? More importantly,
where is the Cetan?"

"I don't know." Narisa had to divert the
woman from her relentless topic. "Please, tell
me, is the battle over? Are the Cetans
beaten?"

"Of course they are. Easy enough for Jurisdiction ships to defeat those barbarians. I
don't know what all the fuss was about." The
doctor stood over her patient with folded
arms and frowning face. Narisa was afraid
she would begin a more rigorous interrogation. In her weakened state she might not be
able to withstand badgering questions for
long. She did not know what drugs the doctor
might have available that would make her
talk whether she wanted to or not. She felt
completely alone and helpless.

"Could I have something hot to drink?" The
thought of a warm cup in her hands was comforting, and the doctor might be distracted for
a little while by the need to order rations for
her patient.

"Certainly not." The doctor looked as
though she had been asked to do something
illegal. "There will be nothing to eat or drink
for you until you have been seen by Leader
Tyre. Some of his interrogation procedures
will be more effective on an empty stomach.
Don't worry, you will be fed afterward, before
you are taken to the Assembly to be condemned and punished. The Jurisdiction is
always humane. Now, I have no more time to
waste with you, *criminal*. I have injured to
take care of, and then I have to inform

Admiral Halvo of my discovery of a fugitive among his crew and make my official claim to the reward for apprehending you. I'll be back to question you more thoroughly later."

With this promise, which Narisa took for a threat, she was left alone, the curtains drawn about her bed to keep her separated from the other patients. She tried unsuccessfully to stop the flood of thoughts that filled her aching head.

She believed she knew what had caused Tyre to issue warrants for her and Suria. The guard Gaidar had so easily rendered unconscious would have supplied Tyre with a full description of the two women who had come to visit the Cetan and then helped him to escape. Kalina's claim that Narisa had been sleeping all of that day would have been reported to Tyre by the Service guards posted at Almaric's house, and Tyre would have recognized it for the ruse it was. Tyre was not a stupid man; he could not have ruled the Assembly for so long if he were. He would discern what Narisa had done, and he would use that information not only to punish her, but to bring down his enemy Almaric. When Almaric returned to the Capital, he and Kalina would be taken into custody along with the indisputable proof of their treason—their companions, Suria and Gaidar. Tyre's triumph would be complete, his position stronger than ever. There would be no hope of removing him from office, no hope of reforming the Assembly. Tarik and Halvo would probably be imprisoned, too. By trying to keep her and Tarik's word to Gaidar, Narisa had given Tyre the opportunity he wanted.

Her anguish was nearly unbearable. Added to it was her physical discomfort. Thirst was fast interfering with her ability to reason. She was desperate for something to drink. The doctor and her associates ignored Narisa's repeated calls.

"Be quiet," the doctor growled through the curtain at one point, refusing to open it and look at her. "We are too busy to bother with you. Be glad you aren't in the brig and stop complaining."

They all went away after a while, dimming the overhead lamps before they left, and the sick bay became quiet. Narisa began to debate with herself the risk of getting out of bed and searching for water on her own. She felt weak and dizzy each time she attempted to raise her head from the bed, and soon realized the doctor had been right about not needing to shackle her. If she could not sit up, she certainly would not be able to stand without help.

Temporarily defeated, she lay back and tried to forget about her aching head and the sick, empty feeling in her stomach and the thirst that was driving her mad. She had to make herself stop thinking about those things and concentrate instead on what she might do to get away before the doctor came back to question her once more. The woman had frightened her badly, and her fears were compounded by her helpless weakness. She listened intently for any sound that might indicate the doctor was returning. There was nothing.

A deep silence had fallen over the ship. The low, barely noticeable vibrations of its engines were stilled. Narisa knew what that meant. They had reached spaceport. Now was her chance to get up, find her uniform or steal someone else's to replace the skimpy hospital gown she was wearing, and get off the ship. If she could hide for a while, then the search for her, which she was certain the reward-hungry doctor would insist upon, would delay any action Tyre could take against Almaric. That delay might give Tarik and Halvo the time they needed to move against Tyre. She saw clearly that this might be the only chance they had. She had to go now, before the doctor came back for her. She had to sit up.

She could have wept from frustration when she tried and immediately fell back, overcome by returning dizziness. She tried again. She couldn't do it. Never before had her body refused to obey her commands. She gave a soft moan of utter despair.

"Narisa?" The whisper could just barely be heard through her accumulating fear and misery. The curtain around her bed moved slightly. It could not be the doctor again, or the guards coming for her, because the sick bay was too quiet and the movement was distinctly furtive. "Narisa?"

"Here." She had recognized the voice. It was Tarik. She did not see him slip inside the curtain; her vision was blurred by tears. As she silently cursed her own weakness, she felt his arms around her, strong and comforting. She raised her own arms, putting them about his neck. He draped the sheet around her near nakedness and lifted her from the bed. "Tarik, the doctor . . . Leader Tyre . . ." She swallowed a sob of fear.

"I know, I was with Halvo when she told him. Don't make any noise that would disturb the other patients," he murmured into her ear. "We'll talk later. Just hold on to me."

It was what she wanted most to do. She clung to him, the aching in her head vastly improved by resting on his shoulder while he carried her from the sick bay. Narisa saw a single attendant in the receiving room, a young woman who stood with her back turned toward them, resolutely inspecting the contents of an instrument cabinet. She did not turn around when Tarik carried Narisa past her.

No one questioned him as Tarik stalked through the ship. He was the admiral's brother, and a commander in his own right, and if he appeared to be doing something strange it must be on Halvo's orders or for his own important purposes. Not one of the Service personnel they met along the way revealed the slightest surprise at the sight of them, and no one tried to stop them.

"Strict discipline does have its uses after all. They are unwilling to challenge me," Tarik said softly as they entered an area unfamiliar to Narisa. "This is the cargo bay, m love. It's small on a warship, but it has one great advantage—its own hatch. In another space-minute or two, the single guard outside it will be called away so we can leave unnoticed."

"Halvo has arranged that?"

"Why, Narisa, what a scandalous thing to suggest," he teased. He carried her to the hatch and stood listening. She was feeling stronger now, and most of her fears had been effectively quelled by the knowledge that Halvo and Tarik were not going to allow her to be turned over to the spaceport guards. She felt absurdly happy. She rubbed her cheek against Tarik's shoulder and sighed.

"My hands are full," he murmured, smiling at her. "If you will push in the numbers as I speak them, we can unseal the hatch and leave the ship."

"Let me stand and free your hands, Tarik."

"I'm not sure you could, not without fainting, and in any case, I don't want to let you go." He hugged her more tightly against him. "Push those numbers, my love."

She did as he asked. She did not really want to leave his embrace. He carried her off the ship and onto a deserted area of the spaceport at the rear of his brother's flagship. A few containers for food and other supplies lay scattered about.

"How are we going to get off spaceport?" Narisa asked.

"We have a personal invitation to ride in Admiral Halvo's private transporter car. Can you sit up alone for a moment or two?" Tarik put her down carefully on top of a container. He then pulled a workman's shirt from under his uniform jacket and hurriedly put it on over the jacket. It effectively hid his Service insignia. "Narisa, I am going to have to wrap you tightly in this sheet and fold you into one of these large empty containers. It's only for a short time, just until we are on Halvo's transporter. We dare not let you be seen. If you are recognized you will be arrested at once. I know you can't feel very well after that terrible blow on your head, and I'm sorry to do this to you, but it's the only thing Halvo and I could think of in a hurry."

"I don't care. Do whatever you want, and do it quickly before someone comes."

He lifted her, bare feet first, into a food container, using the trailing sheet as padding to protect her as best he could. He had to push down on her shoulders to fit her into it and get the lid on properly. Narisa had one last glimpse of his anxious face before the lid was shut and she heard the latches click.

There was no way for fresh air to enter the container, and it smelled foul. Narisa decided it must have previously contained rancid Demarian cheese, and had not been cleaned since. She gritted her teeth, determined not to be sick, telling herself to endure it, that she would not be confined like this for very long.

She was aware of Tarik fastening on the box's carrying straps, which would fit over his shoulders. Her stomach lurched as the container was lifted into the air, or rather, onto Tarik's back. She did not need to see, she could feel every step he took across the cargo area, through a sliding door, then across another space until he stopped. A murmur of voices followed. She could not hear the words clearly through the insulation of the food container.

Her knees were rubbing against her nose. Her legs were so cramped they ached almost as much as her head. She was certain she was going to be sick. The voices stopped, and she could feel Tarik tramping up an incline. It had to be the gangplank to Halvo's transporter. She heard more voices, this time questioning tones, and a laughing answer from Tarik. Was he telling the questioners that Halvo had to have his own supply of Demarian cheeses while staying in the Capitol?

The container hit the deck with a hard thump that reverberated through her aching head. She heard Tarik laugh again. The container felt heavier. By all the stars, Tarik was *sitting* on it! She could sense his weight and hear his voice directly above her head. That was a good way to keep anyone from opening the container, but she could only hope it would hold his weight.

She had an overwhelming urge to giggle and recognized the first signs of hysteria. In another moment she would be laughing and crying at the same time, and her headache would become worse and she would undoubtedly be sick. Furthermore, if she did not soon straighten her left leg and rub the cramped muscles in it, her injured knee might never function again. It was so hot in the container,

and she was so terribly thirsty. And still Tarik
laughed and talked, sitting on the container
lid.

She could bear it no longer. She was going
to scream. He had to open the container and
let her out.

*Think about the planet and Dulan. Think
about the birds.*

She imagined herself standing on the
desert, under a blazing orange sun with the
birds wheeling and soaring above her. It was
so hot there, and her throat was so parched,
but the birds would lead her to water. Tarik
had said so.

Tarik. He was pulling her upright, holding
her against him with one arm. Narisa looked
down and saw his free hand refastening the
latches on the food container. She should be
inside it. Instead, she was being tossed over
Tarik's shoulder and carried through a
passageway. She saw her own hands dangling
near his knees just before she fainted.

She could not have been unconscious for
long. Halvo's transporter car was still docked
at spaceport with its engines off when she
revived to find both Tarik and Halvo bending
over her. They had laid her down across two
seats in the passenger compartment.

"That's better," Halvo said. "I like my
prisoners alert."

"Prisoner?" she responded weakly.

"It's only a technicality," Tarik assured her,
sliding an arm around her shoulder to help
her sit up. She leaned against him, watching

him glare at his brother, who stared back at him coldly.

"It is not a technicality, it is a fact," Halvo stated. He stood stiffly in the aisle, facing Narisa and Tarik. "You are my personal prisoner, Narisa. As an admiral of the Service, I have the authority to hold you in my custody until you are called before the Assembly to answer charges of aiding the escape of a condemned criminal."

"Gaidar isn't a criminal," Narisa protested, "and he was never officially condemned by the Assembly, as you very well know. I thought you understood why Suria and I did what we did." She felt all her earlier fears returning with a chilling rush.

"I do understand." Halvo's icy demeanor changed. He reached forward to take her hand in a gesture remarkably like the one frequently made by his warm-hearted mother. It was an unbending totally unexpected from such a cool and controlled man. "I ask you to understand my position, Narisa. You, too, Tarik. You are too willing to break the law. I am sworn to uphold it at all times."

"I will not allow Tyre to put Narisa on trial," Tarik declared.

"But that is exactly what I want, a completely legal trial," Halvo told them. "I want everything done according to Jurisdiction law."

"No," Tarik said angrily, "I won't hand Narisa over to Tyre, and I won't let you do it, either. You said you would help her."

"Will you be silent, brother, and listen to

me for a moment or two? Your feelngs for
this woman are clouding your judgment."
Halvo sat down on the arm of a passenger seat
across the aisle from Narisa and Tarik. "I
thought we had agreed to bury our differences long enough to overthrow Tyre and his
friends, while keeping the Assembly intact
and functioning with a new and honest
Leader. I believed we were united in wanting
reform rather than full-scale revolution."

"So you said." Tarik watched his brother
through narrowed eyes.

"When we discussed it, you did agree with
me, Tarik. I have a plan that I think will work.
Narisa, I will need your cooperation."

When Tarik would have protested again,
Narisa put a hand on his arm to restrain him.

"What do you want me to do, Halvo?"

"First, I want to take you back to my
father's house, where I will set my own men,
and his, to guard you. There you may rest in
safety until I can demand a full meeting of the
Assembly. Next, I will guarantee to the
Members that you will appear to answer the
charges against you. This ploy will keep you
out of Tyre's clutches while fulfilling the
requirements of Jurisdiction law in such
cases."

"And when I appear in the Red Room, what
will happen then?" Narisa shivered just
thinking about it, but she trusted Halvo
almost as much as she did Tarik.

"I will act as your advocate before the
Assembly, with Tarik as the principal witness
in your defense," Halvo told her. "You will

explain why you released Gaidar, going into great detail about the miserable physical conditions under which he was being held. Tarik will back up your explanation by repeating the story of your discovery of Starthruster and of Gaidar's help to the Jurisdiction. The events of the last few days have proven the truth of that story, so we can claim you were doing your duty to protect the Jurisdiction against its enemies. I believe the charges against you will be dropped."

"And then?" Narisa knew there must be more to Halvo's plan.

"Then," he said solemnly, "I will make a speech demanding Tyre's ouster for neglect of Jurisdiction welfare during a time of crisis."

"And you think the Assembly will agree with you?" Tarik scoffed. "Don't be naive, Halvo. Tyre will have himself well protected by his friends and by those who owe him favors. He will claim an honest mistake, and his cronies will back him. No one will blame him for refusing to believe a Cetan's improbable story about Starthruster. The Assembly will never vote to remove him for such a flimsy reason."

"Flimsy?" Narisa was deeply shaken by Tarik's certainty. She was also angry. "The Jurisdiction could have been destroyed, and that terrible man never lifted a hand to order a defense. If the Assembly votes to keep him as Leader, then they all deserve to be removed from office."

"Thank you for your confidence in me, Narisa." Halvo's smile was grim. "I wish

Tarik were as convinced as you are. I had hoped he and I might work together as brothers and friends, just this once."

"All right," Tarik capitulated suddenly. "I want that, too, Halvo. I don't want to quarrel with you anymore. I think we need to marshal greater force against Tyre than we have in this case, and I am not certain we can change the way the Assembly functions just by replacing Tyre with a better Leader, but I will help you." He put out his hand, and Halvo took it without a space-second of hesitation or reserve.

"What about your ship's doctor?" Narisa asked. "She was determined to turn me over to Tyre and collect the reward he has offered. If she gets to him now and tells him whose ship I was on, she could cause serious problems for all of us."

"I have ordered her confined to her own quarters aboard ship, incommunicado, for forty-eight space-hours while I decide what to do with her. I should be grateful to her," Halvo said, "for discovering that Tyre wanted you so badly. That knowledge will be helpful to us. But she, personally, is a sad spectacle.

"Greed is a terrible thing," Halvo continued, shaking his head. "It made my ship's doctor willing to break her sacred oath to protect her patients and to give each one the best possible care regardless of Race, religion or political situation. Her intent was unethical, to say the least. She can consider herself fortunate if I impose no more punishment than censure and an order to retire on reduced wages."

"She wanted to retire in splendor," Narisa said ruefully. "Speaking of medical care, do you suppose I could have some water? I wasn't allowed any in sick bay."

"For that alone, the woman deserves severe censure." Halvo himself brought her a cup of the distilled water used on the transporter for both humans and the engines. It was tepid and tasteless, but to Narisa it was more delicious than the finest wine. She asked for and drank a second cup. Then, feeling almost restored to health, she leaned back in her seat, resting her head against the padded cushion of the head-rest, while Tarik fastened the safety harness around her.

It was only a short while later that the transporter left spaceport with Halvo, Tarik and Narisa as the only passengers. They circled the Capital several times on their spiral flight down to land in the garden of Almaric's house. Narisa watched the viewing screens, seeing what the Cetan force waves had done.

"I didn't know the Cetans had gotten close enough to blast the city," she said. "What terrible damage. What senseless loss of life."

"I regret it deeply," Halvo replied. "We did not have time to assemble enough ships to protect the Capital as we wanted. We in the Service are grateful for your warning, though. Without it, the entire planet would be rubble."

"As it is," Tarik added thoughtfully, "the Assembly can be held derelict in its duty to protect Jurisdiction citizens. I see a bit of hope in that. It could make our plan easier to accomplish, Halvo. The Members just might choose to make Tyre the scapegoat rather than all of them resigning at once. Especially since six of the most important Cetan warlords have surrendered to you personally and are suing for a peace treaty."

"Surrendered?" Narisa gasped. "Cetans don't surrender."

"I gather they are demoralized by the failure of their battle strategy," Halvo said, "and thoroughly sick of their overlords. That is another factor on our side and against Tyre, who won't treat with Cetans under any circumstances. If we can raise a new and more honorable Leader, I think there is a real chance to make peace with the Cetans and gradually bring them into citizenship in the Jurisdiction."

"That sort of thing has been done before," Tarik told him. "The Jurisdiction did not spring into being with all its worlds joining at once. If you had been taught honest history in your youth, Halvo, you would know it was a gradual and complicated process, taking many space-centuries after the Great Agreement. There is ample precedent for adding new Races to our citizens. You should remind the Assembly of that when the time comes."

If anyone could talk the Assembly into accepting a treaty with the Cetans, it would be

Halvo, Narisa thought. He was clever and far-seeing, and his insistence on doing everything according to Jurisdiction laws was a great strength. If only he were not so coldly rational, if he had the kind of warmth that drew people to him, he would make a great leader. But then, perhaps a great leader had to be cold. Or perhaps, she thought, recalling how he had taken her hand, how he wanted Tarik to willingly join his plan, and how pleased he had looked when Tarik had called it *their* plan a few moments before, perhaps Halvo was not as cold as he appeared to be.

Almaric's house had sustained only minor damage, and the servants had already returned to make the necessary repairs before Almaric and Kalina arrived. To substantiate Halvo's upcoming claim to the Assembly that Narisa had been injured and would need bed rest, Tarik carried her from the transporter to her bedchamber, commenting frequently on her paleness and the concussion she had sustained. When he handed her over to Chatta, it was with strict orders to keep Narisa quiet and allow no visitors.

Narisa sank into her bed and let the little maidservant put cold cloths across her forehead.

"I should call a doctor," Chatta worried. "You need medication."

"The ship's doctor . . ." Narisa cringed inwardly at the thought of that unpleasant woman. "The doctor said rest and time were the best treatments. I'll be better tomorrow, Chatta, just wait and see. What I would like is a pitcher of something cool to drink. I feel as though I've been walking across a desert."

Chatta brought her fruit juices, and after Narisa had swallowed several cups, the maid-servant sat down in another part of the room to let her mistress rest while still being im-mediately available should Narisa need her.

Her thirst quenched at last, Narisa tried to make her mind a blank and not think about what would happen when Halvo's request was granted and the Assembly convened. She fell asleep quickly and woke and slept again until the day was gone. She ate the light evening meal Chatta brought to her and then instantly fell back into a deep, dreamless sleep.

Tarik woke her a little after midnight. She heard the bedchamber door click closed, and by the light that Chatta had left glowing beside her bed, she saw him coming toward her.

Forgetting she was supposed to be recover-ing from an injury, she got out of bed to run to him. A brief spell of dizziness made her stumble, then her head cleared. Tarik had seen her waver. He caught her into his arms, holding her against his chest and kissing her hard. She sank into that kiss, reveling in the touch and smell and taste of him. He was her safe haven from all the dangers threatening them, as she knew she was his. She felt his hands in her hair, felt the smooth texture of his uniform jacket beneath her hands and bare arms. The crisp scent of him filled her nostrils, stirring her senses with memories of his lovemaking and a deep longing for more of it.

When he let her go at last, the first thing she saw was Chatta's sleep-creased face rising from the couch where she had been resting in case Narisa should need her.

"Commander Tarik, what has happened?" she cried. "Have Member Almaric and my Mistress Kalina returned?"

"Not yet. I'm not worried, Chatta. I trust Gaidar and Suria to keep them safe, and I think it's just as well they stay away from the Capital for another day or two. I came to speak privately with Lieutenant Narisa. I will attend to her needs tonight. You may go now." Tarik sealed the door the moment Chatta had left.

"Was that wise?" Narisa asked anxiously. "She will probably tell all the other servants you are spending the night with me."

"How can I be wise when I want you so badly?" He laughed and kissed her cheek. He caught her hand, urging her toward the bed. She wanted to go with him, but she held back, pulling at his hand.

"Tarik, be careful. Remember the eavesdropping system." There was no way of knowing if it had been turned on again after Kalina had disconnected it days before.

"Thanks to a communications officer among Halvo's men, all the eavesdropping devices to this house have been turned off. We

can speak freely in any room. I can tell you
how much I love you without being overheard.''

"How wonderful."

"Wonderful that I love you, or that I can say
it with no one else listening?'' he teased,
sitting down on the side of her bed. Still
holding her hand, he pulled gently and she sat
beside him.

"Both." She leaned her head on his
shoulder, sighing happily as he put an arm
around her. "Won't Leader Tyre grow sus-
picious if he can't hear what we are saying?
Won't he take action against us?''

"He wouldn't dare, not after Halvo's
request for a full meeting of the Assembly has
been approved. We go before them at midday
tomorrow."

"So quickly?" She sat up straight,
frightened in spite of her trust in Halvo. Tarik
drew her back into his arms.

"Halvo wants to make his case to the
Members before our father returns," he said.
"That way no one can accuse him of using
Almaric's influence to make the changes he
wants."

"Halvo thinks of everything, doesn't he?"

"Not quite everything." He grinned down at
her, looking like a small boy keeping a secret
from the grown-ups. "I have a plan of my own,
to take effect after we have finished with
Tyre. It's an idea I think Halvo will agree to,
and that will please the Assembly, also."

"What plan?" She tried to pull away so she
could look directly into his face, but he held

her fast by his side. When she tried again, he fell back across the bed, laughing and taking her with him. "Tell me what you are going to do, Tarik."

"I thought that was obvious." He laughed again, one hand planted firmly on her breast. Then he turned serious. "I need to talk to Halvo first, and then to our father when he returns. Will you be patient, my love, wait a few days and trust me?"

"I trust you with my life," she whispered, "and my future." She turned her face to his, reaching for his mouth.

It was a tender kiss, deep and loving. When it ended, Tarik rolled over, pinning her beneath him, and began to make love to her, his mouth and hands pushing away her thin gown to set her body aflame with desire.

If their confrontation with the Assembly did not go well, by this time tomorrow they and Halvo and his men could all be incarcerated in the tightest security prison the Jurisdiction maintained, convicted of high treason for trying to depose Leader Tyre. She and Tarik might be separated forever.

But until morning they had each other. With her last rational thought before she gave herself up to the storm of their mutual passion, Narisa resolved to rejoice in Tarik's love and return it in good measure with no regrets. Whatever her fate, she would always love Tarik, to death and beyond. The words he was murmuring told her he felt the same way. And more. He told her how proud he was of her, of her courage in rescuing Gaidar, her resolute bravery during the recent battle, her navigational skills, all the things that made her the strong, self-reliant woman she was.

"You are my true mate," he said as they came together. "I want to live with you for all my life. I want you to bear my child. I love you, Narisa . . . love you . . . love you. . . ."

She held him in the pearly rose light of dawn, while he slept deeply and she sent silent prayers to every ancient god whose name she could remember, pleading that they might be allowed to remain together, and knowing deep in her heart the danger of their mission and how unlikely it was that her prayers would be answered.

Chapter Fourteen

They were ushered into the Red Room through the door at the lowest level, the same way Tarik and Narisa had gone once before with Gaidar. They entered the square meeting room at precisely the hour of mid morning, with two of Halvo's personal guards. They were all he was allowed to take with him of the dozen who had accompanied them to the Assembly chambers. Halvo had accepted with quiet dignity the insulting manner of the ushers when they stopped the other ten.

"An admiral deserves a better escort," insisted one of his people.

"Let it be," Halvo responded. "Remain here in the anteroom in case I need you. Now, let us get on with this." He stood before the door to the Red Room, waiting until it was opened for him, then strode boldly forward, the others following.

All of them wore full dress uniform. Halvo's
dark blue jacket glistened with gold and silver
braid on collar and cuffs, and his wide belt
was heavily trimmed with silver. Both sides
of his chest were covered with medals, with
Service ribbons in every possible color, and
with an almost unbelievable number of
honorary decorations from the planets of the
Jurisdiction and beyond. His dark blue cape
had been tossed back over each shoulder to
show its shimmering red lining, and to make
the sixteen-pointed admiral's star on his left
arm easily visible to the Members. His ornate
silver helmet rested in the crook of his left
arm. He was calm, composed, almost regal in
his bearing. Narisa had no doubt he would
impress the Members favorably, recalling to
them his almost legendary exploits in the
Service of the Jurisdiction, thus inclining
them to listen willingly to what he had to say
to them.

She and Tarik walked close to Halvo, where
he had ordered them to be regardless of
Service protocol. Tarik was one pace behind
and slightly to his brother's right, Narisa a
similar distance to his left. Their uniforms
were less resplendent than his, trimmed with
red and silver braid. Their belts were simply
ornamented, their plain silver helmets,
carried in the left arm like Halvo's, were
decorated only with their stars of rank. Both
wore the formal cape thrown back only over
the left shoulder so that the insignia on the
left uniform sleeve could be seen.

Tarik had several medals and ribbons

fastened to his left chest. Narisa had only her Top-of-the-Class Navigator's silver bar and the new medal Halvo had conferred on her that morning, the small five-pointed gold star given to those injured in battle. She had protested that her concussion had been accidental and had hardly been serious enough for commendation, but Halvo had overridden her. She had understood he wanted her make the most imposing appearance possible, and had finally accepted the award.

Halvo marched across the chamber with his head high, the silver streaks of hair at his temples shining as he passed beneath a glowing light fixture. He stopped at the exact center of the open square in the middle of the Red Room. Out of the corner of her eye Narisa saw the young guard on her left stop one pace behind her, as she had done behind Halvo.

They waited while Leader Tyre sat in his chair one level above them and directly across the open space from Halvo. Tyre could not have been happy about this meeting. The issuing of his personal warrant for Narisa's arrest meant that he had planned to deal with her as his private prisoner. Halvo's politically adroit maneuver in making Narisa his own prisoner and then demanding that she be brought before the full Assembly had circumvented Tyre's intentions and would open his actions to question and debate. If Tyre was worried about that possibility he showed no sign of it. He looked supremely confident, his pale, heavily jeweled hands resting across his

abdomen, his posture relaxed yet alert. When
the Members had finally hushed to complete
silence, Tyre lifted his right hand.

"Let the proceedings begin," he said. "You,
Admiral Halvo Gibal of Demaria, have
promised on your word as an officer to
present here for trial Lieutenant Navigator
Narisa raDon of Belta. Have you fulfilled
your promise?"

"I have, Leader Tyre."

"Then step forward, Narisa raDon, and
hear the formal charges against you."

Narisa took three steps toward Leader
Tyre. She stood at strict attention, her chin
up, her eyes fixed forward. Tyre made a
motion with one hand. A secretary rose and
began to read so rapidly that Narisa could not
catch all his words.

"High   treason . . . escape . . . Gaidar   of
Ceta . . ." She did not have to hear it now; she
knew all the charges thanks to Halvo's information gatherers. There would be no
surprises in what the secretary read. She had
only to think of what she and Halvo and Tarik
had agreed she would say when her turn
came. The secretary stopped reading and sat
down again.

"How do you plead, Narisa raDon?" asked
Leader Tyre.

Narisa found she had to swallow hard twice
before she could answer him.

"Leader Tyre, Members of the Assembly, I
plead guilty with extenuating circumstances.
I ask for an immediate trial before the
Assembly so those circumstances can be

made public. Admiral Halvo has agreed to act as my advocate."

There were whispers of shock and surprise from the Members at this last statement. Even Tyre looked startled out of his complacency.

"Admiral Halvo, how say you?" Tyre asked, using the ancient formula for advocates.

"I believe Narisa raDon will be exonerated of all charges against her. She had just cause for what she did. I am honored to be her advocate," Halvo said.

For a moment Narisa thought Tyre would make some objection. Those brought to trial usually had professional advocates to speak for them. The use of an admiral of the Service was highly irregular. Tyre could have refused on grounds of lack of precedent. He did not. He assented graciously. Narisa saw his eyes sparkle and knew Halvo had been correct in his judgment of the man. Tyre, Halvo had told her, would see his chance to entrap the famous Admiral Halvo along with Narisa and Tarik. Once Halvo had lost his power, Almaric, Tyre's chief opponent in the Assembly, would be easier prey.

A three-sided railed structure was now carried out and set down near Narisa. A chair was put into it.

"Narisa raDon, take your place in the witness chair," Tyre ordered. Narisa saw him smiling as he sat back and smoothed his black Member's jacket over his ample paunch. She wondered at that. She thought he ought to have been more worried about what she

would say. She would have been had she been
in his place.

She walked to the witness box, but she did
not sit, she stood in it. Halvo's guard, who had
been standing to her left, took her helmet and
cape, placing them on a bench at one side of
the room before returning to perform the
same service for Halvo. Across the open
space, Halvo's second guard took Tarik's
helmet and cape and escorted him to a seat on
a nearby bench. Above and around them the
Members rustled and murmured, settling
themselves more comfortably while they
waited for the drama to unfold.

Narisa knew the court procedure. Under
Halvo's questioning she would tell her story,
after which Tyre would question her, trying
to catch her lying. Then it would be Tarik's
turn as witness to tell his story and be
questioned by Tyre. Next, Halvo would make
a speech in her favor, followed by Tyre's
response demanding that she be convicted of
the charges against her. Finally, the Members
would vote on her fate.

"Lieutenant Narisa." Halvo turned from
contemplation of the Members' faces to look
directly at her. "Remember that we are all
bound to speak the truth while in this
chamber, with death as punishment for
lying."

"I will remember, sir." She was surprised
at the steadiness of her voice. Now that the
moment to speak had come, all nervousness
had fled. She smiled a little, looking back at
Halvo, and saw approval in his eyes.

"Tell us how you rescued Gaidar of Ceta and your reasons for doing so," Halvo ordered.

"I object," Tyre interrupted, "to your use of the word 'rescued.' The correct term according to the charges is 'escape.' "

"I accept your objection, sir." Halvo bowed in Tyre's direction, a slight smile curving his lips. He turned back to Narisa.

"Tell us why you released Gaidar of Ceta," he said.

"It was because I had received information that Gaidar had secretly been removed from the Assembly chambers and taken to a cell in Leader Tyre's own house. I was told by a person close to Tyre that he planned to kill Gaidar that night. Gaidar's death was to be the first step in a plot to destroy Member Almaric and all his family so that Leader Tyre would have no more opposition left to his rule."

The response to this speech was shocked silence at first, followed by cries of protest from at least half the Members. Glancing at Tyre, Narisa saw by his white, hard face that he had not known she was aware of his plans. He had known Suria had helped in Gaidar's escape—his warrant for Suria's arrest issued along with the one for Narisa was proof of that—but he must not have realized until this moment just how much Suria knew. She half expected him to make some objection to what she had said. Instead he sat staring at her with an expression of hatred so intense she began to tremble. Tyre tore his eyes from her face to look at Halvo and at Tarik. Then he settled back into his chair again, folding his hands over his belly and smiling.

"Will you continue, please, Admiral Halvo?" Tyre said in a silky voice that sent fear to Narisa's heart. Before she could think of what might make him so confident, the Members had quieted and Halvo approached her once more.

"Were you not aware, Lieutenant Narisa," Halvo asked, forestalling a question Tyre would surely ask if he did not, "that by leaving Member Almaric's house you were breaking the agreement he had made with this Assembly to keep you confined?"

"I was," Narisa answered. "Sir, officers of the Jurisdiction Service are trained to follow orders, and under normal circumstances I would never have dreamed of doing what I did. However, we are also taught to use our own judgment in the absence of superior officers during time of crisis. It seemed to me this was such a situation. Member Almaric and Commander Tarik were away from the house and not expected to return until very late, so I could not consult with them. Time seemed most important. Therefore, I made my decision quickly, and acted on it.

"I wish to emphasize," she said, "that neither Member Almaric nor Commander Tarik was aware of what I was doing until well after the rescue was completed. Neither should be held responsible for something I did without their knowledge. They had no part in it at all." She then told the whole story, dwelling in detail on the terrible conditions under which Gaidar had been held, speaking briefly about the mistreatment Suria had suffered at Tyre's hands, and pointing out that although she, Suria and Gaidar had knocked several people unconscious during their flight from Tyre's house, they had not caused serious injury to anyone.

"And so," Halvo summed up when she had finished, "you do truthfully believe your actions were necessary, both to save Gaidar's life and to force Leader Tyre to abort his plan to kill Almaric and his family that same night?"

"I do truthfully so believe," Narisa stated firmly.

"I now invite Leader Tyre to question you." Halvo moved to stand behind the witness box.

Tyre did not rise. He sat smiling benignly at Narisa for a long moment before he spoke.

"First," he said, "I would make a statement. I have no need to justify myself before this Assembly, but an explanation will alleviate any concern about some of my actions. I did indeed move the Cetan to my own house, not to murder him, but to keep him safe. I had reason to fear an attempt would be made to kill him before he had told us all he knew about the Cetan attack plans or their new device called Starthruster."

"As I recall, Leader Tyre," Narisa interrupted, despising the man and unwilling to tolerate his self-serving speech without objection, "in this very chamber you professed complete disbelief in everything Gaidar had to say. Either you were lying then, or you are lying now."

Voices filled with disapproval rose from the Members, most of whom had agreed with Leader Tyre on that previous occasion. From behind her Halvo placed a restraining hand on her shoulder, while across the room Tarik frowned at her.

Tyre seemed unperturbed by the uproar. He raised one ring-encrusted hand for silence. Narisa thought of that hand clutching Suria, bruising her. She could equally well imagine the same hand thrusting a dagger into Gaidar. Or herself. She wanted to tell Halvo she understood what his touch on her shoulder had meant; she knew how dangerous Tyre was, and she would not deviate again from the plan they had made for this trial.

The Members had quieted except for a few whispers. Tyre began to speak once more.

"I will excuse your improper comments, Lieutenant Narisa, because I know you are unaccustomed to the way in which great ruling bodies must function. I am certain the other Members will agree with me, though we have all found your outburst most distressing.

"As I was saying, I had Gaidar taken to my house for his own safety. There was no need for you to help him to leave that safe place. Everything the woman Suria told you was a lie. Since both she and Gaidar are missing, I think we may rightly suspect her real reason for wanting him freed was a perverted and lascivious one.

"Suria's claims of violence on my part are unfounded. I have never hurt anyone. Indeed, my fellow Members have often admonished me for too lenient treatment of convicted criminals. I can see I will have to change my ways at once."

There was no doubt in Narisa's mind that Tyre's last words had been meant as a direct threat.

"You have insisted," Tyre went on, "that neither Member Almaric nor Commander Tarik knew what you were doing. Yet there was one important family member who did know. Mistress Kalina helped you, did she not?"

"She agreed with me that under the circumstances Gaidar should be released in order to save his life."

"I understand that at that same time Service guards were at Almaric's house."

"Yes," Narisa said. "They had been sent to guard Tarik and me."

"Why did you not tell these trustworthy guards of your fears for Gaidar's safety and let them handle the matter?"

"Because we believed they were under your direct and personal orders, not under command of the Assembly," Narisa replied. There was another murmur from the Members at that, and Tyre's eyebrows went up, as though he were surprised at this point of view. He

made no comment, however, and appeared
to drop the subject.

"So under Mistress Kalina's guidance you
and the woman Suria slipped out of Almaric's
house?"

"Yes."

"And while you were gone on your illegal
venture, Mistress Kalina disguised your absence by telling the guards you were
exhausted and sleeping in your bedroom?"

"I—yes, that's true."

"A Demarian woman, wife to a high-ranking
Member, told a direct lie to protect you and to
protect the Cetan?"

There was no sound at all in the Red Room.
Narisa made no answer. There was none she
could make that would not harm Kalina, and
by association, Almaric. Demaria was in-
fluential in the Jurisdiction, its leaders valued
as negotiators in disputes, because they could
be believed. Narisa recalled with pain how
distressed Kalina had been by the need to tell
a lie.

"Will you not answer, Lieutenant Narisa?"
Tyre pressed her. "Will you not tell us by
what means you forced a Demarian woman to
resort to falsehood?"

"I didn't force her," Narisa cried, using the
best answer she could think of—the truth. "I
wasn't even there. She understood how desperate the situation was, and she did what she
thought was best."

"What she thought, or what you thought?"
Tyre's glittering eyes narrowed. He reminded

Narisa of the snake that had once threatened her. Tyre was poised to strike. She had to wait only a space-second or two before she felt the full force of his venom. "Is it not true that you have recently been consorting with telepathic creatures? Were you not able to silently call them to you? Could you not also have influenced Kalina to do your bidding whether she wished it or not? Did you not, in fact, use Mistress Kalina for your own ends?"

"I'm not a telepath!" But she knew where he had gotten that idea. From Jon Tanon, whose mind he had drained. Jon knew all about the birds and Dulan and the lost settlement.

Tyre must have believed she would be so frightened by his accusations that she would give up and admit anything he wanted. She almost did, until she thought of Dulan and the birds. After her experience with them she knew that not all telepaths were evil. She told herself she could not let Tyre twist the beautiful creatures she had found on Dulan's planet into something vile and ugly.

"Telepath! Telepath!"

She clung to the railing of the witness box while the outraged fury of the Assembly washed over her. She heard Halvo swearing softly behind her. She saw Tarik struggling to rise and being held down by Halvo's guard. She shook her head at him to make him stay where he was, and watched him relax, trusting her. Then she drew herself up and waited until the tumult had ended. She knew

what she had to do even if it violated Halvo's
carefully laid plans.

"Leader Tyre, Members of the Assembly,"
she said when she could again be heard, "I am
not a telepath. I was recently forced to spend
time on a planet where telepathic birds
reside, after Cetans had destroyed the Jurisdiction ship *Reliance*. No one knew about
those birds except Commander Tarik, Gaidar
of Ceta and myself. And one other. We told
Jon Tanon, a respected scholar, whom many
of you know. Jon was captured by Leader
Tyre's personal guards and later returned to
Almaric's house by those same guards. His
mind had been drained. We believed then that
it had been done by Leader Tyre's orders, and
now we have proof. That is why Leader Tyre
speaks of telepaths now. He knows the
contents of Jon Tanon's mind. He also knows
that those birds are harmless and that I am
not a telepath.

"I would recall to you, honorable Members,
that mind-draining is illegal. And now, Leader
Tyre, if you have no other questions for me, I
would suggest that we follow the original
order of this trial and let Commander Tarik
speak."

Tyre would have risen, but a Member on
each side of him caught his arms and held him
in place. Except for a few whispers and the
occasional sound of disgust or disbelief the
Red Room was quiet.

"May I step down from the witness box
Admiral Halvo?" Narisa asked.

"You may. Well done, Narisa." He actually patted her on the shoulder as she walked past him. The guard who had been standing by the box escorted her to a bench at one side of the room and stayed with her. She saw Tarik walk across the open space and enter the railed box she had just left.

Pointedly ignoring Tyre, Halvo urged Tarik to tell how he and Narisa had learned of the existence of Starthruster, and how they had successfully used it to return to the Capital. Tarik did so, praising Gaidar for his help, and pointing out that the recent Cetan attack had proven the veracity of the story originally brought before the Assembly by himself, Narisa and Gaidar.

"Leader Tyre, have you any questions for Commander Tarik?" Halvo asked when Tarik had finished.

"Lies!" Tyre shouted, struggling to his feet. "Telepaths! Traitors! A plot against me!" His nearest supporters pulled him down again, cautioning him to silence. Narisa noticed that many of the Members who had once clustered about Tyre, fawning over him and agreeing with everything he said, now were slipping out of their nearby seats and moving to stand as far away from Tyre as they could get. When the Leader's broken cries had stopped, Halvo looked around at the Members.

"Since Leader Tyre has no questions, I will proceed to my final speech," he said. "It has become plain during this trial that Gaidar of Ceta should never have been imprisoned at

all, and that Lieutenant Narisa had sufficient
reason to fear for his life to justify her rescue
of him. Be assured, it was a rescue, not an
escape. Gaidar is no criminal, and Lieutenant
Narisa raDon should be excused of all
charges against her."

A man rose from among the Members. He
was tall and very thin, and Narisa had seen
him seated next to Almaric when she had
been in this room before. When she had asked
Tarik about him later, he had told her the man
was one of Almaric's closest friends. His
name was Kyran of Serania.

"I move," Kyran said in a deep bass voice,
"that the original charges against Lieutenant
Narisa raDon be dropped. However, the
serious question of consorting with telepaths
must be addressed. It is against the law to do
so."

"That information," Halvo responded, "was
obtained by equally illegal mind-draining."

"Because it *was* obtained by mind-draining,
it is unquestionably true," Kyran said. "Shall
I withdraw my motion to drop the original
charges, Admiral Halvo?"

"If you do, I shall make another motion." A
second Member had risen. "Let all charges
against Lieutenant Narisa be dropped, and let
this painful and embarrassing case be closed
and never opened again."

"Agreed. Agreed." The Assembly burst into
applause. After a moment's hesitation, seeing
the direction in which his fellows were going,
Kyran joined them. In fact, only a very few

Members did not register their approval. Tyre remained slumped in his chair, seeming totally unresponsive to what was happening. Narisa saw him pluck at the hem of his jacket with his fingers.

The secretary who had read the charges against Narisa now moved to the center of the floor and held up his hands.

"Unless there is any objection, it shall be recorded," he intoned, "that Lieutenant Narisa raDon is cleared of all charges pending against her and is excused from this chamber."

Narisa rose, holding her breath. There was no objection.

"You may go, Lieutenant Narisa," the secretary said. "Admiral Halvo, Commander Tarik, you are also free to go. Your business with the Assembly is finished."

Narisa let out a long, relieved breath. She saw Tarik coming toward her, grinning. She took one step in his direction.

"Not so fast!" Tyre had risen. He appeared to have regained both vigor and purpose. "There are other charges pending against these people, and I want them answered now. Admiral Halvo, take the witness box."

A new buzzing began among the Members. Narisa and Tarik exchanged a puzzled glance. Halvo stood where he was. None of them knew of any other charges.

"I said, take the witness box!" Tyre pointed an imperious finger at Halvo. "I am your supreme commander, and that is an order."

Halvo walked to the box and entered it.

"That's better. You, Admiral Halvo, four
days ago took it upon yourself to declare open
war upon the Cetans without the required
express permission of the Assembly. Jurisdiction law plainly states the Service is
always to be under the authority of the
Assembly and is not to make policy or war on
its own. You and the officers who obeyed you,
which includes these two standing here, are
therefore guilty of outright insubordination.
By Jurisdiction law, you must all be removed
from your posts, court-martialed and
sentenced to death. How say you to that, Admiral Halvo?" Tyre sat down, looking pleased
with himself for having found a way to get at
Almaric's family after his first attempt had
failed.

Tarik touched Narisa's arm, directing her
toward the witness box where they stood
flanking Halvo. Halvo's closer guard went
with them, but Narisa saw the second guard,
who had been nearer the door they had come
in by, slip out that same door, leaving it ajar
so anyone in the anteroom could easily hear
what was being said. Tyre's men in the Red
Room were few, and all were intent upon the
struggle taking place between Tyre and
Halvo.

"Honorable Members," Halvo said, "Leader
Tyre has invited me to speak. I shall do so
honestly. I accuse Leader Tyre of misleading
this Assembly as to the seriousness of the
Cetan threat, and of refusing to believe Com-

mander Tarik's warning out of personal
animosity toward our father, Member
Almaric. I accuse Leader Tyre of leaving the
Races of the Jurisdiction open to total destruction by the Cetans. I further accuse him of
plotting to murder Almaric's entire family
along with a Cetan prisoner who was legally
entitled to the protection of Jurisdiction law
until he had been tried and sentence had been
passed on him.

"I deny the charge of insubordination. I,
and my fellow officers, were simply carrying
out our primary duty, which is to defend the
Jurisdiction from its enemies. How difficult
that was in this case is witnessed by the great
destruction wrought upon the Capital itself.
But we were successful, and the Cetans have
sued for peace. They are now willing to make
a treaty with us.

"Honorable Members, you are innocent of
wrongdoing in all of this. You have been mis-
guided by a bad Leader, who, in your honesty
and good intentions, you have trusted
implicitly. Tyre has betrayed your trust,
betrayed all the Races of the Jurisdiction.

"In the name of honor and justice, to pre-
serve the unblemished reputation of this
Assembly, Leader Tyre must be deposed!"

What a fine orator Halvo was. His voice,
clear and commanding, carried throughout the
Red Room, thrilling Narisa as it must have
thrilled the Members. Except for Tyre and his
closest adherents, who must have been
terrified. She also realized how clever Halvo's

tactics had been. By accusing only Tyre, and emphasizing that the honest Members had been misled by him, Halvo had made it possible for his audience to accept what he was saying and blame Tyre for everything. She suspected many of them had been weary of Tyre's rule long before this. Watching the faces of the Members as Halvo finished his speech and the applause burst forth, Narisa believed if he had been a Member, the Assembly would have made him its Leader by acclamation.

"My fellow Members!" Almaric's tall friend Kyran was on his feet again, calling for silence, and then saying what most were thinking. "I move that Leader Tyre be deposed and placed in protective confinement until he can be tried upon the charges Admiral Halvo has brought against him."

At that another Member jumped to his feet, not to be outdone in imposing justice on malefactors. "I move that the following Members, all close associates of Leader Tyre, also be removed from their positions in the Assembly and held in custody." He reeled off a list of ten Members to enthusiastic applause.

Narisa saw Tyre make a motion with one hand. His few personal guards positioned in the room began to close in on the little group at the witness box. Halvo and Tarik seemed oblivious to the danger. Before she could warn them, the door to the anteroom opened and Halvo's men marched into the Red Room Outnumbered, Tyre's guards smiled sheepish ly and retired to stand along the wall, until they were called upon a short time later to help Halvo's men escort Tyre and his ten friends to the Assembly's prison chambers. They came readily, knowing Tyre was finished and eager to prove their allegiance to the Assembly. When the doors had closed upon Tyre, Kyran was still standing.

"Honorable Members," he called out, "we need a new Leader. It should be a person of unimpeachable honesty. I nominate Member Almaric Gibal."

"This is highly irregular," protested another Member.

"It is indeed," replied Kyran. "Never before has a Leader been deposed. Never have so many Members been removed at one time. Each of them will have to be replaced by an appointment from a home planet. That will take time. Meanwhile, we who remain should show that we are united and firm in our purpose to serve the Jurisdiction. Our unanimous election of Almaric will prove our good intent. I move we vote at once."

"Yes, yes," came the cry.

"Honorable Members." Halvo raised his voice. "Commander Tarik, Lieutenant Narisa and I will, with your permission, remove ourselves from this chamber, lest we seem to be influencing your votes in favor of Almaric."

"Wait in the anteroom for our decision," ordered Kyran. "We shall not keep you long."

The anteroom was deserted except for three of Halvo's guards, one of them the man who had brought in his men at the crucial moment.

Halvo went to speak with him.

"Eleven new Members," Narisa said to Tarik.

"Not so many among nearly five hundred," he replied. "Still, an infusion of new blood may lead to change. We can hope. I'm proud of you, Narisa. You said exactly the right thing in there." He beamed at her, and she felt like throwing herself into his arms.

The doors to the Red Room were flung open. The secretary appeared, followed by Kyran and a surge of other Members.

"Come with us," Kyran invited. "Halvo, walk beside me, please."

They made their way to a series of levitators and crowded onto the platforms. The doors slammed shut, and within seconds they had been lifted to the uppermost level of the building that housed the Assembly chambers. There they stepped out onto the balcony from which all proclamations to the people were made. The bells had already been rung, and the communication system turned on. They would all be seen, and the words the secretary read would be heard all over the Capital planet. Within a few space-hours, every planet in the Jurisdiction would know of the change in Leaders.

The work of cleaning up and repairing the damaged Capital had stopped when the bells sounded, and far below them a crowd had begun to gather in Assembly Square and along the streets that radiated from it.

By custom, it was the secretary who made

all public announcements for the Assembly. As he began to speak, Narisa listened with growing wonder at what she and Halvo and Tarik had done. Crushed among Members and Halvo's guards as they were, no one noticed when Tarik took her hand in his and held it tight. Narisa let her fingers curl around his.

"Almaric Gibal of Demaria, our new Leader," the secretary read, and had to wait until the cheering had stopped. But it did not stop. It grew louder. It did not take Narisa long to see why. A transporter car of the type used between spaceport and the city had landed on the pad in the middle of Assembly Square. The door slid back. Two Service guards stepped out, hesitated when they saw the cheering crowd, then moved aside and Almaric appeared.

"So," Halvo spoke over the roar, "Tyre had his men waiting at spaceport for my father. And there's my mother, and Suria and Gaidar, too. We needn't wonder what their fates would have been had Tyre still been in power when they arrived in the Assembly chambers."

"I thank all the stars they are safe," Kyran declared. "I was truly worried about them. I don't know what we would have done if Almaric had not returned promptly."

"But with my father's usual inspired timing," Tarik said, "he has returned to the Capital, all unknowing and therefore innocent of complicity in his sons' plans, just after his election is publicly declared. Halvo, you had better send a few of your men down there to protect him from his admirers before they tear him apart with love.''

"It has been taken care of," Kyran said. "See there—an honor guard of Service officers."

By this time the secretary had recovered himself and after a hasty consultation with Kyran began to speak once more to the public.

"Leader Almaric will be formally presented to the Assembly tomorrow at mid morning. All citizens of the Capital are granted two days' holiday beginning immediately." The cheer that followed this announcement was so loud the secretary gave up trying to speak and moved aside to let the Members crowd against the balcony railing to wave to the people below.

"They've begun celebrating already," Tarik said to Narisa, pointing to where several casks had been rolled into the square and were being tapped, while cups and pitchers had mysteriously appeared in many hands. "I wonder how the ordinary citizens always know what is going to happen? I had not fully realized how unpopular Leader Tyre was. It looks as though my parents will return to their house in a triumphal procession."

"I think we should take them there in my personal transporter," Halvo suggested. "It will be easier for them to go by air than through the streets."

"I'll go with you, if I may." Kyran spoke quickly. "Almaric and I have much to discuss."

"Come along then, before all the other Members have the same idea," Halvo urged.

They were taken by levitator to where Halvo's transporter had been left. Most of his guards rejoined him along the way.

"Do you really think," Narisa asked Tarik as they waited for everyone to board, "that Almaric will be able to change some of the most unfair and outdated laws?"

"The Assembly works very slowly. He can't do much about that, but he can use his prestige to influence some changes over time," Tarik replied.

"Two that need to be repealed at once," she declared, "are the Act of Banishment and the Reproduction law."

"Hush, dear rebel, don't even mention that yet." Tarik regarded her with love and laughter in his eyes. "We will talk to my father later."

"And talk to him about your plan, the one you won't discuss with me?" She moved a little closer to him as Halvo's guards crowded into the transporter.

"That, too." He laughed at her, teasing. "Have patience, my love. You will know all in time."

Chapter Fifteen

Unperturbed that their master and mistress had arrived unexpectedly, or that transportation of food supplies to the Capital had been interrupted by warfare, Almaric's jubilant servants provided a surprisingly ample celebration feast for the new Leader and his family. Looking into the eating room, Narisa thought they must have used up most of the food put away in Kalina's storage rooms. Platters and serving dishes piled high with food and pitchers brimming with wine covered the shining surface of the deep red stone table, leaving little space for individual plates and cups and eating utensils.

When Kalina, in one of her typically warm-hearted gestures, decided to invite all of the attendant guards to eat, too, the meal was quickly turned into a buffet. Wandering

diners carried their plates into the entrance
hall or large reception room, or out to the
walled garden, where they sat in small groups
to eat. Almaric himself ate quickly and then
retired to his private library with Kyran,
Halvo and Tarik.

It was in the garden that Narisa found Suria
and Gaidar, both sitting on the grass. Gaidar
held a bowl of vegetable stew topped with
slices of meat in one hand, and a large chunk
of bread in the other. He dipped the bread into
the bowl, scooped out a pile of vegetables and
took a huge bite.

Suria was eating more daintily from a
smaller bowl of fruit and cheese. At her
invitation, Narisa dropped to the ground beside them.

"I haven't had a chance to speak with you
since you returned. Where did you go when
you left the Capital?" she asked them. "I
worried about all of you. Were you able to
avoid the Cetans?"

"Easily. We were far from the battle."
Gaidar laid his bread on one knee so he could
use his fingers to pick a slice of meat out of
his bowl. Narisa refrained from telling him he
should eat with the proper implements as
Jurisdiction citizens did. He would learn in
time. He was too clever not to learn. He
grinned his naughty-little-boy smile, and she
forgave him his lack of social skills.

"Gaidar demonstrated Starthruster for
us," Suria said. "Almaric was most impressed, thanks to me."

"To you?" Gaidar grumbled. "I was piloting the ship."

"A little too enthusiastically, considering Starthruster's potential speed. It's a good thing for you I was your navigator. Without me, we would all be somewhere outside the galaxy, trying to find our way back."

"Don't believe her. We stopped on a planet Almaric wanted to visit," Gaidar told Narisa. "It was in one of the far spiral arms. That is why we were at the edge of the galaxy. It had nothing to do with my piloting. Almaric spent a long time conferring with the planetary leaders, which is why we were late returning after the battle was over. We intercepted a message transmitted from a Service ship saying the Jurisdiction had won, so we knew it was safe to come back whenever we wanted."

"You returned at exactly the right time." Narisa had another important question. "Where is Jon Tanon?"

"Leader Tyre's men took him away the moment we docked at spaceport," Suria said. "But I spoke to Almaric a little while ago, and he has issued orders for Jon to be taken to the medical center. I think he will recover in time, Narisa. He was beginning to notice things again, and to try to speak. He will have the very best care, you may be certain of that. We may also be sure Almaric won't forget what was done to Jon when he is deciding on Tyre's punishment."

"That Styxian lizard deserves to be hung up by his big toes until he rots." This verdict was delivered between slurps as Gaidar lifted the bowl to his lips to drain the last of the stew juices.

"If you wipe your mouth with your sleeve and stain that shirt," Suria told him, "it's you who'll be hung by your toes. Kalina will see to it personally."

"Ah, that one. I'm truly afraid of that woman. This is her precious son Halvo's shirt." Gaidar looked around anxiously, stew dribbling slowly down his chin, until Narisa took pity on him and handed him her own napkin. He cleaned his face with it, then gave it back to her with a comical flourish.

"We'll civilize you yet," Narisa murmured, folding the dirty napkin into her own empty stew bowl. "What will you do now that the war with Ceta has ended?"

"I don't know." He looked glum. "Almaric has asked me to stay here at his house for a while. I think he plans to use me when it's time to negotiate the Cetan treaty, but I don't think that would work well at all. I don't know what to do. Perhaps I'll steal a ship and try to find that lost planet again."

"And you, Suria? Will you be allowed to return to the Service?"

"I'm not sure. Like Gaidar, I've been invited to remain here temporarily. It will take a while for Almaric to begin his own programs in the Assembly. Perhaps I can work for abolishment of the Reproduction Law."

"You Jurisdiction people have a law for everything." Gaidar shook his head in disgust. "I should have known there would be one about reproduction. Do I have to get permission from your Assembly if I want to ask a woman to share my bed?"

"No." Narisa laughed, imagining that scene. "It's not quite that bad." She quickly explained the law and the punishment for breaking it.

"It is a stupid, cruel law." Gaidar nearly choked on indignation. "I don't know why you allow it to continue."

"It is a bad law now," Suria agreed. "But when it was first promulgated, it was a wise idea. The Jurisdiction faced the possibility of extinction through overpopulation. Under the Reproduction Law, permission to have a child is a precious thing and is properly valued. Unwanted children are no longer mistreated or sold into slavery as they too often were space-centuries ago. The civilized Races have prospered and have kept their numbers well within tolerable limits. The situation has changed for the better, and it is time to change the law. I would like to help do that."

Gaidar looked at Suria with more than his usual interest.

"Someone told me that's why you left the Service, to have a child," he said. "Did you have a man, Suria?"

"No. I volunteered for the Genetic Improvement Program."

"Genetic . . . ? By all the stars, you people are mad! Insane! I'll be happy to improve your genes with an infusion of sensible Cetai genes any time you want. Just say the word but make it soon. I haven't had a woman for months."

"Excuse me, please." Narisa stood up. If that had been a proposal of some kind, it was the strangest on record. She could not judge Suria's reaction. Suria was keeping her beautiful face carefully blank. Narisa thought they were best left alone. "I need to speak to Kalina and I'm very tired. My head still aches. I really should rest." She could think of no other excuses to leave them gracefully. She did not think they noticed her going. They were looking into each other's eyes.

Early the next morning Narisa descended to the entrance hall to find Tarik and Halvo there, along with a crowd of Service officers and Members of the Assembly.

"Greetings, Lieutenant Narisa," called Kyran of Serania as she reached the bottom of the wide red stone stairway. His deep bass voice sounded across the hall. "Have you come to wish Almaric well before he leaves for the chambers? This is a joyous day for all citizens of the Jurisdiction."

"You seem especially joyous, Member Kyran." Watching him approach her, she was a little wary, fearing he might raise again the question of the telepathic birds. On the other hand, it was Kyran who had been the first to move that Tyre be deposed. She was grateful to him for that.

"Kyran has reason to be happy," Tarik said, coming up behind her and putting one hand on her shoulder. "Almaric has appointed a Council of Special Members to be his advisors, and has named Kyran its Chief Member."

"It is a great honor," Kyran declared, "though a drastic change from the way Tyre always ruled. For so long everything in the Assembly remained the same, and now, all at once, there are so many changes. So many changes," he repeated.

"Change can sometimes be a good thing," Narisa responded, hoping to encourage him, and relieved that he had not mentioned the birds. "I congratulate you on your new post, Member Kyran."

"I am certain you will prove equal to the tasks ahead of you," Tarik added dryly, and Narisa recalled the unkind remarks he had made in the past about the Assembly never wanting change.

"They will have no choice, will they?" she murmured as Kyran turned away to greet someone else and Tarik steered her toward the eating room. "The Members will be forced to accept a great many changes now."

"It will be good for them," Tarik declared, closing the eating room doors on the sound of voices from the entrance hall. "My father has decided that Halvo and I, along with ten other representatives of the Service, should be at his formal presentation today."

"I thought only Assembly Members were allowed to be there," Narisa said, surprised at this development.

"It was my mother's suggestion." Tarik

grinned knowingly. "She has begun her own program for making changes in the old ways. There will also be a public reception after the official ceremonies are over. She wants you to go to that. She will ask you this morning. Do you feel well enough?"

"Oh, yes. After all Kalina has done for us, I'll do anything she asks of me." She touched his arm with loving concern. "Tarik, you look so tired. Did you sleep at all last night, or were you working?"

"I'll sleep later, after this long day is over. Tomorrow night we'll be together again, my love, and then I'll see to it that it's you who lack for sleep."

"I look forward to it." She put her arms around him and laid her head on his shoulder.

"This is what I wanted before I have to leave," he said, resting his cheek on her hair. "Just a few peaceful moments with you is refreshment enough to last me through all the ceremonies ahead."

They stayed that way, holding each other for a while, until, after a deep kiss that left her wanting more, someone called to him and he had to leave with Almaric. But the warmth of his embrace and the certainty of his love stayed with her all day long.

Narisa was required to wear formal Service uniform for the reception, but Kalina had provided new clothing for her other two guests. Narisa surveyed them as they waited in a corridor next to the Assembly's reception room.

Suria wore a particularly grand version of
the costume of her native planet. She shim-
mered in a glittery green and purple wrapped
top over green trousers. With her flame-red
hair piled on top of her head, and heavy green
stone and gold jewelry at her throat and
wrists, she was gorgeously regal in spite of
her short stature.

Gaidar was in formal Demarian costume,
the velvety golden brown of his trousers and
jacket highlighting his golden eyes.

"He is half Demarian," Kalina explained,
straightening the folds of her own heavy
purple and gold robes. "I thought it best to
emphasize that for this day. Besides, I don't
know what Cetans wear for formal occasions."

"They don't have many," Gaidar told her,
"and when they do, they wear whatever they
can steal."

"You are trying to shock me again, Gaidar,
but you won't succeed." Kalina regarded him
with fondness. "When the Cetan worlds are
admitted into the Jurisdiction, they will learn
more civilized ways and will soon devise the
proper costumes. Now, Gaidar, I will take
your arm, please. Narisa and Suria, I want
you directly behind me. You are all heroes of
the Jurisdiction and you deserve these places
of honor."

They entered a huge, ornate hall that was
draped in the favorite Jurisdiction colors of
dark green and deep, gloomy red enhanced
with much gold and silver trim. There they
joined Almaric, Tarik and Halvo. The rest of

the day was spent in greeting all the Assembly Members and their families, who were admitted to the chambers for this special occasion along with Service officers and many representatives of the ordinary citizens of the Jurisdiction. A surprising number of them wanted to speak to Narisa, to thank her for her part in saving the Capital from Cetan destruction.

As soon as he could, Tarik drew her apart to tell her the news that had all those who had been at Almaric's presentation buzzing with excitement.

"Admiral of the Fleet Momuri," Tarik told her, "sent a message to my father, to congratulate him as the new Leader."

"You said once that Momuri is Tyre's man," Narisa interrupted.

"So he is, heart and soul. I suspect he hoped by his gesture today to escape Tyre's fate of perpetual imprisonment. There's more, Narisa. Momuri has been ill for some time, so, claiming his health prevents him from carrying out his duties, he has applied for immediate retirement. He used the privilege of all retiring admirals to nominate his successor. He chose Halvo."

"That's wonderful! Halvo is just the man the Service needs," Narisa exclaimed. "Did Almaric agree to the suggestion?"

"Indeed he did." Tarik beamed at her. "Of course, being Almaric, he very properly noted that the nomination would have to go through the appropriate Service channels, but he said

if the approved documents come to him, he
will be pleased to sign them."

Narisa laughed at Tarik's description. "I
can just hear him saying that and impressing
all the Members with how different he is from
Tyre. What will happen to Momuri? He wasn't
a bad admiral, you know, even if he was
Tyre's man. Most of the officers I knew
respected him."

"I told Almaric," Tarik said, "that if
Momuri were harshly punished, Halvo's
appointment would split the Service into
quarreling factions. I thank all the stars my
father was willing to listen to me for once.
Momuri will be permitted to retire with
honor, the Service personnel who backed him
will thus be pacified and Halvo will inherit a
united Service."

"Thanks to your good sense," Narisa added.

"I believe my father is not without sense,
either," Tarik said, adding in a voice filled
with wonder, "He listened to me and seriously considered what I said. It's the first time
that has ever happened."

Almaric signaled to him then, and Tarik left
her to rejoin his father, but Narisa was not
alone for long. There were still more people
who wanted to speak with her, humans and
non-humans alike expressing gratitude for
deliverance from the Cetans and Tyre's
corrupt rule.

The day ended with an official banquet that
lasted far into the night. By the time they
were all finally back in Almaric's house,

Narisa was so tired she could barely climb the stairs to her room. She was grateful for Chatta's help in undressing, and was asleep even as she fell into bed.

She slept until well after midday, and awakened completely refreshed with no trace of headache from her injury.

"You are to join Leader Almaric in his library," Chatta informed her as Narisa ate the fresh fruit and bread the maid-servant had brought. Narisa heard awe in Chatta's voice, and knew the girl was deeply honored to be a member of the Leader's household.

She found Halvo and Tarik with their father. Kalina joined them a moment after Narisa had arrived.

"You will be interested to hear," Almaric told Narisa in his formal way, "that the Assembly has this morning agreed to accept the Cetan warlords who surrendered to Halvo as honored guests rather than as prisoners. They will remain in the Capital while we work out the terms of a treaty with them. We hope other Cetan leaders, learning how fairly we have dealt with these, will consent to join their fellows as signers of the treaty."

"All of the Assembly agreed to this?" Narisa asked, surprised.

"There were some objectors, those who deal with space armaments, or who have other profitable reasons for wanting bad relations with the Cetans to continue. They were shouted down. The time for war against the Cetans is over."

   "I'm glad," Narisa said quietly. "There will
be no more dead planets. No more Beltas."
Her own hatred of the Cetans was gone, wiped
away by victory and her growing friendship
with Gaidar. Cetans were not all monsters,
any more than citizens of the Jurisdiction
were all good and honorable.

   "However," Halvo said, breaking into her
thoughts, "we cannot begin to trust such old
and crafty enemies as the Cetans without a
certain initial wariness. Tarik has made a
pertinent suggestion for dealing with this
problem, which I will let him explain."

   "I have not heard about this," Almaric
complained. "Are you taking matters into
your own hands again so soon, Tarik?"

   "Perhaps it's only that you have been too
busy for him to talk with you about it, my
dear," Kalina soothed. "I haven't heard
Tarik's idea, either, so let us both listen to
him before we begin criticizing him."

   "I believe," Tarik said, "that a small, secret
group of colonists should settle where they
can keep a watch on the Cetans. I suggest
these people leave the Capital in advance of
serious negotiations. They cannot in the
future be counted in violation of any treaty
provisions if they are established in their
new home before the treaty is made."

   "An interesting idea," Almaric mused. "I
will consider it."

   "Do it now, Father," Tarik urged. "Let me
lead the colonists."

   "Impossible. I need you here with me."

   "No, you don't, Father. I'm not a man for

the day-to-day details of administration. That's Halvo's talent, not mine. It's one reason he's such a successful admiral. I would never be content living here at the Capital. You know I'm speaking the truth. I will not stay here. I have always done what you expected of me, but now, before it's too late, I want to choose for myself the form my life will take."

"Have you been quarreling with Halvo again?" Almaric looked at his younger son in irritation. "Is that why you are so eager to leave us? Let me tell you what I think of your indifference to Service regulations."

"No, Father." Halvo interrupted Almaric's imminent tirade. "We have not quarreled. In fact, we are in greater agreement than we have ever been. I endorse Tarik's suggestion completely. Here, he would quickly become useless. As the leader of such a colony, he would be invaluable to you and of great benefit to the Jurisdiction. We could trust him as we could trust no one else."

Narisa had been listening to this conversation with growing excitement. She was certain this was the plan that Tarik had hinted about to her, and she thought she knew the planet he had in mind. She decided it was time to tell Tarik's parents what she planned to do. They had to know sooner or later. Better now, in private.

"I want to go, too," she said, "and I want permission to have Tarik's child. I am prepared to resign from the Service immediately."

There was a quickly smothered gasp from Kalina. Almaric looked shocked. More importantly to Narisa, Tarik smiled and nodded his agreement with her statement. She thought he was going to say something, but his brother spoke first.

"Too bad," Halvo drawled. "You were about to be promoted to lieutenant commander. Are you certain you won't reconsider?"

"I will," she told him, "if I am assigned to Tarik's expedition and if I am permitted to have his child. Only then would I consent to remain in the Service."

"Well done, beloved rebel," Tarik said, not caring who heard. "How much you have changed."

"Remain in the Service and have a child?" Kalina's tone revealed her concern, and, not surprisingly for that strong woman, a certain admiration. "Would you defy every custom and law about motherhood?"

"I care not at all if I remain in the Service or leave it, so long as I am with the man I love," Narisa said. "Where Tarik goes, I will go. You have been by Almaric's side for most of your life, Kalina, and you were permitted to have two children, a rare indulgence for the Jurisdiction. I want to have at least one."

"Then, if you are so determined, I will support you in this." Kalina's hand was warm and comforting on Narisa's own. "I remember what happened to Suria. I want you to avoid that fate. You and she are right, my dear, it is time for change."

Almaric cleared his throat. Narisa saw bright moisture in his eyes.

"I wanted my sons with me to lend me their strength with this difficult burden I have undertaken in my old age. It grieves me to let Tarik go." He cleared his throat again, and his voice became firmer. "Nevertheless, the suggestion Tarik has made is a valuable one. I think we badly need such an outpost. Have you a planet in mind?"

"It's in the Empty Sector," Tarik said, "and rather near to the Cetan worlds. It will be easy to stay hidden there."

"Ah, your lost planet." Almaric nodded. "A dangerous location in that sector, but a necessary risk, no doubt. When would you leave?"

"As soon as possible. Halvo will have the Cetan ship we arrived in refitted and provisioned as soon as you give your official consent."

"You will have Starthruster."

"I will leave the plans for it with Halvo. Jurisdiction engineers can build more. Or our new Cetan allies can provide some for us to copy. Make that a provision of the treaty."

"You will need other colonists. Who will you ask?"

"Gaidar and Suria," Naris suggested.

"Is that all?" Kalina exclaimed. "You need more people to begin a colony, Tarik, people with diversified skills."

"It's a small planet, Mother."

"At least eight people, then, possibly ten."

"She's right, as usual." Halvo laughed. "I

know of a few cadets and some officers who aren't really suited to Service life and who would flourish given the independence and freedom from regulation that you will offer. Why don't we begin by asking your first choices and hearing how they respond? After that, I'll send for a few likely candidates."

Gaidar came first, and listened in silence to Tarik's explanation of what was intended.

"You may remain here," Almaric told him when Tarik had finished. "You could be very useful to me as an intermediary with the Cetans while we negotiate the treaty. Or you may go with Tarik. The choice is yours. You are no longer a prisoner. The Jurisdiction owes you too much to want to punish you."

"It's because of that I'd be no help to you at all," Gaidar replied without hesitation. "The Cetans will see me as a traitor and have nothing to do with me. I could only harm your efforts to make a lasting peace. I'm neither Cetan nor Demarian; I don't belong in either society. I need to find a new world to live in, where I can make my own place. With my knowledge of Cetans, I can be useful to Tarik. I will go with him."

Suria was called into the room next, and the project explained to her.

"You may rejoin the Service with your former rank," Halvo assured her. "You have been unjustly punished, Suria."

"I still want to have a child," she responded, "so I won't go back to the Service. I want to go with Tarik, but I need Narisa's consent first."

"Mine?" Narisa was astonished. "Why my

consent?"

"May I speak with you in private?" Suria asked.

"Use the anteroom," Kalina suggested.

Suria flashed her a look of gratitude and rose, Narisa joining her.

"The men would be embarrassed by this," Suria said, closing the door so they could not be overheard. "Narisa, what was between Tarik and me was finished more than a space-year ago, but we remain friends and always will be. Can you accept that and be my friend, too? If I join this colony, we would be living too closely for angry thoughts or the hatred that comes from jealousy. In the short time I've known you, I have come to admire you. I believe I could live in close proximity with you, but not if I make you uncomfortable."

"I was jealous of you once," Narisa admitted, "but no more. I know Tarik loves me, and I believe you have begun to care for Gaidar."

"I have." Suria smiled. "He would father a strong, beautiful child, would he not? And I don't think he would be terribly difficult to civilize. He's eager to learn."

Narisa laughed. "Come with us, Suria. Be Gaidar's mate and my friend, and anything else you want to be. A world under Tarik's rule will allow you those choices."

"I will." Suria was smiling happily now. "You are going to need me, Narisa. I am a midwife, remember."

"I hadn't forgotten." Narisa could feel herself blushing. "How did you know I . . . I only told Tarik's family an hour ago. . . . I mean. . . ."

"When a woman loves a man as you love Tarik, she wants to bear his child. When a man loves as Tarik does, he wants the same thing. We are going to a world where he will be the final authority. We both know how little he cares for strict regulations when they are applied without regard for individual needs. The two of you will have your child regardless of what the Reproductive Agency decides, or whether the Assembly changes the law. I will be your midwife when your time comes, if you will help me when I bear Gaidar's child. I will have the child I want, too, when the time is right."

"Agreed." They shook hands, and then, impulsively, they hugged each other. When they flung open the door and returned to Almaric's library, there was no need to announce the outcome of their talk.

"You now have four colonists. I will find another four or six people to go with you," Halvo, ever practical, promised his brother. "We had better get started on the lists of provisions you will need. All of you can help with that."

"I'll never see you again." Kalina's gray eyes brimmed with tears. "Never see my grandchild, if you have one. The Leader is not allowed to leave the Capital."

"No such law applies to the Leader's wife. I might create you my personal ambassador," Almaric suggested. "You could make tours of inspection at various planets, and bring back to me information the official reports don't contain."

"I'll give you the coordinates for Dulan's planet," Narisa promised. "I have memorized them. The Empty Sector is in constant flux, but if I provide a guide and Halvo will lend you his best navigator when you make your tour, it will be easier to find us."

Tarik appeared in Narisa's room late that night, talking excitedly about his many plans. She had never seen him so happy.

"For the first time in my life," he told her, "my father approves of something I want badly. He believes I am the best person to carry out this assignment. And Halvo, too. There hasn't been an angry word among the three of us all day. They listen to what I have to say about Dulan's Planet. We have agreed to make that the official name. I thought you would be pleased."

"I am. And I am so glad for you. I know it hurt you that you and your father were so often at odds." She smiled at him with just a touch of mischief in her expression. "As for myself, I can't wait to return to Dulan's Planet. Do you know, Tarik, I haven't heard one word of poetry from you since we left here?"

"The Capital is not a place that inspires poetry. But you shall hear it again," he promised. "When we are home. And when we are home again, I shall see the sight I have missed. You, my love, coming out of the lake, laughing and dripping wet, like Venus rising from the sea, holding out your arms to me, wanting my love.

"I want you to be my wife," he said, embracing her. "I want a permanent union between us, not one of those temporary arrangements some people make."

"Yes," she whispered, "oh, yes, my dear and only love."

He swept her off her feet and started for the bed. She lay cradled in his arms, thinking her heart would burst with joy. He put her down on the bed and stretched out beside her.

They undressed each other slowly, savoring the touch and taste and scent of each other's body, teasing and stroking and kissing along arms and legs and torsos, moving inexorably closer to the now throbbingly sensitive centers of their passion. As if to prolong their tormented pleasure, they delayed their coming together until Tarik's breath rose from his chest in harsh gasps and Narisa was whimpering in her half-crazed need of him. Only then did they join in a union so profound they were as one in body and soul and mind and for a little while the galaxy slowed and stopped for them, and time itself stood still.

"Did you know your mother is busy re writing the Reproduction Law?" Narisa asked much later as she lay with Tarik in th dark. Hearing his deep chuckle and mur mured response that his mother could do any thing, she went on, "She has been at it a afternoon and evening, in consultation wit

Suria and me and two elderly creatures who are some kind of legal advisors to the Assembly. Neither of them is human, which Kalina says is important, because the non-human Races have a right to say what they think, too. The one called Nirn came in a pressure bubble because our air is unbreathable to it. I rather like the creature. There is a sense of humor behind that bubble, as well as a wonderful mind. The other is a male Jugarian, an irritating creature, but brilliant."

"What did this high council of Kalina's decide?" Tarik slid down in the bed to nibble at her right shoulder.

"Kalina wants each world or planetary system to decide for itself whether to insist on the yearly injection. Only those on active duty with the Service and those who travel in deep space will still be required to comply with the old law. She says that is for their own safety and the well-being of any children they might have."

"Sounds sensible enough to me," he mumbled.

"What will you want for Dulan's Planet?"

"Hmmm." He had progressed from her shoulder to her right breast, and he did not answer for a long time. Narisa began to lose her hold on rational thought.

"Tarik?"

"Let the colonists vote on it," he muttered, his voice thick with desire. "We've made our choice. I move we implement it at once."

Epilogue

It took one space-week to provision the Cetan ship, which Gaidar had renamed the *Kalina*. Two new shuttles were added for a total of three, plus a heavy load of medical supplies, food, clothing and farming equipment.

True to his word, Halvo found additional people willing to undertake a possibly dangerous assignment far from their familiar worlds. There were six candidates, three male and three female. At Halvo's insistence, they were all human.

"It will be easier to withstand the tensions of such a venture if you have that basic community of thought," Halvo counselled. "I have seen often enough how humans and non-humans can disagree over the most fundamental necessities. You need compatible people to go with you. I have chosen six Interview them and decide on four."

But after Tarik, Narisa, Gaidar and Suria
had met with the six, they decided to allow all
of them to go.

"We need each one of them," Narisa said,
and Halvo saw to the required legalities.

Their prospective colony now had two communications officers, a male physician to
supplement Suria's midwifery, an agricul-
tural expert, an historian-archivist, whom
Tarik insisted was vitally necessary, and a
young woman with advanced degrees in both
botany and interplanetary zoology.

On the day they were to leave, Almaric's
family, with Suria and Gaidar, gathered on
the terrace just outside the eating room.
There, as the late day sun of the Capital planet
streamed down upon them, Almaric said the
words that offically bound Tarik and Narisa
together through all of life.

Narisa wore a formal Beltan costume, of
silver fabric with gold and copper braid trim
that Kalina had given her. Tarik wore his
Service uniform for the last time. At Narisa's
suggestion they exchanged the simple silver
rings that were the ancient Beltan symbol of
an unbreakable union. Such outward signs
were seldom used in the Jurisdiction anymore, but Tarik had agreed readily when she
had asked him.

Then, with Kalina and Halvo acting as wit-
nesses, Almaric retired Tarik from active
duty in the Service and appointed him Leader
of the new colony on the world known in
secret Jurisdiction records as Dulan's Planet.

Narisa had her promotion after all. She was

made a lieutenant commander in the Service,
then promptly retired at that rank and
appointed as Tarik's second-in-command.
Gaidar was placed in charge of security, Suria
of housing and provisions.

Kalina had ordered a feast prepared, but no
one ate much of it. All were thinking of the
newly outfitted ship waiting for them at
spaceport. The leave-taking was difficult.
Kalina's tears brushed everyone's cheeks, and
even the usually controlled Almaric was hard
put to maintain his smooth composure.

They left at last in Halvo's transporter car
with only Halvo accompanying them. At
spaceport, after all the others had boarded
the *Kalina,* Narisa looked back from the entrance hatch to see the stern Admiral Halvo and
his younger brother in a tearful final embrace.

The planet was not where it should have
been. Using Narisa's and Suria's best
navigational efforts, it took them three space-
days of searching to find it again.

"That's the way it is in the Empty Sector,"
Tarik said patiently. "Narisa, are you certain
that's the right planet?"

"Thanks to Halvo, we have the latest
viewing screens," she responded, touching a
button. "See, there is the lake, and there the
island. Shall we take a shuttle down?"

"We'll take two. You and I will go in one,
Gaidar and Suria in the other, and we will
load each with as much equipment and
supplies as possible. We'll run the shuttles
back and forth between planet and ship until

all the people and supplies are unloaded. We can land on the lake and unload on the beach."

But this was the Empty Sector, where navigation was frequently difficult. The first shuttle to leave the *Kalina* had landed safely on the lake, that much Tarik and Narisa heard before communications became impossible because of the static generated by an electromagnetic storm. Their own shuttle spiraled downward, Tarik at the controls, Narisa beside him checking the navigation panels.

"We are off course," Narisa reported, "but I can't tell by exactly how much. The viewer screens aren't working properly, either."

The shuttle crashed against something hard. Narisa heard the sound of ripping metal. She was thrown back in her seat, the safety harness holding her securely. She could see Tarik struggling with the craft's controls, fighting against the restraints of his own safety harness, trying to reach the manual levers.

There was another crash. Narisa felt as though all of the shuttle beneath her feet had been torn away. A gentler bump, a long, screeching slide, and with a final bounce the craft came to a halt. The entrance hatch popped open, and hot orange-gold sunlight flooded the cockpit.

Narisa released the clasp on her safety harness. Tarik looked to be unharmed. He was checking the last of the gauges on the instrument panel, putting the little ship to rest like the good spaceman he was. Narisa knew he would not want to be disturbed for the next few minutes. She finished with her own panels, then climbed out of her seat and through the hatch.

The shuttle had crashed in the middle of a desert. From horizon to horizon the pebble-strewn land lay flat and lifeless under the blazing orange sun. The cloudless sky was a dark purple-blue bowl. Narisa shielded her eyes with one hand and turned slowly, scanning the horizon, searching for some sign of life. She took a deep breath of the thin, clean air.

From far away, low across the desert floor, came a lustrous, brilliant blue creature with outspread wings. It was rising now to circle over the ruined shuttle, its graceful shape blotting out the harsh sun, lending blessed shade against the hot glare.

"Communications with the *Kalina* are impossible until the electromagnetic storm subsides," Tarik declared, appearing at the hatch. "That may take several days. We will have to find Gaidar and Suria. We need their shuttle to remove our cargo."

Narisa wasn't listening. She was watching the bird. She knew which one it was by the scratch on its beak. Behind her, Tarik put one hand on her shoulder.

"We'll have to do it on foot," he said.

She looked up at the circling shape above her. Then she smiled at her husband and love

"I know the way," she told him. And taking his hand, she began to walk.